Seven Nights
in the
Dying Castle

Seven Nights in the Dying Castle

Copyright © 2023 by Sara Dahmen

ISBN   978-1-77374-107-9

Promontory Press | www.promontorypress.com

Cover Design by Deranged Doctor Design

Typset by Loose Leaf

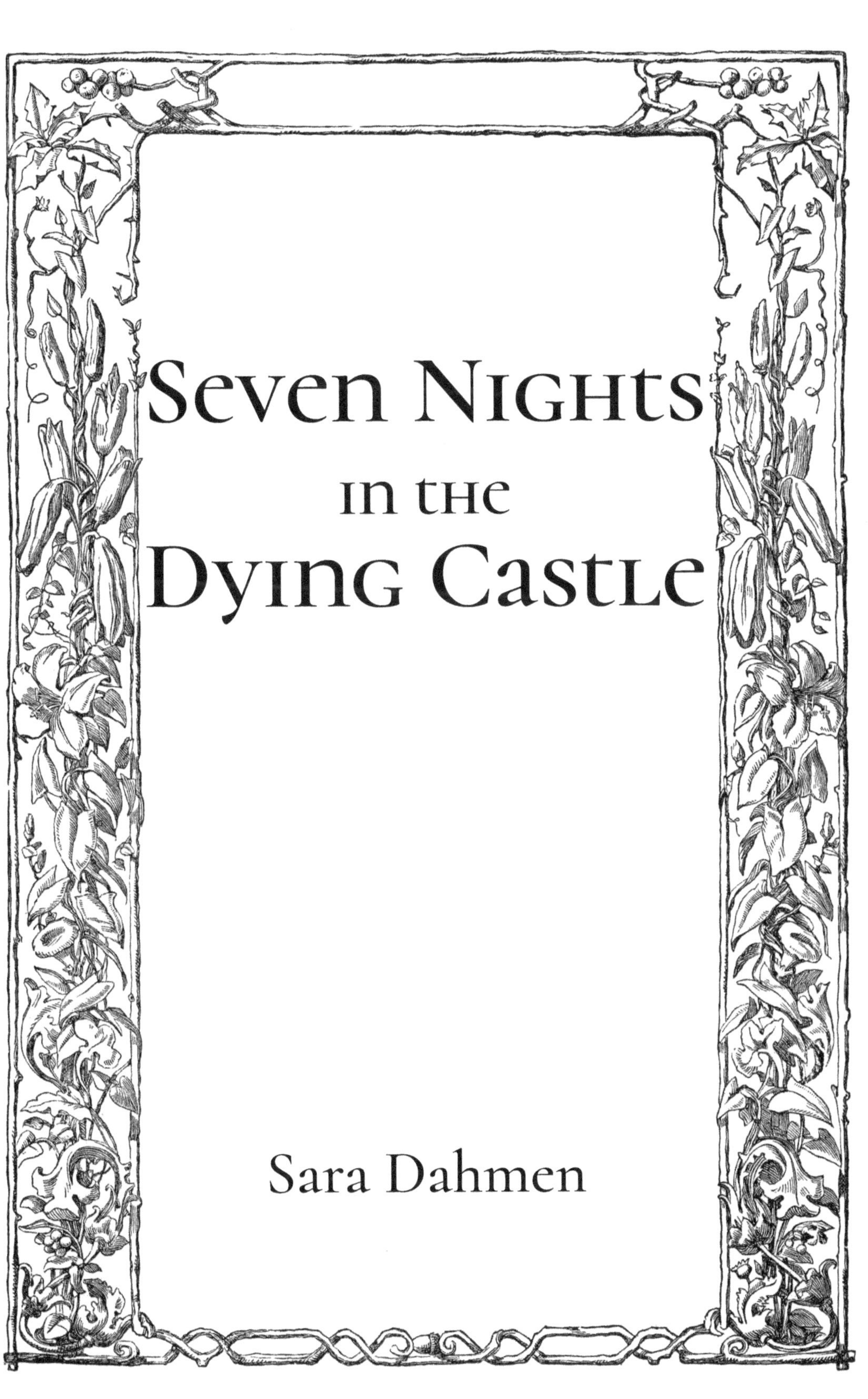

Seven Nights in the Dying Castle

Sara Dahmen

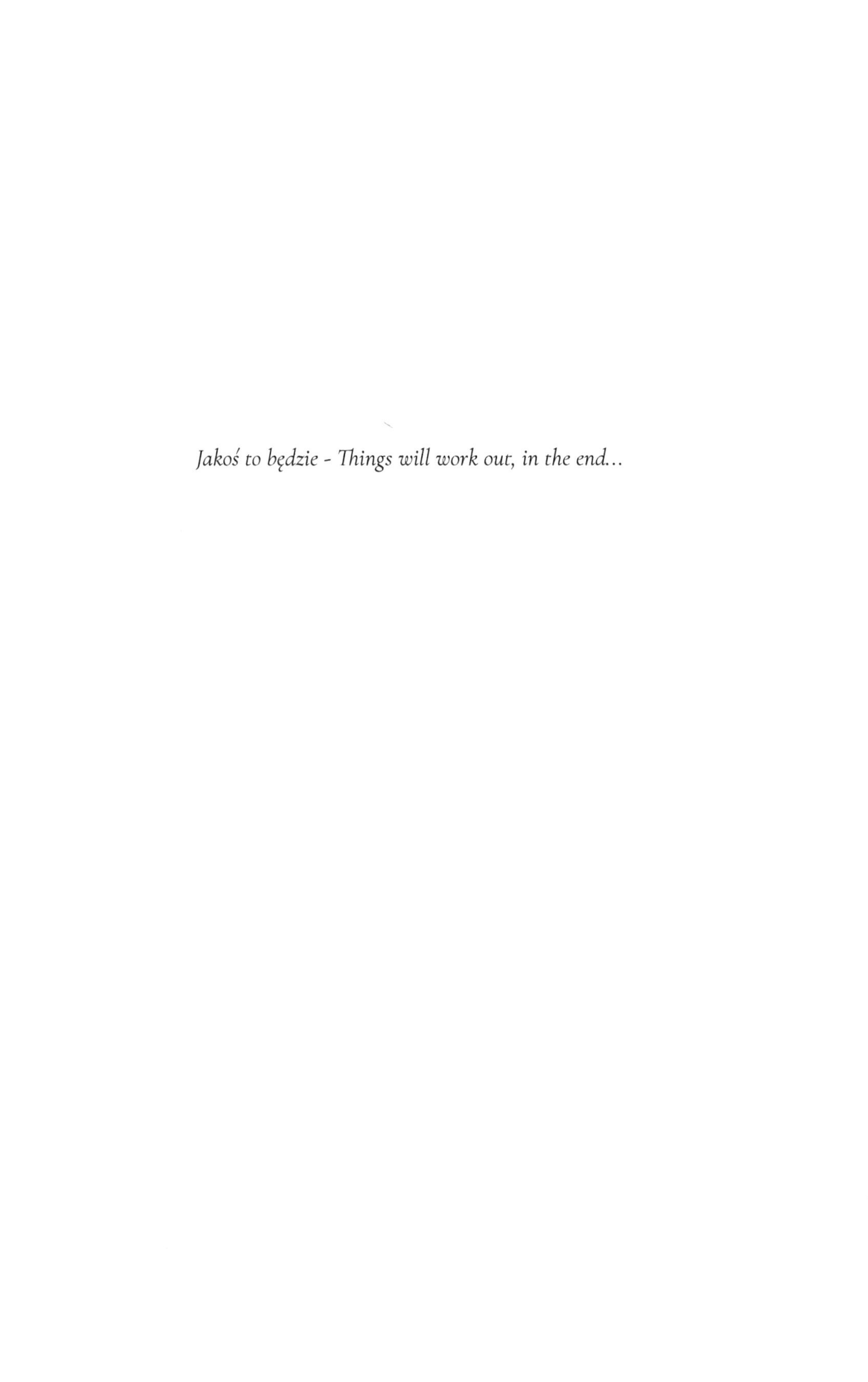

Jakoś to będzie - Things will work out, in the end...

A fire roared in the hearth, and a cauldron set to boil. And then the
creatures approached the bed and pulled her to it.

What a fine maid we'll dine on tonight! said they.

She thought she'd perish in fear, but she remembered the crow's words,
and never uttered a sound.

-- from the old story, *Zaklęty w wronę*

Part 1:
The Meadow

MIÓDSHIRE

THERE WERE RUMORS IN THE *hills...*

They had always existed, as if the hills and the wood and the meadow were linked to the stories, one and the same. Perhaps it started as an old tale, a fireside fright to keep the little ones from getting lost in the thick green pines and the never-ending black forest. She knew tall tales and fairy stories, for she'd recited many from hoarded childhood memory to the children she'd taught in the city. If anyone knew the guts of any piece of lore, it was Zaklina. And she knew they were only fables, without substance and weight.

She had never heard stories spoken with reverence.

And yet, anyone new to the village could sense the truth in the words of these other tales, the repetition giving them life and legitimacy.

She was surprised at the immediacy of the rumors; how quickly she heard of them on her second day to market. The villagers seemed to buzz with the sentences, even unspoken, as if they were necessary to repeat, remind and warn. As if neglecting the stories for a day would be as if they were forgotten, and the forgetting would be more frightening, for their identity would then be lost as well.

It was a sticky sort of story, a web of tales that wound and rewound.

Miódshire nestled near the edge of the wood, which sat like a smoke smudge along the far edges of the great meadow—the meadow of impossible flowers stretching outward, as if it wished to claw itself out from the village. Or maybe the meadow kept the forest at bay. She couldn't decide. The yanking between forest and hill, field and flower was a tight coil, an unseen tangle and fight that pulsed in the sound of footsteps on the stone paths and echoed in the bone. She decided on the third day she would leave as soon as she could, but her sister was soon to give birth and as next of kin since their mother passed—and alone now, too—she needed to give Milena the comforts of a kept home in the month of confinement. It was a nice change, at least – far from the city by the sea, where the mists were heavy and the salt wilted her skirts and pulled her hair into soggy braids. It was a change from the memories at every corner along the quay, where she'd once strolled and laughed, thinking herself settled in love.

"Do you miss them?"

She turned from the door, where, trance-like, she was staring at the wildflowers inching along the far side of the dirt track that served as one of the main roads.

"Who?"

Milena smiled from her bed. "See, my sweet Zaklina, a few days here and already you forget your charges."

"I was thinking of...Mother, and thought you meant our parents. But no, I don't miss being a governess."

"You didn't need to work so much for me."

"It was for me, too. What else was I to do?"

Milena looked down, and picked at the pilling on the old quilt, where faded calico married gnarled wool. Words circled their heads, floating above in the dim rafters, where cobwebs wafted and stuck to tufts of dust and last year's moldy leaves. They were words Milena only asked once, and though likely her curiosity was not sated, she did not ask more.

Zaklina did not dare speak too much beyond the platitudes, for as much as she loved her little sister, the depth of the sacrifices she made of which Milena had reaped the benefit were too many to count anymore. And even as she attempted to do what was right, she always seemed to ruin the outcome somehow anyway.

"Will they take you back in a few months, do you think?"

"I spoke of this in my letter to you. Did you not read it?"

Milena's eyes went wide. "No." And then her cheeks flushed pale cherry, a rose-pink of fresh youth untarnished by fretting and too much salt air. "But I suppose the postmistress forgot to re-seal it and send it home with Marek."

Zaklina sat on the edge of the bed and brushed the coarse fibers of her overskirt. "Ah, so my trials are on display to all of Miódshire."

"It's a small town, and you were always writing from the seaside."

"I see."

"Everyone felt very sad for you."

"They didn't put the blame on me?" Zaklina snorted. "I find that difficult to believe."

"Well, they may not have read every single letter. Sometimes I could intercept the mail cart before it delivered the sacks."

Zaklina could only hope the earlier notes, the ones filled with more shame than sorrow, were the ones Milena had hidden away. She went with the hope. "So this spying accounts for why all in the village seem to accept my arrival without issue? I am the odd, exotic sister. If only they knew..." She would not trouble her sister with the lengthy unspooling of the many difficulties she'd endured to make a meager wage in the previous years, ever since her life had been slashed in half.

Long before her latest disgrace, when she was still a green girl-child and Milena a tiny babe, there were the years of work first as a seamstress in mean quarters and poor light. Then as a hat girl, modeling both men and women's designs as she sewed ribbons and feathers. And then afterwards, when she was discarded and unloved, through a lucky acquaintance, she'd taken on the role of governess. Sleeping upstairs in the cramped attic – hot in summer and freezing in winter – was at the very least better than with the servants in the basement, who shared their beds with cockroaches and their pillows with rats.

"Everyone is kind and friendly to you, I hope?" Milena asked, her voice high like a child's at the end of the question. "You've been welcomed?"

"And more," she said, without offering how. It was near uncanny, the way rumors and stories of Miódshire poured into her from the beginning, but it was all so fast the words fell like drops of iron water into her ears, so that she heard but in hearing became deaf to the true meaning of the tales.

Even now, Zaklina was not sure she could recite these new stories. It was as if they did not attach themselves to her.

As if she were immune.

Only yesterday she went to buy rosehips for tea, and old Mrs. Staryski approached her, a massive basket sagging on her arm, full of importance and an obvious secret air. She offered a cuppa at her house with the un-original idea of handing over a salve for Milena's stretched stomach. It was far-fetched – nearly as far off as Mrs. Staryski's house on the very edge of town, where the meadow met the forest and the village green in a trifecta of grass.

But the morning had been chilly, and it was only Zaklina's second day. She had not known about all the rumors then, or the dangers under them.

Stepping into the cozy front kitchen, where the beams rustled with countless herbs, the stones underfoot were worn to pits, and something dark and oily bubbled in the old cast iron pot with spindle legs, she felt as if this might be what the Jezi Baba's house might be like, though without the chicken legs below.

Mrs. Staryski bustled with importance, setting down her big basket of market goods and wilting greens to put on the tea. There was no air, as she took all of it.

"And I said to Marek when your poor sister took with the babe that the timing was ill, I said to him, as it's too close to harvest, and heaven knows we need every able-bodied person to grab hold of the winter rocks, as they creep so fast into the fields and gardens. But we will take any babe, all babies, always. Did you have a garden in the city? Of course not, how could you, the salt in the air would choke anything green, so I hear – I hope you do like nettle tea? It's good for the whole spirit and the body alike, you know, though don't ask how I know, no one ever asks – oh, and the wild-flowers in the meadow, have you seen? So early, they're always blooming early, and now going strong even with the harvest looming, but still—"

As they both sat over the tea, the loss of sound was suddenly heavy.

Mrs. Staryski heaved her great bosom, inhaling so the busks of her stays creaked and groaned under the cramp-printed calico. "Zaklina, there is something you must know." She spoke with relish and the ease of practice, and the words poured into Zaklina's mind, and were erased almost at the same time, as if unable to stick. Unwilling to let Mrs. Staryski know that she prattled almost brainlessly, she glanced at her tea to hide her boredom, and watched the darkness of the herbs turn moldy.

A spiked caterpillar floated to the top.

When she looked up again, Mrs. Staryski had aged ten-fold, her skin withered but glowing, as if she had eaten gold, but it was rotten. The rumors poured from her blackened teeth, and Zaklina was stuck to the chair, as if tied or subdued by magic.

The hills were old, said Mrs. Staryski, her voice raspy with age and use and broken vocal chords. And the meadow as old if not older, and also the forest older still. The flowers kept the meadow alive, but only just, for within the wilds roamed a beast of such untamed nature that all lived in fear of him. He had not been seen for centuries or more, but surely he did exist for once he was seen leaping from roof to roof, causing little mischief but never-ending horror.

"Long ago?" Zaklina asked, and Mrs. Staryski started, as if forgetting Zaklina sat in the kitchen, too.

"The grandfathers of Miódshire say they heard his roar once, when they were boys hunting in the meadow for toads. Only the once. But we all know of him, for he has lived here always."

Zaklina wondered why people feared him so, if he did no harm. It was the wrong thing to ask. Another worm floated to the top of her tea. She felt an irrational desire to drink it, but also to retch into her apron. Mrs. Staryski pressed forward, hurrying to explain, as if she left an incorrect impression in a youthful mind, and the fear might not take hold properly. Zaklina wanted to explain it would never work, that she feared the tea more than this beast, but her own words seemed muddled and stuck to the roof of her mouth, where they curdled and turned into seeds rolling in her gums.

"You must know, sweet Zaklina—what a funny name it is—that once, long ago, in the time of the grandfathers of the grandfathers, the beast made a demand of the village, that a young maid go to him. We did not allow it, of course," Mrs. Staryski said proudly, overeagerly, with a burning light in her eyes. "And the anger of the hills and the village grew and grew so that none could breathe with it. The air was thick with fear. All were tortured, and water was like grit and the sky was dark as night every day. And then, one morning, the young maid was found dead in her bed, with her heart torn out. It was him, of course. The beast, taking his revenge. And then the sun returned."

Zaklina did not trouble Milena with the story at all, the old protectiveness swelling in her chest. She almost did not believe it really happened anyway. Had she daydreamed the moldy, wormy tea, and the way Mrs. Staryski turned into a hag at her kitchen table? Did the older woman think such a tale would inspire the same fear and worry? Perhaps Mrs.

Staryski thought she had done her duty and warned Zaklina of an ancient scare, much like mothers tell their children of creatures in the night to make them mind.

And it was an odd story, backwards and upside down. It was not the tale of the winds and the maid, or the witches who lived as ducks, or the hyena-man. The tale was not that of the child-bride sent to live with a bear, or the mother who lost her snake-husband, or the swan woman.

There were no spirits, and not a hint of magic.

So she came home with the rosehips and rubbed the special salve on Milena's poor stretched skin and did not think of the rumors again.

Instead, she cooked and told her sister the well-worn tale of the young shepherd and the wila, and then the one of the girl and the crow-prince.

That night, the dream came.

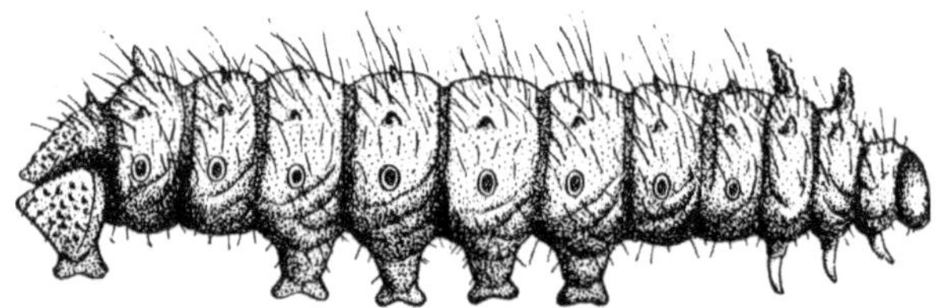

The ramparts of a castle fortress, crumbling yet serene.
> The buttresses crawling with twisted gargoyles.
> Cold.
> Rain.
> Low, heavy clouds scuttled across the sky, black and bleak.
> The stones were lonely.

She felt the coolness of the sleet on her face and the whip of the wind around her skirts and for once they felt thick and rich, unlike the careworn wool of her day dress.

The land around the castle crowded with trees so dark green they were almost midnight, and there was no sound.

None.

As she watched, floating as nothing more than an air sprite, one of the large gargoyles near her uncurled and then unfurled great ebony wings and long planes of muscle and sinew. All of him was the grey and purple of scurried stone—but living.

He stretched and grew, and she saw the power of his wings, the cage of his ribs and how his stomach sunk below his lungs. Her skin felt hot, and her hips heavy, and yet she could not help but feast on his form, breathtaking and sensual though he was a monster.

Claws grew from the bones of his hands and suddenly he towered and seemed ten feet tall. As his overlong arms reached to the heavens, he threw back his head...and roared.

Zaklina jerked awake, sitting up in the bumpy mattress so fast the blood rushed into her forehead and made her eyes cross. Blind and blinking, she squinted in the gloom only to see Milena and Marek bolt upright in their large featherbed.

The roar echoing in her dream was also there, in the night, in the room, in the air.

It bellowed in the wild woods near the village.

It was here.

All she felt was surprise and wonder, and no fear could take hold. The dream itself, and the roar, spoke mostly to her of loneliness.

Milena's pale face shimmered in the gloom of the banked fire and Marek reached under the bed for the long gun, his fingers trembling.

And she knew she was foolish to be unafraid.

A dream did not save a girl from getting her heart ripped out, after all.

"You hear it too," she said instead, to make sure she was awake.

"It's impossible," Marek gasped, his throat and words choking. "It's only an old story, a rumor. Nothing more."

"It is a bear," Milena said, without any conviction.

Marek peered out the square smeared window near the door, shoulders hunched against the night. Milena lit a candle on the nightstand. Zaklina, feeling strangely at loose ends, went to put on some tea though the hour was small.

While the water heated, she stood next to Marek to peer out. In every home across the cobbled street, lights flickered as lamps and wicks were put to flame against the roar that still seemed to knock inside one's head. Soon every house in Miódshire shone from their bone and glass windows. Shadows and grey forms moved back and forth. Zaklina saw the shriveled, wrinkle-drawn faces of Aldona and Gnegon, the closest neighbors, as they too gazed into the dark.

No one ventured outside, even as they stared across yards and into one another's homes. Marek moved, trace-like, and barred the door instead. And as Zaklina watched, the darkness oozed ever closer, snaking along the stones of the roads, flowing and undulating, and soon blocking out the lights, one by one, until all she saw was Aldona's candle. And suddenly, that too, was gone, leaving only a strangling darkness outside, as far as one could gaze.

There was a meeting at the village square the next morning. Everyone gathered as if they had sent a messenger through the town. Yet she knew they had not – or so Zaklina thought, for no child had gone calling through the lanes of a time or place. At noon, everyone drifted toward the center of Miódshire by some unspoken agreement. Zaklina would have missed it, but for Marek standing up from the midday meal and walking out the door without a word.

She grabbed his sleeve just in time, and when he turned, it seemed at first he didn't see her.

"Where are you going? You left all your potatoes."

He didn't glance at the half-full plate at the table, nor even at Milena, who sat placidly eating without lifting her head to listen.

"They are calling a meeting at the square," he said, plainly, as if it were obvious, and kept moving into the wan sunlight.

Zaklina watched Milena, who did not look up at this oddness. Torn at first between her sister and home duties and a buried curiosity, she untied her apron and put on a faded, floppy hat long given over to holes. When she stepped outside, the sun seemed to brighten and then dim, shining through a strange pale haze. She hurried in Marek's footsteps, arriving at the village square and standing on her toes to see over the heads of most.

In the center of the square, on the short stone dais in front of the church steps, stood Mrs. Staryski. Zaklina squinted against the whiteness of the weak sunlight. Mrs. Staryski seemed thinner than the other day, as if the roar had made her peel off layers of flesh in fright. Next to her stood stooped Tanek, the oldest man in town, who worked his black gums with spittle-flecked lips and scratched the dark sunspots on his neck. He stared out at the crowd with his droopy eyes, and as he looked toward her, Zaklina put all her attention on the tips of her shoes. Around her the rumors flew like the buzzing of blackflies, worried of blood and terror, of a coming night that would not end, of the end of summer and flowers and a faded harvest. Zaklina could not understand it—if this beast was so evil a being as they said, he would not walk among them now, in sun and morning dew.

Nothing cruel or twisted enjoyed the beauty of daylight.

Did it?

Mrs. Staryski raised her arms and the bubbling murmurs fell silent, trailing off until only the cadence of a thousand breaths could be heard. Zaklina found herself holding hers.

"We all heard it last night. You were not mistaken. He is returned."

A shudder went through the crowd, one whole rippling movement starting in the center and worked outwards. By the time the tremor reached Zaklina, she felt it quivering on the air and washing over her, but not through her.

"Only a few of you elders remember much, and only Tanek recalls a time when the beast could be heard so near the houses. It is maybe not a worry quite yet," Mrs. Staryski said, but her voice shook, and she glanced across the square at the flower-filled meadow beyond. Her gaze flickered, feather-light and fluttery, as if she counted the number of blooms in an instant, reassuring herself of their nearness.

Zaklina followed her gaze and frowned. Was not the meadow full of flowers? But no – on the skirts of it, along the edge where the forest met the land, the flowers were gone, replaced only by dark emerald grasses that waved to a contrary wind.

The flowers were being eaten. By time or wind, or sheer contrariness of the forest grass. Zaklina felt an odd impulse to run to the new-green lime of the tall fronds, and run her fingertips through the smooth silk of the slippery tips.

But Mrs. Staryski's words broke the shuddering, stuttering silence, and new words and stories whirled in a soft hum in her pause.

"Perhaps it is an ancestral curse. We are doomed."

"He has come back to retaliate."

"It is our fault. We have forgotten the old ways."

"He is hungry – all beasts get hungry."

"It is our honor at stake. Our very souls."

"We cannot allow another to die – it would be a sacrifice! And he will wish more!"

"We cannot stop him. We have no power over the land!"

"But why? Why now?"

"What has disrupted us? What has changed?"

The thoughts and fears came hot and fast, and tripped on each other, and Mrs. Staryski did not speak again, only folded her arms around her middle and watched with bright eyes and slowly fattening hips.

Zaklina pressed her lips over her teeth and no words of speculation came off her tongue. In the middle of a group of young men, Marek stood with others, his best friend Ludoslaw shaking his fist, his neck hot and blotchy-flushed under the ears.

He caught her eye and grinned, but the grin looked manic and full of unquenchable fire, and Zaklina took a step backwards. Ludoslaw made to follow her, but Marek grabbed his shoulder and said something urgent. In the moment of distraction, she turned and scurried through the back lanes toward Milena's house and fought herself so she did not look back. Not so much because of the obvious and unnecessary heat in Ludoslaw's eyes.

Mainly, she did not want to see who watched her depart the crowd.

She baked the rest of the day, watching the sun slowly cover itself with a misty cloak, so it soon was only a blur against a slate sky. Milena knitted with contentment in the bed, her stomach rising like a mountain in front of her and the needles clicking like bones newly stripped of flesh. The sisters did not speak, so every clack of thin steel against wool, or bang of the iron oven door sounded like a crack of lightning.

Zaklina snuck glances at Milena under her lashes. She was glad Milena had married for love, and in the time past, she did not begrudge her sister the silent years of strife, the poor bread and hardened calluses. It was her duty to see her little sister to adulthood and married well, and she had done so. It was her one pride, the singular thing Zaklina had not ruined. Three years had passed since she'd last seen her sister and sent her off to the wilds with Marek as a newly minted husband, with Zaklina's long-hidden savings in their pockets. It was an ill-begotten fortune, forged of moments stolen from under a disapproving husband's eyes, and in the end Zaklina was glad it had not been there, hidden under the rough mattress, for Narcyz to use as one more black mark against her. Part of her believed he had been right in his ire, and she deserved the loss of love and his esteem. She had brought it upon herself, after all. She hardly believed her fortune when he had wed her, and felt little shock when he soon grew disgusted with her presence and mind.

Only after Milena had left for Miódshire had Zaklina finally examined her own life, open for her own pleasing in the void left by the man she had loved and lost, and realized her time had passed. Too old to marry again and ruined at that. She was now a lost cause, a cast-off spinster-woman, good for nothing but the whorehouses and hard labor. With very few respectable avenues open, she'd taken the gentler path of childcare. The children, at least, did not mind when she devoured their schoolbooks with as much delight as they did, and they certainly gobbled the stories of fairy folk and wizard ways Zaklina pulled from old memory and crackling books borrowed from the great libraries in their homes. Many nights were spent in front of a fading fire as she ate the lessons buried in the lore, and memorized the lines of familiar tales. She knew them by heart, both the ones from her past and the new ones recently discovered. Proud of her memory, she shared the tales with glee to any of the children who sat on her lap. They sat with broad eyes and quivering energy as she retold about the cindergirl and her troublesome father, the one of the tinderbox, and the queen of the ocean who lost her love. She retold them all, hiding her own sorrows under the layers of the stories, and able to forget reality in an idea of mystery. But only to the children. She never spoke aloud to the men who hired her, and kept her sentences clipped to the women whose children she raised. Zaklina knew well the slant-eyed distrust given to a woman who displayed her smarts. Had not her beloved Narcyz looked at her the same way, when she had shown him the wiliness of her mind?

She had turned to any task with great care, attempting to squash the curiosity and desires so inherent to woman and so despised in women by men. And it never did good to dwell on the emptiness of her own womb and arms and bed.

Now her sister glowed with all the trimmings of womanhood, while Zaklina still stood over the oven with fire-flushed cheeks and hot burnt fingers and a single bed filled with pokey straw and a lumpy pillow and only the echoes of what had once been.

Sometimes it was impossible not to compare, and at times even harder not to care.

Marek came in, sweat beading off his forehead and his yellowed shirt sticking to the undersides of his arms and the middle of his back.

"Was it a warm day in the fields, husband?" Milena asked, sweet worry in her gentle voice as he splashed water over his face and let it drip over the sideboard.

"Yes," he said, but did not look at her as he wiped down his neck, which prickled with curled hairs, all of which needed a trim.

Zaklina peeked outside the open front door to the hidden sun and wondered if it was hotter than it looked, for the sun's paleness gave off cool silver-gold light instead of the usual late summer heat. She kept her thoughts inside her mind as she served Marek, so her questions did not trouble him further. His hands still shook and his fingers trembled as he tore apart the steamy bread and began to sup, his lunch long forgotten in the earlier meeting of the town.

Zaklina prepared a tray for Milena and took it over, balancing it beside her sister's hips as her belly still grew and got in the way of everything.

"Everyone is unsettled yet," Marek said from the table, and he growled the words, his voice overcome with emotion. "It only gets worse as we do not know what to do."

Zaklina looked at him, where he hunched over the table like a dog guarding his food and home. "Surely we can simply wait and listen."

"And just wait for doom? For him to demand a maid? We will utterly not allow it!"

"But then...the stories say he will come and rip her apart anyway. Why not deliver a woman if she be willing? Maybe he will have no need to tear her apart then," Zaklina reasoned, hoping the quick warmth in her cheekbones went unseen in the eaves by the bed.

"Deliver a woman to a monster!" Marek shot to his feet, his narrow, earth-crusted nails ripping into the crackling sourdough. "What do you take us for? We are not some mindless men, offering up our girls and maids to be devoured if we can stop it!"

The vehemence in his voice shook the house, amplified by the new hoarseness in it. Milena put a hand out to placate him, offering her slim fingers as a lifeline toward her husband. He came slowly to the bed, and took her palm in one of his. As they touched, some of the pent power in his muscles seeped out, and he deflated. After a moment, he bent his head to the bulge of their unborn child and rested his ear against the pulled skin. The tight pinch around his mouth softened, and he looked like the youth who had swept Melina off her feet those years ago, when she was an untried maid, and Zaklina brightly wed.

Zaklina dropped her eyes at the simple display of affection, and instead gazed at her newly baked bread in Marek's hands. The spongy crumb was dirty from his worrying it, and small orange worms, covered in a glistening slime, uncurled and undulated inside each hole.

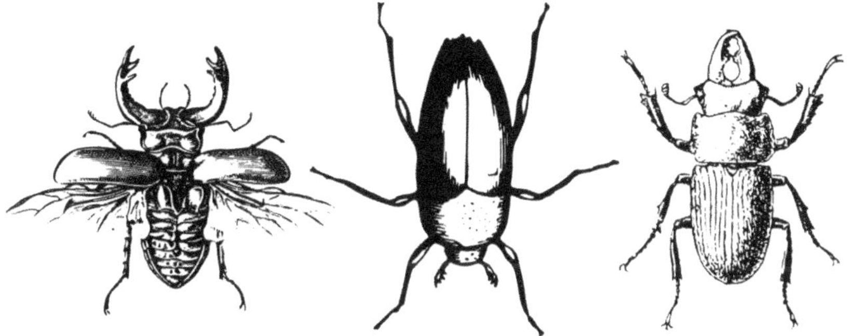

The next days passed in the same smeared blur, except the townsfolk she passed in the market wore deeper lines on their jowls and sunken eyes. Perhaps people did not sleep for worry? The rumors swirled at the market, and she could not buy much as it was often infested with flies or squirming larva or scuttling roaches. Others did not notice the vermin and went about with soured mouths and raised shoulders.

She saw Mrs. Staryski often, drifting between housewives and twisted elders, her eyes less bright and thinner each time. Mrs. Staryski did not look at Zaklina in any recognition, as if their little chat over tea had never happened, and often put moldy fruit in her basket with an unseeing glazed stare.

Zaklina dug into the root cellar for unblemished turnips and small round potatoes while waiting for the garden to ripen in a fall season that dragged too long. She worried over Milena and wished the babe would come early for at least then that unknown would be complete. Marek grew worse with every night, and the other menfolk took to walking the streets with pitchforks and rakes, or hoes and primed long guns.

She watched three youths march past the garden with straight faces, their steps in unison and the flat hard leather soles slapping against the worn stones of the lane with with a strangely soothing ring and beat.

There was nothing yet to take in for dinner, and Zaklina felt at a loss.

For the first time since her arrival, she felt like an outsider, and longed for the soggy air and screaming gulls that grabbed at her crackers and tore at the felt hat she would wear to the wharves with her little charges.

She stared past Aldona and Gnegon's house and their stringy garden to the rich meadow beyond Miódshire. The oily, greasy dark grass crept closer every day, overtaking the bright straw-yellow stalks of wheat mixed with heavy-topped poppies and juicy wild roses and countless other soft flowers and blooms.

Perhaps there...

Unthinking of anything but flavoring a dish with something other than turnips in the vegetable broth that smelled of mildew, she left the garden, clutching her herb knife. As she passed Aldona's house, the old woman's head popped from the small kitchen window. The suddenness of the long, horsey face and dark eyes behind the wavy glass made Zaklina jerk with surprise. Her heart pounded once, twice, and then stuttered as Aldona stared out. She made no noise or motion, and Zaklina inched past, feeling the slither of Aldona's stare on her shoulder blades.

As she passed, she noticed Aldona's carrots and squash rotted purple and yellow and a bruised brown. The pumpkins rolled with pink pustules, and the beans spilled from their sockets, already shriveled. Gnegon pushed scraggly vines this way and that in the back of the garden, uncaring and unconcerned with his ruined harvest. When she moved along, he glanced up, and his eyes were as empty as Marek's each night – or at least, how Marek looked until the worry poured out of him at Milena's silken touch.

The first step into the piss-yellow grass crunched loud – a snap and crack of brittleness underfoot. She stopped. The lads playing leapfrog in the fringes didn't pause their game, and she took that as a sign to go on. Beyond the bent crones in their dripping black rags and their moldy noses as they hunted under the folded lupine and poisonous foxglove for bumpy truffles, she wandered the golden straw as the heady waft of sweetgrass and bee balm crushed below her heel. The powerful scents made her quite listless and slow, and her steps faltered. She began to forget the notion of spices and herbs, and the plan for dinner slipped from her mind, as oily as spoiled lard on a hot day.

As she reached the end of the flowered edge, she paused where the meadow gave way to hunter and hooker green. The grass waved in a breeze of its own, knee-high and thick stalked, wide and sharp-tipped on the ends. In the depths of it, the earth looked black and smoky, rolling as if the entire ground teemed with worms just below the surface.

Zaklina took a deep breath, and in that moment the heady stench of a million flowers cleared as she inhaled the loamy froth of fresh dirt and the clean crispness of simple grass, touched by pine and crusty bark. It was the brightest thing she'd smelled in her life, as if the very rocks were washed with rain and the scent of it lived in the air. Her lungs cleared of fog and salt and expanded so the busks and whalebone of her stays snapped below the faded wool of her bodice.

She took one more stride, and found a private glory in the sudden quiet. As she took each step further into the green, she felt she floated over the rolling hills. It was as if she was chasing the sun, where it disappeared beyond the towering trees on the edge of the meadow, which no longer seemed dark and forbidding, but open and free.

The wind changed direction and blew stronger the further she went from Miódshire, but the meadow was not so hilly as to obstruct the view. The grey and brown thatched houses and their greasy smoke were visible still, as were the shrinking figures of townspeople as they hunted in the straw and flowers on the end of the village.

And as she walked ever closer to the forest, the feeling in her marrow changed once more.

First it was if her blood curdled in her bones, and then ran clear, and then everything felt hollow. The sap-veins of the nearest trees pulsed with her lifeblood. The stalks of each blade of grass bounced with delight as she passed. And yet, it was all alone. She felt the loneliness of the dreamy castle in her limbs, as it seemed to pull at her and pick at her eyes.

Was she in her dream?

Was she not in the meadow?

She clung to herself, and hugged her arms to her chest, squeezing the careful strength in her biceps and the ligaments of her fingers under the rock of her elbow. She was still she: Zaklina, the elder daughter who served, who did what it took no matter the cost, who did not care for sacrifice, who was determined and strong and did not shirk from any task. Who had loved and lost, and yet still survived the heartache.

Who was too much, and never enough, and yet still somehow found the strength to live.

She paused for breath.

And in that breath, everything went upside down. Or was it right-side up?

The axis of the world tilted under the pinched lasts of her shoes, and for a moment she thought she might fall over and faint, though she had never done so before. Perhaps it was the power swirling around her. The sun darkened and the clouds twirled low and heavy and grey. The wind changed once again and came in sudden forceful gusts. It tore at her many layered skirts and yanked the pins from her wilted hair, curling the edges so the edges stabbed her eyes. For the briefest of seconds, she reveled in the wild. The change of light made the colors bleed, and the grass turned emerald from lime and then a deeper green and the forest curdled to such an unrelenting black so she finally knew where the woods begot its name.

And in the silence between the gusts, she felt him, as if she could sense him crouching on the edge of the trees. Considering, weighing...and then he was there. Behind her. In the daytime.

She shuddered, because she suddenly knew in a moment the towns-folk would see them, and come screaming and shouting and with their big powdered, goose-greased long guns. And she didn't want anyone to see this – not this first moment when her dream became a reality. For as they stood there, unspeaking, she could taste his sorrow and the long days weighing on his shoulders like iron. She felt the hardness of his being and yet understood he could be soft, too, and that his roar was only one of frustration, not hate. But—how could she be so sure of it? Zaklina wanted time to stop, so she could examine this unwieldy truth, which did not follow logic, and had never been scratched in any book.

Because she did not immediately turn, she did not shirk or scream. She took a gulp of air and lowered her eyes. In the oft-shifting winds, his scent came to her, and it was not unfamiliar – wet stone and rock and earth.

She spoke softly, then, into the air and still away from him. "Milord?"

"I am no Lord; you know this."

At the sound of his voice, she felt warmth creep into her – an unusual reaction, as she had not realized she shivered. His tone was surprisingly mellifluous, deep and throaty and tinged with an unknowable accent. The timber of it unfroze her, and she could move and look up to finally see his face in the gloom and haze of the lowering clouds.

Had her dream not warned her, she would have recoiled no matter the gentleness of his voice. She now only gazed quietly at the dark fur-hair cascading down his shoulders, hanging heavily as a mane, yet somehow, strangely immobile. He was still as broad as she remembered, and his height certainly taller than a man, but he was no giant, and he had no gargoyle wings.

"You must know I am a monster," he continued solemnly. "Do you not scream?" His eyes were obsidian and unreadable, and his face too foreign in shape with the strange jaw line and deep sockets.

The oddness of it all made her speak out of turn, and unlike a lady. "Why should I scream when you have been a vision to me already? Surely you sent the dream."

Shock oozed into his cheeks and the long line of his mouth – that at least she could read as if he were human. His mouth opened, revealing blue-white teeth, and he inhaled carefully.

A shot rang out behind them and whizzed past their ears in a rusty rush.

She spun to face the next, her hands raised against the bullets, but no more came, only the shouts and yells echoing across the distance. Two and two dozen of the town slashed through the petals of flowers, fully shredding heavy blooms, with Mrs. Staryski coming last, wailing a loud, renting scream.

She had not heard any of them, had not seen them out of the corner of her eye as they sprinted to rescue her.

He turned away. For the first time, she saw him move as an animal might—swift and immediate and cat-like. In a half-moment he was gone, disappearing first into the trees and then beyond into the deep recesses of the gnarled branches. The long grey cape swirled with him as he left, wing-like indeed.

Zaklina squinted after him, as if she might see him in the gloom, but it was without luck and the fastest of the boys reached her breathless, his gun still half-loaded.

"Miss Zaklina! Did he hurt you? Was he to steal you away?"

She was dumb, numb, and the lad's voice scratched at her ears. She shook her head to clear it, and he seemed to take it as answer, though dubiously so.

And then all silence was breached, for it was as though half of Miódshire came to her aid, all manner of weapons in their hands from pitchforks to dented muskets.

In the midst of them all stood the sobbing Mrs. Staryski, her wide apron covering her wizened head and drooping hair as she moaned over and over. "I have lost my touch—I forgot! I forgot to warn her! It is my fault, I did not warn of the meadow. Oh heavens, oh my heart!"

Some looked at Mrs. Staryski with troubled frowns, shaking their heads as if to dislodge the words. Others did not seem to hear her wailing, and crowded Zaklina's space and touched her fingers and hands carefully, like the whispers of a spider's web, until she trembled and wished to scream, too. Raising her arms, so all had to step away, she moved toward Mrs. Staryski. The men parted before her like water before a rock, and when Mrs. Staryski took down her snot-covered apron, her eyes were red-rimmed and dirt crusted in the corners of her eyes.

Zaklina blinked once. Twice.

At first she saw the robust woman, round and fat who gave her tea not a few days earlier. Another blink showed her the twisted woman more near a skeletal hag. And then once more, a woman in black, with skin shriveled and yellowed rags twisted round and round...

All versions held worry and fear, as if somehow Zaklina held power, but that could not be true. She was only just arrived at Miódshire, and did not know its people or its ways. With a thousand questions burning in her throat, she instead put a hand out to Mrs. Staryski and then carefully laid a palm on the short woman's shoulder. The visions settled into one – the Mrs. Staryski of yesterday. A rotund woman gone to seed, losing the flesh of youth, with grizzled hair and deep lines around her mouth.

"It is no fault of yours," Zaklina said, and her voice rang like a bell across them all, carried on the wild, whippy wind. "I wandered alone, so unseemly for a young woman. Please do not worry. As you can see—as you can all see—I am unharmed."

Mrs. Staryski collapsed inward, her chest shrinking, but it seemed more with relief than anything else. Zaklina frowned, uncertain what she said to change the dynamic.

Had there just been a test?

If so, she felt she had failed.

With her words, everyone surged forward again, propelling each other back toward Miódshire as if a wave onto themselves. Zaklina was carried forward on it, and soon the crunch of the yellowed grass and fat flowers met her nose. Within the crush of humanity, and the stink of putrid teeth and clogged bowels, mumblings and hiccups of superstition floated.

"You see, the sun still does not return. Has he hexed it?"

"Will our crops now wither? We will starve!"

"He will be wanting her, to be sure."

"We must stand firm!"

"Suppose he wrecks hell upon the village now? It is the beginning of the curse again!"

"It is her fault – she wandered into the deep grass and woke him for the first time in an era."

"The roar was before this – he has been awake these days."

"She has brought this upon us!"

"He is anxious."

At this, Zaklina could not help but answer. Frustration simmered in her blood. "He is not anxious. He is lonely." She was right, she knew it. There were creatures and monsters always. Every story said so. They were not always evil, and some actually good. They all simply wanted the company of a maiden.

Her declaration was met impassively, and with no small amount of disbelief. Old Gnegon shook his head at her, sorrowful and dull. Marek's friend Ludoslaw gave her a sad sort of smile, as if troubled she could not grasp the issue.

"He is a monster," Ludoslaw said, as the group waded out of the brassy grass and back into weedy lawns. "We all saw him. We are amazed at your bravery, to be sure. But you are not from here; you cannot understand."

He took her elbow and squeezed, and the muttering of fear and anger washed over her. She turned once more to refute it, but the hunched backs of the men were all about, and none would meet her eye.

Only Mrs. Staryski did, and she stood a little taller and her cheeks bloomed a new pink. She grinned, displaying grey-black teeth, and gave Zaklina a leering wink.

Ludoslaw stayed long enough to eat supper with Marek, and the two men sank into their beers. As their talk grew lower and their eyes turned to slits, the bread between their hands turned green with fuzzy mold, and soon enough flies buzzed about and laid their larvae in the holes of it.

Often, they glanced at Zaklina, and every time they did, they looked more surly and they curled ever lower to the table and their dark ideas grew so they seemed to take shape in the coiled smoke of Ludoslaw's pipe.

Zaklina took Milena stale soup in chipped crockery. She had forgotten to choose herbs in the trance of the meadow and then of the gargoyle creature, but her sister did not complain.

Milena met Zaklina's gaze as she picked up the spoon. "Did it truly happen? What the men say?"

"They all gossip like old women," Zaklina said. "It only served to make Marek upset, and he's already wound so tight. They all are."

"I can feel it," Milena said quietly, looking down at the broth. "Every time the door opens, it is like drowning. He brings it to me, and I feel I must somehow make it go, or else it will infect the babe." She put a slender finger in the center of her hill-like belly.

"It's good of you to draw it out."

Milena looked at her with eyes wide and brown. "I never knew it, I swear, sister. I did not understand what I undertook when I wed him, or what a life here meant. I did not realize I would become one with them all, that my thoughts and feelings—"

The door burst open, as if the flaking forged hinges broke in their own brittleness. Marek and Ludoslaw rose up slightly from the table, but did not say a word against the womanly intrusion. Mrs. Staryski stood on the threshold, a basket wilting on her flesh-droopy arm.

"I've come to see how our sweet mother fares," she crooned, and stepped into the short house without concern, as if she had done so dozens of times before. "We must take care of each child like it is our own, don't we? After all, it takes a village to raise one, so."

She waddled over and heaved the basket onto the bed, near crushing Milena's feet. Black dirt crumbled onto the bedding. Zaklina made to brush it off, but Mrs. Staryski's bulk moved in the way.

"Now then," she said, sounding more jovial than she had in days, almost like the jolly woman who invited Zaklina for tea. "What will it be to ease your womb?"

Milena put both palms over the rise of her stomach. Mrs. Staryski gently moved them, then placed both of her own over the great mount. Zaklina stood by, apart and unable to speak a word in comparison. How could she? She had never carried a child nor borne one, and likely never would. That privilege passed to Milena alone, and Zaklina would not begrudge the only family left to her, no matter how her curiosity ached to know the mysteries of womanhood. She would not tell Milena the dark wonders of her heart, in the deep night when the gentle sighs and grunts belied the lovemaking of her sister and her husband.

She would not dare give voice to the lusty wanderings of her fingers and soft suggestion of what she had lost.

To any man—and woman—she had given up such delight when she had strayed too far from her own hearth to books and stories, allowing an ambition and a hunger to learn cloud her.

Yet now, even in her ignorance, she detested the way Mrs. Staryski touched Milena's stomach, with ownership and surety. Zaklina's arms quivered and she held them behind her back, so she would not grab the older woman and thrust her outside. As Mrs. Staryski prodded Milena's belly, it turned purple, then golden bruised, like a too-ripe peach.

"What have you done to her?" Zaklina cried out. Loud. The men at the table paused their mutterings and all eyes were on her. Her skin shivered and then burst into goosebumps, as if small wiggling worms niggled just under her flesh. She hugged herself, and refused to leave her sister's side.

Mrs. Staryski offered the same crotchety grin and opened her hands, so the over-concerned Marek could see for himself. Even Milena sat up to look. The skin looked normal, unblemished.

Zaklina blinked many times, clearing her sight.

It had been there. She was sure.

"I have done nothing but worry on the unborn babe, and to check the mother's needs." Mrs. Staryski picked up her basket, which now burst with yarn and knobbly knitting. "But I see your sister-in-law has it in hand and I'm not needed." She nodded at Marek and fair pranced to the door. The air thickened. Zaklina was afraid to look at anyone, feeling that somehow she had put herself in an untenable position.

"She's not from here. She doesn't know you're the midwife," Marek said, sounding choked, his eyes lined with broken blood vessels as he leapt to block Mrs. Staryski from departing. "Please, be sure my wife is comforted."

Mrs. Staryski minced backwards toward Milena's side. "Well. If you're certain." The smell of sugar rot and eggy sulfur wrapped around Zaklina as she passed.

"You're needed," Marek said, breathless with relief, sagging on the door-frame. "Of course you're needed."

Zaklina watched as attention poured into Milena. She did not watch where Mrs. Staryski touched, afraid to see what she might. Instead, she could only be aware of how thin her sister's arms seemed to be, the flesh sucking toward the bone, leaving the fragile blue veins bulging and criss-crossing in her translucent forehead.

"It's nearing your time," Mrs. Staryski said at the last, patting Milena's hand. "Any time now, I would think. A few days at most. How thrilling to have more children underfoot. A village thrives on its babies, you know. It is what keeps us young and alive."

"Alive?"

Zaklina had not meant to speak out again, but it was too late. The gazes bored holes into her skin. She rubbed her elbows and stared at the table, where all her hard-worked potatoes and bread festered under blue-and-white bumpy mold, and a long-legged spider danced.

"What is it you worry on, dear?" Mrs. Staryski crooned. "You are afraid of the monster in the hills? The beast in the forest? Do not worry. He won't come too far into the meadow, and he has never tried to steal a baby." She glanced at the menfolk, who looked wary and fearful. A small smile fit into the corners of her thick cheeks as she turned back to Zaklina. "I suppose you must be fearful, though – he has singled you out. I shouldn't wonder – you are new to these parts and don't know the ways of it. He thinks you are easy prey."

"I won't have it!" Marek said, spittle forming on his gums. "She is my wife's sister, the only blood left to her family. On my honor, Zaklina will be guarded."

"And I will help," Ludoslaw stood. "It will be my honor as well."

Zaklina's stomach curdled with bile as she tried not to feel Ludoslaw's intense gaze on her face. "I'm not afraid of the beast," she said, looking straight into Mrs. Staryski's eyes. "I am afraid of dying from lack of food to eat. And Milena, too. She's wasting to bones."

"But it's near harvest," Mrs. Staryski said calmly. "And there is always plenty to eat. We never want for anything here, as long as everyone works and is willing to do their part to protect one another and share what we have. This is not such a novel notion."

Zaklina forced herself to silence, though the questions and frustrations pounded inside her head as she shuttered her very nature. She felt the green-and-brown bile still sitting in her gullet, clawing up and stinging her throat. If she looked at the table, she would be unable to stop from mentioning the decaying food and inedible produce.

Mrs. Staryski gazed back for a long moment, and Zaklina was certain no one breathed in the space of it. And then Mrs. Staryski grinned, and was more round and merry than before.

"That settles it, then," she said calmly. "You will be guarded by the menfolk, so that your heart is not torn from your ribs. We will not let it happen again."

Zaklina opened her mouth to speak against the idea, but as she did, it was as if cotton stuck to the back of her throat. The words, like the old rumors, spun around the room and felt solid. Marek and Ludoslaw nodded and Milena did, too, though her brow creased down the middle as she did so. Mrs. Staryski left without another sound, and the room filled with the scent of freshly bloomed honeysuckle, though it was well out of season. Everyone's sinew seemed to melt with relief, and even Zaklina was unable to resist the calmness, even if it was tinged with something tight she could not name.

It was only later, when the menfolk went to the local tavern to likely overeagerly spread the word of Zaklina's guard, and Milena slept fitfully and her stomach growled, that the spell of honeysuckle withered on the night air. Zaklina turned back to the table to discover all the food had curdled black and grey. When she touched the newly baked bread, it crumbled under her fingertip, and turned to nothing but dust on the chipped china plate.

The hours crawled and the weather sagged beneath boiling iron skies. Far above the black trees, a line of white separated the rippling pearly clouds from bruised ones. The wind rose, then fell. In the stillness, a body would smell the headiness of peonies and poppies, roses and aster, and all manner of riotous buds in the yellow meadow grass, long overdue to die.

Zaklina stared at them from the back garden through the narrow slates of the gate. Beyond the bristling straw of the flowered meadow was the oily green of the grass that kissed the shadow of the trees. And though nothing bloomed there, Zaklina found herself yearning for it. She imagined climbing the gentle hills of the meadow, until her toes curled in the rich simpleness of the grass, and thought if only she could get there that she would finally fill her lungs once more.

And maybe...perhaps he would come to her again.

But she would never leave the tiny patch of land belonging to Marek and Milena now. Not without a clutch of guards. Children – most of them—many only old enough to carry a sharpened stick, which made the entire pantomime feel like nothing but a game. Yet a game they all took seriously, for if she took one step out to the street, they teemed about her so that she was always surrounded by bodies and makeshift weapons.

Zaklina could not understand it, could not make them see that such a guard was nothing more than a farce. Should a monster truly roam, these young ones would be easily ripped apart.

When the harvest could spare menfolk later in the day, they would take a turn at her side. Even Marek would stand guard inside the house, prowling the corners as if the mice and cobwebs were a danger waiting to destroy her. She could not ignore the rising ire that floated in the very eyeballs of all she looked at. It was as if they could not see her. It was as if they could only see her as a threat, or perhaps the Gargoyle himself as one.

She did not know if they knew the difference.

All she knew was that she was forbidden from wandering beyond the confines of Miódshire's borders. Her guards would point their weapons or sticks at her if she attempted to get close to the tall grasses and blooms, even if she begged it. It would only be for Milena, she pleaded. For herbs for her sister's wasting body. For Zaklina's own stomach, which cramped and shriveled with the lack of food.

None seemed to care. Or to hear her.

With the passing of another night, and day, it soon became clear that all were starving. They ate the molded bread and crunched the pitted carrots, but it was not uncommon to see people turning to retch in the market right after they stuffed a rotten tomato into their wobbly teeth. The many children who stood around Zaklina as she pried with a dull knife into the earth for a clean potato for Milena to eat came with bloated bellies of air and dusky circles under their eyes.

"Are you hungry?" she asked them.

"Everyone's hungry, but there's plenty to eat," said the eldest, a child called Edek.

"That doesn't make any sense," she pointed out. "It is a contradiction in a sentence. You say there is food everywhere, but look at this. It is unable to nourish. It is all rotten and fouled. No one can eat this and be well." She pulled up an entire potato plant, which came easily out of the loam. The ends of the roots, where potatoes had once lumped underground, were nothing but withered stumps, with fluffy white chunks of pus clinging to it.

The children blinked. Edek reach out, his hand curled as if expecting to hold a massive potato in his hand, which only came away slimed with the white, gooey mold. He stared at his palm and swallowed so loudly it made Zaklina shudder.

"Do you see?" she asked, not unkindly. It was not the children's fault their parents had given them this strange task. "This is the way of all the vittles. It has been—"

"Like this since the beast appeared to you, yes."

Zaklina jumped to her feet. The potato vines crumbled under her boots.

Mrs. Staryski stood by the fence, looking thinner than the day before, but more robust than anyone else just the same. She gave Zaklina a careful look, one that held no emotion at all. "You see, it is the monster's doing. He wishes you for himself. He wishes to destroy you, and as we are now protecting you, he attempts to blight our crop."

"So you admit there is nothing to eat."

"I did not say that. Only that he tries to do this. There is, of course, plenty to eat."

"If you wish to eat bread that turns green and fruit filled with maggots," Zaklina said, punching her fists on her hips. She felt her heart speed up, as if it was thrilled with the challenge, and for the first time in many weeks, her mind felt her own. "It is food, yes, and there is plenty, but it goes off and putrid at once, and no one can eat that."

"It seems it is a matter of taste, then. Perhaps you are so city-fine that you are too good for the simple fare of our little village."

"Suppose we ought to speak to the beast. He may tell us what is really going on in Miódshire. It seems it would only take some simple words, a conversation, a discussion. So much worry, unnecessary..." Zaklina floated her hand over the children's heads.

Mrs. Staryski deflated as Zaklina spoke, but as she glanced at the little ones, she gave a heave of her sagging bosom and shook her head. "Well. You cannot reason with a monster." She moved off, a strange new limp to her gait.

"Then we will starve!" Zaklina called softly.

Mrs. Staryski froze between steps, and when she turned, she near fell over with imbalance. Her eyes slowly sunk into her skull, and age lines lightly edged the roundness of her nose. "There is a time for sacrifice. Be grateful you are protected."

"But I don't need—want it!" Zaklina protested. "All this takes is some thinking, a plan. There is nothing to be afraid of."

"Do not be foolish," Mrs. Staryski said, looking suddenly very grey and tired. "Of course there is. Look around you. Can you not feel the fear?"

Zaklina looked beyond Mrs. Staryski, at the people of Miódshire slowly dragging in the harvest to their homes. Baskets leaked with burst peaches, where hornets swarmed and suckled. Squashes dotted with spongy brown spots tumbled with mushy apples, and the turnips wore rusty rings of mildew. Though everyone exclaimed over their bounty, it was done with a muted fear, and Zaklina shook her head.

"They don't fear the monster. They fear they will starve. It is separate."

"It is not separate!" Mrs. Staryski hissed, her eyes cracking with yellowy jaundice. "It is linked!"

"I think it is a lie. The stories don't match. It is all just rumors, in the end, and they will do more harm than anything else."

"It is you who causes any trouble, what with your ideas and accusations. You'll see!" Mrs. Staryski suddenly spun and half-walked, half-limped away, her head high and basket swinging.

The children let out a sigh, and went back to surrounding Zaklina, the potatoes forgotten. And from the vines at her feet poured a thousand tiny black bugs, running in circles and spreading out, infecting every crevasse of the garden. She cried out without meaning to do so, and Edek turned in circles, his stick raised.

"What is it? Did you see the beast?" he asked, his voice higher with hidden agony. "Is he coming across the meadow for you?"

"No." Zaklina peered under the garden's blight-frosted leaves. "It is only all the hive beetles. There are so very many..."

Edek's fear seemed to infect the others, and when the parents came to collect their children, the fear bled into them, too. So they all looked sideways at Zaklina, and the menfolk muttered and played a quick game of dice to see who must stay near her over the next hour.

It was Ludoslaw who drew the lot, and while he didn't seem angry, he was not pleased, either. Still, she thought to attempt a new direction with him. She had to try something, or risk letting Milena starve, and herself as well. And Ludoslaw had—until this moment—looked at her with something that hinted at interest.

"You are much stronger than the children," she said, when they were alone, walking to the late afternoon market. It was a futile exercise, as she already knew there'd be nothing there to take home to eat, but it allowed her to leave Marek's house and stretch her knees and hips. A garden could only be managed so long before one started to see worms even where they did not exist.

"That is an apt description of me," Ludoslaw said, his mouth twisting. "I should think you would be safe with me."

"Certainly. And if I am guarded...and if we could go search for fresh herbs...then I might make both you and my sister a good broth tonight. If you...wish to stay for dinner again." As she made the offer, the bones cracked in her clenched fist. She had not meant it to sound like a girlish proposition, with strings and romance attached. But too late. Ludoslaw turned to her with sparkling eyes.

"You are offering?" He seemed genuinely interested, and if she minded her ill-gotten and newly unmarried status overmuch, she would have been glad for the attention. Instead, the notion crawled on her spine, and she wished she could eat the words back.

"I am saying I would like to make a good new soup. But we'd need herbs, freshly cut, to make it worthwhile. Will you wander with me?"

She took a step to the side, the cobblestones and mud slippery under the lasts of her boots, but she dug in her heel and took another. Ludoslaw followed without looking, and she smiled up at him. If he would play the game, she would use it. Her stomach squeezed, and she thought of the lifeblood draining out of Milena and her unborn niece or nephew and took a deep breath.

It had only been a few days under watchful eyes, and already she felt herself shrinking under the constant attention. What were they waiting for? The Gargoyle to appear and rip out her heart? To starve? To build themselves to a frenzy of bloodlust, which they were doing already? Or for her to make a dash for the meadow and the cool tall green of the far hills?

And escape...

...if only to find clean zucchinis and glistening berries.

"I think the harvest seems to worry people, same as the monster who roams. Perhaps there is just some game afoot, and if we can find the root of it, we will know the truth of it all. Maybe it's only a misunderstanding that rots our beets and pumpkins and crumbles the corn in its husk. Maybe—"

She took one more step, and her foot crunched the dry yellow of the meadow. Ludoslaw seemed transfixed to the spot, and for a moment she thought she had broken through his blindness.

And then she took another step. A single rose smashed under her, and the musk of it surrounded them. Ludoslaw's face clouded over, and he looked thin and haggard as he leapt to grab her. "Watch out!"

His shout drowned in the roar blasting through the hills and along the grass, like a bell that rang with rage. The town folk around them cowered, and Ludoslaw gripped his long gun with trembling hands and went down on a knee.

Zaklina stared about, then up at the leaden sky as if Gargoyle himself would drop out of it.

But no – it was something else.

They were as a swarm.

She was suddenly surrounded by several of the men, and their wives in wilting kerchiefs, and the children with their pointed sticks. The hysteria of their breathing, the buzzing of their mutters, the flurry of their hands as they raised and lowered their arms sent her senses reeling, and she sniffed the air as if looking for something unmentionable but missing. All she could smell was the fetid, food-crowded teeth of her neighbors and the heavy staleness of weeklong sweat, made more pointed with the fear.

The mass became a mob. As they reached for her under the pretense to protect, they tore at each other's cheeks and rent their arms with crusty nails. They pawed her skirts and ripped a hole in her sleeve, and a chunk of hair was yanked from behind her ear. They clawed at their weapons and scratched their own skin with black iron shovels and gleaming gun butts as the roar continued to ebb and echo, pulsing just under the surface of their muscles and sinews. Even Zaklina felt the frenzy, though she stood apart from it as questions poured through her marrow and erased all the warnings in Mrs. Staryski's stories.

A cry rent the breathing and the mutters. It was Edek, blood and liquid pouring to his neck. A ruby hole glistened where his eye was punctured from one of the other children's sticks.

The sight of blood arrested them all.

The children fell to each other with the sharpened ends, pushing and kicking as they chose sides in a fight that they believed was Zaklina's, but really seemed to be between one another. The parents tore the children apart, screaming both against the monster and Zaklina, against any child not their own.

In the middle of the melee stood Edek, whose high wails rose above the murmurs. And his mother, whose screams were louder than the shouts of the men and women who bound Zaklina with their bodies.

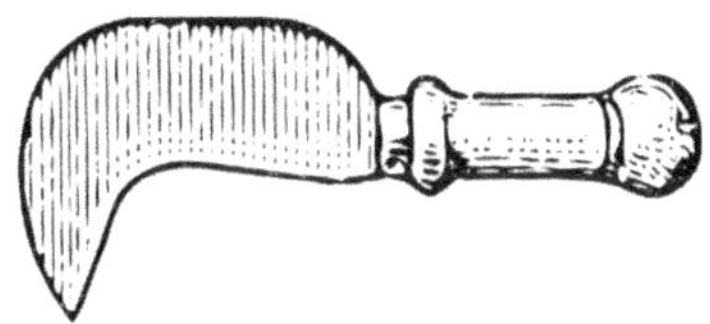

Old Gnegon walked her home, and she was relieved Ludoslaw did not join them. Without the herbs she had mentioned, there would be no new broth anyway. The hunger ate at her insides, stabbing into her stomach so swiftly it stole her breath. Gnegon plodded on, gripping his old garden hoe, and did not notice her staggering.

"You be alright, then?" Gnegon asked, pausing at Marek's house.

"Of course I shall."

"But you have no guard now, not til young Marek returns. I should go and get Ludoslaw back."

"Oh, he is to be back, never fear," she said smoothly, surprised at the honeyed ease of the lie sliding out. "I promised him a meal at the hearth."

"Did you?" Gnegon glanced inside the gloomy house, peering through the thick windows. "I suppose he's on his way then."

"Yes. Or Marek will be here before then, too, surely. I don't want to keep you from your own home. It'll be alright. Besides, the sun is still awake. Nothing truly evil can happen in the daytime, can it?"

The reasoning felt sour as she spoke it, but the old argument still seemed to make sense and have sway. He turned after a beat then, and muttered to himself as he walked across the street. Aldona waited for him at the door, her arms twisted together tightly and pressed against the dough of her used stomach. When Gnegon entered, Aldona glared over at Zaklina.

The look poured a river of discomfort through her, and she quickly shut Milena's door.

"Nothing at the market, then?" Milena's carefully gentle voice trickled through the dusk piling in all edges of the house. "Not a bite? Will you bake some new bread then, at least, sister?"

"No. I won't." Zaklina glanced out the window once, then scurried to Milena's side. "There is no use. It will only turn to dust." She took her sister's hand and squeezed the narrow fingers, which were ice and fire at the same time.

"What?" Milena blinked up at her. "There is nothing to eat?" Her spare hand trailed a pattern of curls and leaves across the overstretched skin of her belly, the pale linen not able to hide the bulge or the dark streak dividing it.

Zaklina reached across and touched the top of the unborn child. Under her fingertips, the skin felt like pebbled rock, and the cloth slithered so it seemed the babe roiled in Milena's womb.

"We must hurry," Zaklina whispered, glancing back at the quiet door again, her blood half-frozen and her muscles ready to spring. "We must work together, or we will die, the lot of us. You, me, the child."

"No!" Milena's eyes went dark. "Not this child! Everyone wants it, all are celebrating another birth. There have been too few..."

"There won't be a birth without vittles, and there will be no vittles while the town's crop decays on the vine. I must go to this monster – I must deliver myself to him, to barter for food, for an end to his anger."

"He will tear out your heart!" Milena gasped. "You cannot go!"

"I don't believe it," Zaklina said. "I won't. I've no intention of allowing him to hurt you or your child, and no intention of sitting here and doing nothing. I will go to him, and let him do with me as he will. It's all linked, somehow, though the true reason eludes me. If I go, there will be plenty, and you will not die."

"You cannot mean this."

"I must discover for myself what it is – if it is he who holds power over the crops and blights the harvest, or if it is something else. You must help me escape. You must help me keep Marek and Ludoslaw and the other men from seeing me depart."

"You always do this," Milena said softly. "I do not understand why you were given the mind of a man. It suits you, though it harms you. Why do you chase it?"

Zaklina could not find the words to explain. She did not rightly know, either. Was it because questions poked at her mind even when she did not seek them? Was it because she could not hear rumors and believe them so wholeheartedly? Because she resisted a crowd, and preferred to go the opposite way always? Was it because she had filled her mind with other stories, and had layers of folklore printed on her soul? Was it because Mrs. Staryski's tales did not stick in her mind, and bled out of her memory so only a wondering was left?

Was it because she was unnatural?

She stood and looked behind them once more at the window and door. Beyond the fat, plastered walls came the calls of the men and field workers, and the clattering of tiny donkey hooves tripping past. Time grew short.

"I don't think the monster will plunder or rape me. If anything, I think he wishes companionship. Had he wished to abduct me, he had ample time in the meadow."

Milena stared. "But...you have heard the stories. The young maid with her heart torn out...you would be like the innocent bride..." She looked up at Zaklina's face, and her mouth opened further, surprise and disbelief etching across her forehead. "But you are eager for this! I can see it in the strange glow of your face! You are serious, this idea is like your wedding day. Sister! This monster has bewitched you!"

"It is not I who I believe bewitched," Zaklina said, the heat of a flush spidering across her chest and up her neck. She rubbed behind her ear, where the patch of flesh oozed with the loss of hair from earlier. A soft, unbidden thought crisscrossed her mind. The monster might not want her. She may not be beautiful enough. What a very ridiculous thought, indeed – it was as if Milena was more astute even than herself. Was she hoping to be lovely for a gargoyle?

Such questions seemed too much to fathom.

"He plagues Miódshire ...perhaps if I deliver myself, he will leave you all alone."

"You don't know what you are asking."

"Even though I was shunned and cast from my own marriage bed, I have not forgotten the early pleasures. I know what I might ask." Zaklina gripped the mound of the baby suddenly with both hands, the pads of her fingers digging into Milena's tender, splitting skin. "I am asking you to save your child. Save yourself. Save me! If ever you wish to repay me for what I have sacrificed for you, help me now."

A rumble of boots bounced outside the door, and Marek's voice hailed Gnegon in his garden.

Zaklina stared into Milena's eyes.

And slowly, slowly, her sister nodded once. Twice.

"Behind the hop vines and under the squash, you will find enough of what you need."

She told Marek she needed one last ingredient to make a fine soup that would be sure to strengthen his bones and make his child take deep breaths upon birth. It was enough to let him allow her in the garden without his beady eyes. And it would not be false if she could find the proper ingredients. Marek did not know there were none to be had in all the village. It seemed only Zaklina knew that.

She sifted toward the back of the narrow plot, pushing past the pink bleeding heart, until the sharp edges of the dried hops jabbed at her eyelids.

In the dimness of early dusk, she knelt in the overripe earth, and her palms cupped the soft velvet heads and spongy bottoms of what she sought.

She did not loiter, though she wished to do so. In the gloaming, the houses were cast in navy and twilight, a soft purpled blue that went rosy with the slant of the sunset and the lamplights in windows. Her shoulders strained under the faded brown cotton, and, if she was truthful, an ache unfurled within her womb, like ribbons of lust and longing.

For what? For whom?

Dare she put a name to it, even in the quiet confines of her own mind?

As she entered the murky house, she was struck by the simplicity of the wattle and daub of the walls, the musk of the mildewed straw in the rafters above, and the hardness of the old dirt packed below their feet. She shuddered at the dusty dryness of the kindling as she re-stoked the fire in the hearth and how the rust from the goose-arm flaked into the hungry flames when she put the old iron kettle on.

Marek stood as she chopped, but he did not bother to watch over her shoulder. She knew enough of him – of all men, it seemed – to know he would not worry himself over a woman's place or what her hands did. It was the one secret they all carried, Zaklina realized.

She supposed that was why poison was considered a woman's curse.

It was so easy to do.

Marek sat with a grunt as she served him, and glared at the meager table. "Where is the bread? What good are you, if you cannot put a full meal on the table?"

"There was no wheat to spare today," she said, refusing to mention the melee in the street. "And no time to grind it at the stones, as I am guarded unceasingly by children."

"For good reason," he said darkly, and fell to the broth she ladled for him, thick with a flour roux and stuffed with the garden's cumbersome and unmentionable harvest.

He shoved the broth in without comment, and Zaklina watched with bated breath. She wondered...had Milena told her false? Did her sister's love extend so deeply to this man that she would not be true to her only blood? She glanced at her sister swiftly, suddenly filled with uncertainty. Zaklina was not wed, and her one experience tainted with loss. She did not know the true bond of a loving husband and wife. Perhaps she asked too much, overmuch.

But surely, her sister would want to save the life of her child?

All of this was only to bring back the harvest, and roll back the rot, as Zaklina could not help but think her very presence had once again ruined a careful balance. She had made another mess and must go. All so her sister would not starve.

At least, that is what Zaklina told herself, whenever she felt her thoughts straying to the moments in the meadow, when the greasy grass had tickled her ankles and her entire body felt as if it had cleaved and bound itself to a creature of myth and power. It was as if the fairy tales of her past had caught up with her fantasies, as if the man of her dreams had manifested into a twisted version of masculinity.

Marek sat back and wiped his mouth. He glanced at Zaklina and then Milena and shook his head. "You forgot my wife. You should have served her at the first, with the babe in her belly."

"Yes! Yes of course." Zaklina's hands twitched. She had forgotten to make a second pot! She hurried to the hearth and carefully skimmed off the top, careful to only catch a few spoonfuls of the water itself and nothing more.

The spoon clattered against the earthenware bowl as she carried it, steaming and hissing, to Milena's bedside.

"Let me serve you, sister," she said, soft but yet loud enough that Marek could hear.

Milena seemed choked, and Zaklina said lowly, "It is only the water, but do not drink."

And so she spoon-fed her sister, who carefully drooled the tainted water out of the corner of her mouth, wiping it away with the edge of the worn quilt.

Throughout the farce, Zaklina's heart hammered and raced at turns, as if it was trying to suffocate her. She was eager, it was true, but was it to remove herself from this village and its ways, to escape a smothering she could not understand? Or was it because she felt tethered to the monster of her dreams? She could not decide which it was, and over it all was a worry that perhaps the soup did not suffice.

Perhaps it would not be enough...

"He still does not sleep!" she whispered to Milena.

"Give it time," her sister said, her body quivering under the quilts.

Marek burped behind them and rubbed his stomach. "It was well done, for once. A thick and heavy stew to be sure."

Milena and Zaklina glanced at one another, brief and breathless. It was only water and mushrooms, but neither woman made to correct him.

Zaklina went back to the hearth least she be tempted to say something too loud and unforgiving to Milena and stirred the contents of the black kettle. Amanita muscaria. An old mushroom, linked to faeries and old tales, fantasies and death. It had many names and was worshiped by some in the eastern parts of the continent, this she knew. A toxic fungi, but perhaps no worse than what everyone had eaten over the past days as their own crops shrunk with slugs and wormholes. It was not a deadly choice, like the chalice de la mort, and lost much of its inherent potency when she sliced and boiled the flesh in the weakly seasoned broth. But it would cause enough dreams for Marek and any others who ate it, and certainly leave them ill in their beds for a day or two.

And she needed only the night.

She hoped.

"Suppose he is vile and unkind?"

Milena's worries itched at Zaklina's mind, like the buzzing of angry bees. She shook her head and wound her stockings into tight balls before burrowing them into the small bag on the bed. Next to Milena, Marek snored heavily, though likely that would not last through the night before the broth kicked up in his guts and made him wretched.

Milena cast a worried glance at his bulk, brief and with some care.

"He will be fine."

"I know. But this monster. Will he be awful?"

"He will be no worse than the menfolk here in Miódshire," Zaklina said. "He is...he is as a man, only...roughly made and...taller. Much taller." She thought again of the gray stone armor of her first dream, and realized she had not even looked at his clothing when they were together in the meadow. And then, as if already inching toward such romantic visions, she was reminded of his profile.

"You are blushing!" Milena interrupted, her voice ripe with hushed astonishment.

Zaklina's hands went to her cheeks, which felt overwarm indeed. She turned away and looked out into the night. They'd been fortunate that none other than Ludislaw had arrived for food, and even then, she worried he would fall asleep before he reached his home. A man asleep in the street would rouse suspicion. It would be over before it began.

All she knew was she must go to him of her own accord. It would break something. A cycle. An expectation. A holdfast.

"I must go," she said softly to Milena. "You understand? I cannot wait for him to fetch me, for he won't. And you know no one here will understand. They will drive him away, they will devour themselves with fear and bloodthirst. They will forbid me to go outside, and we all will starve. It will be under the belief that they must protect me from him...from myself. But I do not think I need protection."

Marek snored in his sickly sleep, and they both jerked and paused.

In the muddy dusk, Milena tried desperately to hold her gaze and find her eye, and read her as only sisters do, but it had been too long since they lived together under a roof, and their circumstances had changed them both. Finally, Milena shook her head.

"It is in your nature to nurture, Zaklina," she said, naming the obvious trait and ignoring the one that had brought Zaklina so much trouble. "If you sense this monster is lonely, so much so that you cannot bear it, and if you are certain you are not afraid...I know enough not to dissuade you."

"You had already decided," Zaklina said, gesturing to the now-cold soup.

Milena sunk further under the covers, and raised a skeletal, trembling finger.

"If it is to be your bridal night, then you must have a little trousseau."

"If the men find I have left, they may be unhappy, and I don't wish to carry a burden. But I will press my raw silk skirt and sleeves, for it becomes my hair."

She opened the small trunk, buried under her meager straw mattress, and smoothed the fabric with her calloused palms. Her skin caught on the fine threads and snagged on the lines, but she pushed at the wrinkles anyway in hopes to make herself fine enough.

As an offering? A sacrifice?

"What shall tell if...when..." Milena's eyes moved to Marek's bare back. He shifted and let gas go, which filled the room with the scent of maggot meat.

"Tell them I am out foraging. Hunting for something. Anything. Mushrooms or leeks."

"Perhaps...not mushrooms," Milena said, a hint of an old wryness in her voice.

"Perhaps not."

"And if they are angry? If all the men in the village come to me and scream that you have gone mad, that I let you go without escort?"

"Then they will be glad to be rid of me, I should think. And serve them some sugar water. It may put them at ease." The idea came swift, surprising Zaklina as she spoke the words, but they rang true even as she said them. How could she know this? What could something sweet do against the evil festering in the corners of every cranny?

Milena swiveled her head around the small house. "There cannot be such a thing left in all of Miódshire."

Zaklina opened the small molasses barrel, which sat in the farthest corner of the shelf. She crawled her hand through the heavy syrup until her hand submerged and the sludge swallowed her wrist. She scrabbled and scratched, and her nails filled with the grains so that when she pulled up her fist, she held the fermented brown sugar long hidden at the bottom.

"This is still good. I will leave a pitcher with it, so you can keep the trouble of my disappearance from your bedside, if only for a night." She did so as she spoke, ever aware of Milena's eyes on the crease between her shoulder blades.

"You...I may never see you again."

Zaklina turned from her sugar water and frowned. "But we have crossed these words before. When you wed and left the city, I did not think I'd ever see you again, either."

"But you came anyway," Milena said, her voice mingling a worry and sorrow together, so it only sounded bittersweet.

"It is an imbalance in my nature to be so active," Zaklina agreed. "It is why I cannot sit and let us starve, and why I cannot wait for the frenzy of Miódshire to take me. You understand."

Milena's eyes searched Zaklina's, and in the quiet, Zaklina could see her sister did not. Not really. She never had a mind for the stories, the romance, the possibilities.

But they were sisters. Milena reached carefully to a box next to the bed. "Take my ribbons. They will match your silk."

In the dead hour, when the moon was already gone and the daylight seemed an impossibility, Zaklina stood at the threshold of the small house and squinted into the night. The stars could not pierce the thick clouds that had never left since the Gargoyle appeared in the meadow, but she did not fear the darkness. It would be her shield.

"Are you sure?" Milena asked one last time, a butterfly whisper.

"You must tell them I am a willful woman, who ran out too early to stop. I may have returned to the city."

"Mrs. Staryski will not believe that."

"Remind them of my terrible nature, and that it is no wonder a man does not wish to stay wed to me. That it is best I am gone."

"You do yourself a disservice to speak so."

"I speak a truth."

"They do not realize they are afraid," Milena said, and it was so honest and clear Zaklina wished she was strong enough to carry Milena with her.

She bent instead and kissed her younger sister on her damp and clammy forehead. "Do not let Mrs. Staryski hear you say things. It would not do for her to know you see the fear for what it is, and what it can become."

Zaklina's boots did not make a sound as she padded on the cobblestones, and she was glad she had not had the coin to purchase new ones before she came. They would have clattered and slapped the rocks, and surely woken old Aldona as she slipped past their home.

At the edge of the meadow, the yellow straw grasses seemed to hiss at her with the rising wind, and she paused with her toes just kissing the edge of the hills.

It was not the fear that stopped her, but her blood, coursing with unexpected, joyful euphoria. An anticipation.

A strange desire.

It was as if she was princess in the tales, the queen off to seek her fortune. The maid who would tame the monster.

But that was foolishness, of course. She was no maid. And the stories were not hers.

Without the stars or the moon, the night bled into the earth, and yet she could see a faint mist swirling among the far trees of the forest. The darkness smuggled through the meadow, eating at the fog, and yet the mist of it seemed to reach for her with long, gnarled fingers. She hoisted her small bag under her arm and picked up the rustling skirts, and took a step outward.

Was it a gasp?

A hum?

Had anyone woken?

She should not have been so vain as to wear her fine clothes – the raw silk crackled overmuch in the best of times, and even without the insistent breeze, perhaps she had woken Gnegon after all.

There was no time to look or wonder. It was time to move or be trapped.

Trapped in a web, a cocoon, a honeycomb of tangled magic.

Something so old, so tied to the earth, so primal that she felt the tug of it on the corners of her body, even as she knew she had been resisting it from the start.

How long before Milena would be completely immune to it? If Zaklina was not there to find fresh food and clean water for her sister, would she succumb faster? Was she escaping, only to leave her sister to a doom? Was she not actually fixing the trouble in her hunt? Would there be salvation and safety in a Gargoyle or was she allowing a wild dream and a midday encounter to cloud her thoughts and her desires?

As she walked, the misty fog curled around her knees, and she thought it a boon, for all it would likely wilt her fine clothes. The wetness masked the pungent crush of flowers under her feet, and made her feel as if she was protected. As if the very dewdrops and clouds could keep her safe from the ire and fearfulness of the village.

As if water might wash away the old rumors, the ones as old as the hills she now walked.

It was strange, she thought. Strange that she felt so certain he could save her, though she did not know what she was fleeing, not really. It was… survival. That she could sense, in the way a wolf scents a wounded doe.

The sense of adventure became more pronounced in every heartbeat as she approached the end of the flowers and where the yellow gave way to piney grasses. With the first step onto the slick stalks of green, the air sliced with spiced vanilla. She inhaled and held it a long moment and when she let it out, the breeze smelled of snow.

Zaklina paused on the top of the furthest hill as the wind rose quickly, with hurried frenzy, as if it had meant to start earlier and was catching itself up. It whipped her skirts and she held up a hand to her forehead as her long tresses were once again torn from their pins.

Her heart beat louder, and she was certain she heard calls in the village, and a shout that carried in the wind. Afraid to turn, lest she see anyone charging after her to yank her back to Miódshire and Marek's stifling kitchen, she instead faced the blackened trees and dangling boughs. Was that movement within them? Something out hunting, perhaps – a simple animal or an owl still awake.

For the first time, Zaklina felt the fear.

But was it for the unknown ahead of her, or the unknown behind?

She felt emptiness, the vulnerability and loneliness creeping into her skin, and she wasn't sure if it was hers, the villagers' or the Gargoyle's.

Did she finally understand what Mrs. Staryski had warned? Was there a presence in the hills? Something old and ruinous and terrifying, that would come out in these early hours to devour her heart?

And if so, would Miódshire go back to the sweet country village she recalled from her first day? Would her death save them all, more than just Milena and the unborn babe? Or was whatever festered there too deep to tear out, and would never be cured?

The sound came again, a rustle to her left. But then there was something else, and Zaklina looked behind her without thinking.

She regretted it at once.

The houses of Miódshire were ablaze with candles. Fires crackled on fat torches, and a boiling mass of men gathered in the town square. They were far off, but not so far that the vision was impossible to see. Her throat closed, and yet she could still give a short, hoarse scream into the rising, roaring wind.

"Please! Where are you?"

In an instant, she felt him behind her again, as if he appeared out of a rent in the meadow, sprung forth from the earth without a sound. As he stood just over her shoulder, he spoke quietly and with great urgency.

"Why are you here again? Do you not know the meadow is dangerous?"

She turned and looked up at him. He flinched as she gazed upon his form, but did not move. She took another step closer. "It is not so if you are here. Do you not know, Milord, that I have come to be taken? I do so of my own free will, so the anger of the village – and your anger, too – does not grow. So that my heart is not pulled from me."

His hand twitched, but he hesitated again. "Taken. By what? Whom?"

"By you."

His breath sucked in, a loud gush of heat, and then before anything else, before the menfolk in the town square could look toward them, before she could ask the myriad questions burning in the back of her mind, his arm was around her and they moved.

A breathless speed, a violent journey. It was an impossibility. As she kept her arms and legs rigid, he tucked her close and leapt. Up, up into the trees and across their tops, with that cape of his behaving as if it were wings indeed. Zaklina dared not open her eyes more than the first time, for she feared the heights and had no interest in knowing how far he jumped between treetops.

She clamped her teeth so she could not squawk and clenched every muscle and sinew in her body so she would not flail as he hurdled them across a vast distance, going so fast that the breeze slashed at her cheeks and chapped her throat, and she was certain the silk of her dress would be ripped to fragments.

He was silence itself as they moved, without a stutter to his movements or a grunt as he vaulted. His arm was iron. His body like rock. Was he truly a stone gargoyle come to life, or strength personified? Was he taking her to a prison, where she would be locked apart from the world forever? Would he eat her heart anyway? Zaklina tried not to shiver, nor think of what awaited her at the end of the journey. There was nothing to be done. What choice did she have? Stay with Milena until she died or was consumed by the stories Mrs. Staryski and the others wove and retold? Lose her mind to the thoughts and feelings of the others? Return to the city and continue her brittle existence in servitude, hiding from the painful memories of the past? Live in the shallow retelling of her favorite fairy tales?

Or this. This adventure. This curious, compelling idea to go with the Gargoyle everyone fretted over, though she still did not understand the rules binding all. She had unwittingly stepped into a strange story. It was the old magic, come alive. It was a story she had never heard, one that tickled the edges of her mind. The lore, long stored in her mind, seemed to wiggle, wobble, and blurr. She squeezed her eyes tighter.

Only a brave fool would go against the authorities who forbade them. Zaklina thought perhaps Mrs. Staryski simply did not like that Zaklina would prefer reason or ration over the old tales, which had kept Miódshire safe or bound all the many years, safe from whatever evil or magic had lodged itself in the festering of hidden fear. She could not help pushing back anyway, though all knew a woman never should dare to be ambitious, be more than a goodwife or a spinster. A woman ought never be curious.

There was danger in that, too.

Part 2: The Gargoyle

THE CASTLE

THEY SEEMED TO TRAVEL LEAGUES, with the forest floor fathoms below. The light did not waver, the sun stuck just below the horizon, and the wind blew ever colder. The frost crackled the creases in the silk and chewed at the tips of her toes and fingers. The Gargoyle did not seem to notice. In truth, he did not seem to notice anything save a distant goal, far beyond what she wanted to guess.

The dew of the morning still edged into her shoes, and was not yet dry when she was set on her feet, and the hot arm of her uncertain host slipped away from her waist.

As she slowly opened her eyes, the vertigo hit her so fast she could not stop the nausea if she tried. She swayed violently, spinning and tilting, and felt the earth tip once more on its rod before she crashed to her knees on unforgiving stones and lost what little she'd put in her stomach in Miódshire across them.

More came out of her mouth than she had eaten, boiling and curling, as if worms had lived in the pit of her gut. She retched again at the sight of the roiling mass, and again so quickly that acid seared the back of her throat and lanced her tongue and gums, burning her nose and eyes with it.

And then, at the last, blood.

It dripped from her nose as she curled over and came out of the depths of her body in a last purge, dark ruby and spotted with honey-colored globules. A clogged nose hid the sweet-iron stench. She gasped and put her hands to her eyes to stem the dizziness and the sight of her illness and to dab at the tears. But it was not tears – more blood came from her eyes.

It was too much.

She fell away from it all, slithering, scrambling and forever ruining the carefully pressed skirts.

As she pushed back, her shoulders hit an immoveable wall, cool and warm, and she froze, her breath coming in fast, hard pants.

There was a whisper of a cape, and the smell of wet earth, and then the

Gargoyle bent over her. Wordless, soundless, he handed her a square of cloth. Grey and marbled, but edged in what seemed to be old lace, worn so thin it was near a spider's web.

"It's coming from your ears as well," he said, without a trace of worry in his gravelly voice. "Would you like to clean it yourself, or allow me?"

She took the handkerchief—only belatedly wondering what it might mean for a monster to hold with such gentlemanly ways—and put it to her ears. When she looked at it, the blood looked black on the grey, and then slowly disappeared, as if the fabric would clean itself of dirt. Zaklina quickly dabbed at her nose and the corners of her eyes, wiping it at the last across her mouth.

"Am I dying, do you suppose?" she asked.

"I do not think acutely," he responded, crisp and grave at the same time. "But I think you were wise to leave as you did, when you did."

She stood on trembling legs, using the side of the ramparts and ignoring how the rocks dug into her palm. Looking out across the land, she saw they had come to the shortest walk of the shortest tower of a castle that spun above, chewing into the side of a mountain, with its boulders scurrying so high that the topmost were lost in the clouds. She felt as though she might tumble backward if she continued to gaze so far above, and nearly did anyway as she brought her gaze down.

The Gargoyle's hand came to her elbow as she stumbled on her heel, and she looked at him. His face was dark and unreadable and unnatural. Unfamiliar, and yet somehow safer than what she willingly left behind in Miódshire. She still wondered at her lack of fear. There was a part of her, perhaps still connected to the dream, that wished to feel the breadth of him, and lay her head against his heart. Or was it because she had read so many silly tales of dragon-princes and...snake-swan-monkey... She put a hand to her forehead and turned her thoughts away from the stories, which seemed oddly fragmented.

Was she bewitched? Beguiled?

He seemed disinclined to make a suggestion to go elsewhere. Maybe he wished to enjoy the careful creep of a hidden sunrise. As they stood there in the overcast morning, she blinked and took in more of her surroundings. Slower, this time, and without moving too quickly.

Ahead of them were the tips of the trees, evergreens all, near equal to eye view. Branches along the tops of those nearest were broken and cracked. Several more were beyond, and she realized it was the path of their half-flight, stretching into the mist far off. The stones under her hands dripped with cold water, and the moss in between the tiny rivers was fat and dense. She did not dare look up at the soaring precipices of the whole, crumbling castle again, and instead looked at the creature at her side.

His clothing was not as stone-like as she had once mused, but a thick, coarse material that looked molded to his every curve and angle and sculpted from the hide of some forgotten animal. She drew away her gaze before he would think her unseemly and forward, and instead glanced out again at the vast green spreading from the mountain. There were hills here, too, though hidden by the rustling needles of the pines. And there was not a tendril of woodsmoke to be seen in the foggy distance.

"Where are we?"

He looked down at her. "Home."

Home.

The word, like the notion of the castle, clattered around in her mind. It was unsettling.

Home for him? Or for her, now, too?

And...*castle.*

He did not say she was his prisoner, but surely such a thing did not need to be spoken, for where else could she go but die in the vast forest below? And yet...she did not feel locked and imprisoned. She had been saved. Hadn't she? She'd fled. Been...fleeing. And suddenly the sick curdling of her stomach lurched, and she slapped a hand to her gut. The sound sprayed and echoed across the land, and a dark bird blasted up from a tree. She could not tell if it was a raven or a crow, though she thought the difference important and significant.

The queasiness continued as she recalled the utter fear she felt in the hilly meadow before the Gargoyle had come, and she shuddered. His hand on her elbow gripped harder, and through the thin fabric of her sleeve, she felt the power in the palm and the hard grooves of short nail-claws.

"I had been afraid, before. Afraid you wouldn't come. And then, more than afraid..."

"Afraid of me?" His voice was so gravelly it sounded like a stone rolling.

She shook her head and breathed out carefully and in small puffs, trying to dispel the leftover anguish and worry. "No. Not of you, Milord. Of... something. I could not put a name to it, but it is something great and undeniable. Or perhaps it is only a silly girl's fear of the dark."

She turned to him at last, looking up in his face without that fear, full of self-depreciation. Maybe he would say it was indeed only that. Maybe he could explain the blood and darkness she'd purged only moments ago. Maybe it was, indeed, all a dream...

There was no humor in the long planes of his face.

"You are no silly girl, and I do not think you fear the dark, for then you would not have sought me out. No. You feel the fear of man rightfully felt on that meadow these years. It is against the...fear...that I battle."

She stared up at him, wondering questions crowding into the space the word home had left behind. It was a relief to feel the curiosity bubble up, and it was then she realized how long it had been since she truly voiced a question in full, and had allowed her mind the freedom to push back.

"Then does that make you a warrior king? A guardian? One made of gargoyle stone, who protects those who ask it?"

He looked away, along the line of their travel, and dropped his hand from her elbow. She missed the warmth, as the chill of their morning's journey had seeped through every layer and the dew half-soaked her hair.

"Come," he said, turning away. "You will want to change from your damp dress."

Zaklina had a half-thought to ask him if he liked its color, the pink against her skin and hair, but it felt as if was a thing an overeager woman would ask, and he might think her brazen from the start. So she buried the thought and followed him across the uneven walkway without a backward glance.

He took her through a dizzying number of stairs and steps and wide pavilions. Each went higher than the last, for they never went down—only up. Some of the rooms were completely blocked up, filled with rubble and wet rock. Several of the stairs had missing stones or rotten mortar, and twice she was certain she heard the collapse of another part of the castle.

Zaklina stopped really looking after a while and followed him blindly. When she lagged, he took her hand. She was too overwhelmed to think on the intimacy of the gesture, as she'd just discovered their view out the narrow windows of the latest staircase showed nothing but white.

"What has happened to the forest?" she asked, stopping and staring out. She felt as if she might fall down the stairs what with the otherworldly blur outside.

"It is still there," he said. "Only below the clouds."

She whipped to gape at him. "And we are not?"

"Not anymore. Do not fret. We will not be inside them for long."

The next round of stairs and halls were followed by corridors, raggedy gardens dripping with fog and fat chunks of water that hovered on the edge of heavy leaves and too-large foliage. It was as if the clouds fed the greenery and they grew to unmentionable size. She reached to touch one leaf that was twice as long as her arm, and wider than her shoulders.

"There used to be gardeners for these higher pavilions. The fountains ran with the clearest and coldest water in the castle. It was once said on cloudless nights, the stars would fill the water with their brilliance, and the women who drank of it then would glow for a year and a day." The Gargoyle touched another leaf, and a shower of sprinkles cascaded on his hair and garments. "But that was long ago, when the world was different. The stories were, too."

He nudged her along, until the air became less sodden and the stairs less slippery. She wanted to tell him of the wolves who sat in the stars, as the story went, but she found she had forgotten how it went.

Was it the bears in the sky?

Or the coyote who built the ladder? The story slipped away, and Zaklina took a deep fill of air and glanced outside to clear her mind, trying not worry about the fact that she could not recall. It seemed unlike her...

And once again, she paused, and forced the Gargoyle to wait.

The sun shone on the fluff of the cloudy day. As far as Zaklina could see, it was a blanket of white and pearl and silver. Above was the bell of the sky, forget-me-not blue and pulsing with the sunlight. She stretched a hand out of the window, forgetting for a moment how very high they were, and let the heat burn away at the chill brought on by gray days and poor food.

As the sun poured into her blood, she forgot about the story of the wolves and bears, and it evaporated in the sparkle and lure of the warmth.

Finally, they stopped at a door. It was a strange jewel in a castle of wet, crumbling masonry, for this door was inlaid with gold and rubies, studded with mother-of-pearl and a white rock shot through with bright rainbow lightning. As the Gargoyle pushed it open, steam gushed and bellowed around them.

She looked up at the tall shadow of him, half-hidden in the staircase. "Shall I dress for...for what? Dinner?" Zaklina twisted her mouth at the offer. Where had such a thing come from? Perhaps a leftover civility from her days in the city, when such a thing was done. Had she not dressed for the husband she had lost?

The Gargoyle shrugged slightly, a human motion that set her teeth on edge. "It is still morning. You might wish to breakfast in your garden."

"Will you join me?" she asked, the words sliding out without thought.

He paused, and if she could read him right, it was incredulity that rolled from him. Disbelief in her sincerity, maybe. She found this rose her ire, too, and she clenched her fists around her damp bag of belongings.

"I will join you, if that is your wish." He gave a slight bow and turned away, moving so quickly he was down half a flight of stairs before she found her voice.

"I would very much desire it!" She flung the words down, and he stopped. "And now? Now where do you go? Will you be quite far away from me?"

He went completely still. "Is that what you wish?"

Exasperation burst from her. "No, of course not, Milord! I ask because I wish for exactly what I ask. Will you join me for breakfast—I wish it. Will you be far? I hope not, for I wish your nearness in this labyrinth. I mean exactly what I ask. There are no hidden meanings."

He moved so swift and silent that he stood in front of her, before her words ceased bouncing off the walls. In a moment, he had taken both of her hands in both of his, and his eyes glittered in the slant of sunlight from the slitted window of the hall.

"Then I am grateful."

And with that, he left her. There was nothing to be done then but to stride full force into the moist center of her new quarters.

It was a glorious space.

So glaringly, brilliantly glorious it was the most dreamlike of anything she had seen yet, and that was after she had nearly flown for unending, endless miles, flittering from the tops of pines and elms in the clutches of a monster.

It was lavish. Perhaps hedonistic. She did not know what word to use, only that any of the most decadent would still fall short. From gleaming gold-veined marble underfoot to the walls that glimmered with silver leaf and inset emeralds between the black rock, the translucent glass bathtub filled with aqua water and topped with incandescent, shattering bubbles to the crowned ceiling leaking gold and painted frescos, it was an attempt at light and air and fairy-sweet. The only thing giving away the illusion of grandeur was the icy stone around the windowsills, which could not be hidden for all the cake-like wonders of her new rooms.

Who did he think she was?

Some long-lost noblewoman, who required the finest? Or a fainting lass who would swoon with the gleam of fine metals and gems?

Clearly, the Gargoyle was not able to read minds or souls, that much was certain.

What would he say to her past? To her mind? To her basic questions?

For all she could not pull up the details of the story of the polar bear and his curious peasant wife, she never forgot the sting of her own reality before Miódshire, when Narcyz turned away. The rejection of her nature burned into her very soul.

Would another male think her too much, and yet not enough? Would this be yet another cruel twist of fate that she would land, for the third time, in a place where she was unwanted and considered uneasy?

She would guard herself against the offering, then.

She would accept, but only just.

If he wished her to smell like roses and lavender and wash her hair, she would, but only because there seemed little else to do with the time before her.

And she would comfort herself with the hope that by disappearing from Miódshire, Milena would be safe. There would be no more fury cast on Marek's house, and they would cease to care about the echoing roar of a long-lost beast. Maybe there would be more food now, and the harvest end up swelling and thick with heavy grain and chunky carrots. Without the fear of the mob of men, the fields would not molder with slime. They could turn to their crops without lurching at every sound. They could smell the flowers of the long-overdue blossoms.

Then again, maybe the rot was only a dream...

Zaklina wandered the suite, trailing her hand along the thick, cream brocade of the couches and the blue velvet of the pillows. Green tassels dripped from the enormous bed canopy. Window seats carved into every nook, half hidden by curtains of satin and silk, patterned softly with wide flowers. She tried not to shudder as she touched them, thinking of the old hills and yellow meadow of the morning.

Tapestries covered the chocolate wood and polished rock of the walls. Most of them were of flowers and trees, birds and animals flitting through a forest without a care. There were no people on any, no sign of humanity at all, except for the last, which she found in the furthest corner.

It was a finely woven piece, but old and with a hint of moth holes in the edges. It smelled of honey and of catnip, with a touch of white clover. In the middle was a woven skep, straw-colored and pale. From it flew many hundreds of tiny insects, black and ocher, into a swirl, as if mad. And in the middle of the skep, sitting upon the top, with a tiny crown made of gold thread, was a larger bee, with a pointed stomach and waving arms, conducting the swarm as it whirled in a cloud of smoke.

Zaklina reached to touch it, and when she ran her fingers along the old threads, several of them broke under her hand, coming away in powder and falling without a sound on the polished floor at her toes.

A crackle startled her, and she turned so fast she left a mark on the marble with her old leathered sole.

It was only a fire, suddenly hopping merrily in a hearth that had been cold but a moment earlier. She approached it hungrily, reaching out her hands so they felt fuzzy with heat in short order.

When she looked at the glass washtub, she noticed a wet sheet under the water, silky edges dribbling from the basin's lip, near transparent with finely spun thread.

There was nothing for it but to bathe. There was no stove to stoke, no wood to find, and certainly no garden or market to cull for something edible. The thought of food made her stomach clench at its emptiness, and she closed her eyes against the memory of the sickness she'd spewed when her feet had touched the castle.

Castle. The word clattered inside her stretched mind.

It was a dream. Or a story. Or somehow, she had slipped... into one of the tales. The fairy-folk-tall-tale. But which one?

One of them. All of them. None of them...

When she opened her eyes, she was astounded to see a hundred candles lit around the room, each of them dripping as if they'd been lit for hours.

She peeled off her layers, suddenly ashamed of the dirt hiding in the seams of the underpetticoats and below the cracks of her nails. As she plunged a foot into the water, the splash slapped against her skin. She suddenly realized how unearthly quiet it was in the room, save for the fire and her own movements.

"If I could sing," she said aloud, if only to make sure she had not lost her voice. "I would do the one about the brother who killed the hawk-enchantress. Or perhaps the one about the crow-prince. Or maybe the lament of the rich man."

She said the words, and tried to start each song, only to realize she didn't know the words of the tunes. The words stuttered on her tongue and pricked at the corners of her mouth.

Could magic erase memory?

Was it worth the price if it did?

She lowered herself, a soft bellied crab and utterly vulnerable, into the water. She went neck deep, for modesty's sake, though she did not think the Gargoyle a spy or a voyeur, and there was no one else to see her.

Zaklina had never expected much from life.

She only expected the reality of her sex. A youthful marriage, a simple kitchen, a bit of coin for the market each week, and children. All had happened for her, too, just not in the way Milena had experienced. It had been backwards early on and disjointed from the start. The marriage disintegrated, and the ink of his departure barely dry when she realized everything had disappeared.

She had lost the husband—he said it was due to her over curious mind, her unending questions, her thirst to learn about the world, and her ability to remember everything she heard and read. He had regretted teaching her to read during their courtship, he said, and thought he had created a monster of a wife because of it.

There was more than that, she knew, for she heard the whispers in the market, as much as she turned her face and her ear away. But she had heeded the snippets of disgust enough in the depths of her heart to hurry the marriage of Marek to Milena and stop her little sister from hurting with the possible taint of Zaklina's match. Perhaps she should not have rushed Milena. But how was she to know Marek would take Milena back to his childhood home, where it festered with too many broken stories and threats?

With the loss of the marriage, she lost the cramped kitchen, where crumbs had rotted in the corners of the floors and in the knots of the wood under the stove. She lost the embrace of a man she...had given all. She lost of the promise of forever. She lost the crusty pans and the faded, limp dishtowels. She had not mourned such losses, but only the shell of its protection. Without the kitchen, the coin, and the market, she had no purpose. Without the man, she was nothing—and worse, for she had no virginity to offer as a prize to another.

And there certainly were no children.

She filled that void with others' offspring, and the position of nanny and teacher, caretaker and nursemaid, was enough to fill her days and her purse and gave her a new, cramped room that did not have a kitchen. It was not terrible, but it was not what she had expected. Her greatest relief and only real joy was that her employers were always begrudgingly glad she held so much knowledge in her mind and could teach their children an excessive number of facts.

And stories.

There had always been the stories...

As Zaklina filled her palms with glistening bubbles, she marveled at the silkiness of them, how they felt like air but were clearly of substance. What made bubbles? What allowed for the mixture of soap and water that caused such delight, instead of the caustic burning of lye?

Always questions. They never stopped.

They were often such a curse.

The sheet sucked itself to her body when she rose, clinging to every curve and bump of her muscle and skin. She shivered once, and turned to the fireplace. Next to it, a table, made of spindly green cane and cut glass, held a mountain of white and gold cloth.

"I suppose that settles the question of magic," she murmured, and shivered again. "I must assume it is a power made to serve, as this is all very kindly."

Once dry, she sat by the fire again for a long while, letting the warmth dry her hair and overheating her feet. Her stomach rumbled again, and she suddenly realized the Gargoyle was waiting for her for breakfast.

"How long I've taken!" She jumped up, then looked at the robe around her chest. "I surely cannot go to the...garden...or solar dressed like this."

She turned around. At first, she thought she would laugh, but she had not laughed in so long she did not recall how to do it. Instead, a corner of her mouth lifted, and she stepped forward to touch the delicate silver rack that held three dresses. They were simple, of plain but richly woven cloth, with only bits of embroidery on the necks and sleeves, and Zaklina reminded herself that she should not be surprised they fit, as if invisible tailors had taken her measurements while she sat, fully visible to all in that glass bathtub.

She stepped out into the narrow stairway hall, wearing a dress in palest blue, with tiny vines clustered around the bodice, and waited as the finely decorated door creak closed behind her. At once, she missed the heady steam from within, but she had promised to meet him, and did not want to anger him on her very first morning.

It was a gloomy corridor, now that she stepped down alone, and she worried the folds of the dress as she realized she did not know where her "garden" was located in the vast castle. How did one find anything in the whole place, which was the size of many villages put together, mashed into the face of the soaring mountain?

As she reached a small landing, she almost turned back to go back up. Would she ever find her glorious little cage again?

"Milord?" she called, suddenly, and with a gripping uncertainty. She had not dreamed him, surely. The word bounced on the cold stones, but as it disappeared down into the darkness below, she noticed a door she had not seen in the gloom.

Tentatively taking a step toward it, she repeated, "Milord?"

The door swung open, and he towered through it, black as late dusk, blocked by the white light beyond. "I have told you. I am no lord."

He stood aside and waited, still as rock. She crossed into the space and gaped as the sunlight blasted onto her scalp.

It was a garden carved from stone, with fat carpet stretched wall to wall. Squares and rectangles cut into the carpet, where riotous plants and trees shot out and reached for the heavens, their glossy greens and colors so bright it hurt her eyes. Some of the gardens were arranged with lilac or linden trees, with a little pond in the middle. The biggest one had a stream and waterfall of silver and pale aqua, which was fed from the jagged rock reaching for the sun. Zaklina shielded her eyes and bent back to look up, where she was certain the end of the castle must be but was struck by golden rays. She looked back down, blinking quickly against tears.

"Don't bother," the Gargoyle said, and shut the door, locking out the chilly castle stairs. "I have attempted to find the top of the castle all my days, and have never found it. You'll blind yourself trying."

His voice seemed smaller in the garden, tighter and bumpy. She kept him visible as she peered in each garden and discovered a cedar table and two gilt and velvet chairs in the center, buried by orange trees and bunched mistletoe. It was set for two, with crystal forks and copper goblets, plates of pearl heaped with glistening ham and sparkling pastries.

"That is...." Zaklina could stand on ceremony no longer. She sat without clearing the crinkles of her new skirt, forgetting a linen to cover her lap, and grabbed the smallest fork. The meat melted under the roof of her mouth, and the tarts were a blessed mix of sweet and sour, sugary and fluff all at once. She ate so quickly, so ravenously, filling a belly that had not been full in weeks, that for a few moments her manners fled.

A prick on her lip, sharp and red-hot, made her pause, and she looked up at the Gargoyle, appalled at herself and her lack of decorum. What would he think of her?

"I am so very sorry." She half-rose from her seat. "Do not stand on ceremony for me. I am no gentle woman, as you can see plainly," she added ruefully. "I did not even wait for you to join me."

"I do not have it in me for very grand gestures," he said, and sat slowly across from her. "Not anymore."

He picked up his napkin, a sheer, ethereal material shot with bronze, and handed it to her, motioning at her face with his gnarled hand.

She took it from him, dumb, and he picked up one of the larger cut crystal forks. "You're bleeding. These can be overly sharp and slice easily if you're not careful."

Zaklina quickly put the cloth to her lip. It came back with seven spots of vermilion, and she couldn't help but shudder, recalling the gush of black bile and blood from the morning. Suddenly, her appetite decreased, and she felt she might be sick again.

"Don't worry." He watched her closely. "It could have been much worse."

"Worse?"

"At least you did not bleed from your every orifice."

She froze, staring at him. He seemed embarrassed, though she still struggled to read emotion on his face, and he turned quickly to begin to fill his own plate.

"Every? Have you seen such—"

"Yes."

She waited for him to pick up his goblet, but instead he only ate the pastries and ham. There would be no toasting of their morning meeting, then, and of her rescue.

And how many had he rescued—if that was the word—over the eons? Where were these people now? Locked in the many different wings of this massive castle?

Or long since departed...

She took a breath and began to attend to the tea service, pouring both for him and herself as he ate soundlessly, delicately inserting the knife and fork between his long, thin mouth. Zaklina was proud of herself, when she handed over the milkbone saucer to him without it clattering. As she sipped her tea, she looked at him again through slitted eyes.

She ought to be scared of him. He looked exactly as a monster should in some ways, but in his manners and motions, he was human. Deep lines etched into the sides of his nose and along the gash of his lips. She did not think he was very young at all. Was he a half-myth, like the whispers of faraway legends? A blood-thirsty beast waiting to pounce until she was well-fed?

The quiet of the garden was broken only by the soft trickle of the soft waterfall or a gulping plop of a fish in one of the small ponds as it broke the skin of the water. There was not even a breeze to move any of the greenery, and they were too high in the sky for birdsong.

She thought she might go mad with the silence.

How could he stand it?

"I had more to fear this morning in the meadow, did I not?" Zaklina suddenly asked, and he jerked as if surprised to hear her voice. "You saved me. You are not what should be feared."

She wanted to say more, but it was stuck.

The magic here stifled her with tantalizing but unspoken rules. She knew she was on the cusp of grasping the reality of it, yet still it remained elusive. There was a current, pulling on the edges of her eyes. There was a story linked to him, she was sure. Something different than what Mrs. Staryski said. Some timeless tale, re-told across cultures and lands.

Always about a beast.

Or was it a maiden? A frog-princess? A swan?

Something about a castle...hidden? Enchanted? The palace East of the Sun and West of the Moon. Or was it...

The Gargoyle slowly set his cup down with extreme delicacy, and she was reminded of his arm about her during the journey of the morning, and his excessive strength.

He was quiet for so many long minutes she worried she might have angered him. There was no way to know for certain what had happened in Miódshire before she left, nor what was happening now that they saw her depart in his clutches. What had transpired when Mrs. Staryski discovered Zaklina had defied her well-crafted and upside down stories and rumors, and not succumbed to the rot and tangled words spun in the village and tied to the flower-heavy meadow?

If only...if he knew. If the Gargoyle had done this before, perhaps he could tell her what to expect. And perhaps it was not very civilized to ask such questions outright. It was unbecoming a woman of any stature, but she hoped he would forgive her forthright manner at least for the first day, when her appearance in the castle was new.

Still he remained silent, and yet when she looked at him, he seemed downcast more than cross. Impulsively, she went to kneel at his knee, touching the coarse fabric of it without thought, and he stirred and found her eyes. She noticed a softness about him, here in the garden. Unlike in the wilderness or the windswept meadow, he did not seem so visceral now. It was as if, in the castle, some of his very essence was diminished.

His arm lifted, as he made a half-hearted and fruitless effort to lift her up. She did not move and pressed her case. If she did not speak now, she thought she might be more anxious with each passing day. If he believed from the start that she was a curious thing, who over-asked and was of an inquiring mind, perhaps he would allow questions always.

"I would prefer a response. An answer. Any answer. About any of this. I...anyone would be best adapted when one knows what is to be faced."

His great head moved in the negative. "It is something I cannot tell you. It is...it is to do with magic."

"That much I could decipher."

"Then you will know the rules of magic, as they are in so many places, do not allow one to speak of spells, curses or hexes, or even the outcome of a quest."

It seemed a flimsy explanation for his lack of one, and she frowned and finally stood as he continued to sit, though he did not resume eating.

Had this been how it always was? Magic of unspoken rules.

Magic unknown?

Did the heroines of all the tales stumble about in such blindness?

Did the peasant-bride lose her husband to the knives? Or was her loss due to lack of knowledge?

She frowned, attempting to remember how the stories always went. Was he in correct form, or was it she who was to transform? Did the man burn the clothes of the woman, or did she kiss him to break a spell? It was all muddled, all gone, spirited away as splinters of tales even as she thought them, as if such memory was forbidden.

How could all she know splinter so fast?

To hide the tendrils of panic, which rose in her throat like a spike, she stood and walked a few paces away. Taking a deep breath, she fingered a waxy red flower, phallic and too-showy, stuck between frothy and overly tall hibiscus. Nearby, skinny palms mingled with date trees, and a pear stood between copper boxes filled with oddly standard kitchen herbs. She wondered who made the food, and who filled the bath. If no one did, then this magic was by far more powerful than any story known to her. Even the ones of gods and demons did not have such sway.

Zaklina spun on her new shoes, which caught and dug into the carpet below. "Perhaps...if I guess at the curse or the magic, even in a roundabout way, I could know what is to be done? Or what is to come? There must be some expectations, and I must owe some debt for my rescue."

He did not move and stared at her from dark brown eyes under heavy brows. Again, he seemed to be made of absolutely stone, the same as that of the castle's, and she recalled her very first dream, when he had uncurled, and she had woken to his roar.

She continued, hoping something would open his tongue. "For certainly, I do not fear you. You are not vile or dangerous. You would not have killed the girl in the village, from the long-lost story. You did not rip her to shreds to eat her heart. I cannot feel that it is your nature."

Finally, he stirred and stood. She stood her ground and gazed up at him, hope bouncing into her throat.

"Did I hit upon it, then?"

"Not quite," he said, and though he spoke softly, his voice was a deep rumble, and the leaves around them seemed to quiver and twitch with the timbre. "But you have hit upon the fact that I myself have brought you here for a purpose. It was particularly lucky for you that it also saved you from a different fate."

"Then, you can answer—"

"No." He shook his head again. "I am afraid I cannot answer all your questions, but that I must ask you one. It is one I feel...required to ask."

Her eyes followed his, where they flitted to the side, and then back to meet her face openly, with a strange resignation.

"Miss...." He stopped and gave a grimace, which seemed to be a mix of ruefulness and shock. "I am afraid that with the unusual...circumstances of the morning, I have not properly introduced myself, nor learned your name. You may call me Gargulec, for that is what I am, and be done with the ridiculous 'Milord'."

"My name is Zaklina," she said.

"Zaklina," he repeated, and there was a lilt in his voice as he said it, before he concluded, most unexpectedly, "I ask that you marry me."

She stared at him, unbelieving, half-shocked and more so when the spice of anticipation ripped through her loins. Then coldness blasted shortly after the heat of excitement, because of course, he did not love her, nor did he ask from his own desires.

It must be a part of the magic and the curse of his seclusion. That could be the only answer, for no one, not even a monster, would wish to bind himself for life to one he did not know.

And surely, once he realized what kind of a woman she was, he would not want her heart.

"Ask? Or demand?" she whispered, holding his gaze.

"Ask only," he swore solemnly.

"Then...I ask that you give me time to think," she said slowly. "I have only just arrived, and would like to ponder logically on it."

There was utter silence in the garden as she said this, and the sun itself seemed to pause in its long trek across the sky.

"Then...you do not immediately refuse?"

She shrugged. "There is...something else. I cannot honestly refuse you, for a part of me does not wish to close the opportunity forthright. Perhaps if we speak more in coming days and weeks? Or walk about the garden so

I might learn of your nature?" She refused to speak the other side of such a sentence—that he would learn of hers, and have the time to retract his request.

He stared at her, as if filled with utter confusion, before shaking himself. "I...yes, we can speak. But not now, for I am afraid I must leave you for a while. There are duties I cannot shirk, even for you, Zaklina."

The Gargoyle bowed briefly, then turned and nearly fled the garden, leaving her to sink back to her seat and stare at the sunlight piercing the crystal of her fork, and at the small drop of dried blood on the edge of the last tine.

What was there to do, but to wander?

Zaklina filled her day with it, wandering from one room to the next, but keeping only to the staircase she knew would take her, eventually, back to the rooms where she was to stay. What would become of her if she was truly lost? Would the Gargoyle—Gargulec—come to her rescue again? It seemed foolish to expect him to be so available, and to aid her every trouble. He had already pulled her from the edge of Miódshire. What more could she ask?

Most rooms were empty.

None were locked.

It was unsurprising to find many filled with rubble from walls caving or ceilings that gave out. Only one held furniture, but most of it was broken, and all of it covered with a fine powder, as if a mason had blown all his stone dust into the room and departed.

Had she traded the decomposing Miódshire for a disintegrating castle?

Was she doomed to forever only know things that decayed?

Her marriage. Her livelihood.

Even her brushes with magic were marred by corrosion.

It followed, in Zaklina's mind, that she was the trouble.

She was the problem.

Perhaps Narcyz had been right. She was not enough to satisfy anyone or anything. A problem. Unlovable. An uneasy type of woman, who would shame any man or trouble any place she touched.

She was not like the rescued girls in the old stories. She was not the virgin sacrifice, nor the brave warrior-queen. Nothing seemed to fit in this magical reality. A castle, certainly. But the other tales? What had they said? Animals of many shapes, who could speak and perform many wonderous tasks. But the Gargoyle was no animal, nor did he seem a knight or prince. He simply...was. A being that did not belong in any of the folktales...

And neither did she.

Maybe they *were* well suited.

As she thought of those old stories, buried in the journal left behind in Milena's safekeeping, they fractured further in her mind, shattered into a hundred pieces and unable to be glued together even as she tried to recall. Nothing made sense, and she had an overwhelming worry that she might forget them all if this place wormed into her head any more.

And then she realized, too, it was the first time in many long weeks that she had not been surrounded by rancid food, foul-tempered souls and cloying flowers.

Had she depended on these corrupted things to keep her mind sane?

As she wondered, not even certain what she was looking to find, she thought of the garden that he said was hers – one she longed for by the afternoon, after staring in empty rooms and stairways, and how she'd left Milena's garden in disrepair herself. Who would tend the squashes and hops? Would they continue to rot? Would Milena and the baby starve, or would Mrs. Staryski attend to them now, in her own, horrifying fashion?

Zaklina tried to tell herself it was for the best. Her appearance only seemed to create trouble.

The thought returned her to her musings, all of them a lash to her self-worth.

When she returned to her garden, it was a relief. She'd survived a whole day, as desperately long and tedious as it had been, and had not gone mad in the silence or the loneliness. Yet her hands felt strangely empty and clunky, so to move them, she began to snap off the leaves of the plants in the copper boxes, known to her for their properties to heal and to season a soup. As she sank her hands into the juicy chives and twisted the oil-sweet springs of lavender, she breathed in and out, reminding herself of the ways of the hearth. She did not want to forget that at least, for it was certain at some point she would depart the castle and go back to the quiet life of a discarded woman.

A wasted woman in her own right.

It was a short climb to the golden door of her room, made brighter by the slant of the unopposed, setting sun outside the narrow window across from it. It made half the jewels wink as it slowly dipped under the layer of fat clouds below, and likely below even that, in the world of people and hovels, pine trees and meadows. She supposed she could walk all the way down, taking a ball of thread with her as the one tale used to say, and find a room below the clouds, to gaze out across the land, and remind herself of her future.

Inside her quarters, the fires burned low and comfortably, and she set the herbs on the nearest table. They appeared limp and puny, an earthy uselessness in all the finery. It felt silly to leave them to waste, so she took the ribbons holding up her hair and bound the flowers and leaves by type, hanging them just over the smallest hearth to dry. At once they filled the air with musky spice, so thick and home-like she was sure they cast colors of green and purple and silver into the air.

There was a knock at the door, and she turned, filled with an eagerness she quickly tapped down. He'd left her with a question, true, but he could not expect an answer. She had begged for time, and he had not offered a limit. But perhaps he would dine with her? She was surprised how alone she felt, and how often her thoughts turned to Milena and even to Marek and Ludoslaw. She even missed the neighbors Aldona and Gnegon and their pinched judging faces. How had he withstood so many years of quiet? The question ran in circles around her head, crowded with many others.

"Please. Enter!" she called, and the door swung open on golden hinges at once.

The Gargoyle bent into her room, but stood on the threshold, and held his hands behind his back. "There is another place I could show you this afternoon," he said slowly. "It is part orchard, and part cavern, but I did not think you would mind as it holds many wonders."

"I would not mind."

"Then...." He stepped to the side and waited. Zaklina stepped up to him, and, after a beat, slipped her hand onto his forearm. He did not draw away, which she half-expected, and she was encouraged. Perhaps he would be able to answer more of her questions. Could he understand that a truly intelligent woman would be forced to ask them?

Anyone who simply accepted the unnatural power of the magic here was either a sorcerer or a fool.

They walked side by side down the stairway, at a slower pace than the morning, and he seemed careful to take smaller steps to accommodate her. As they moved, her thoughts slowly formed into sentences, though she kept them bottled so she would not ruin the mood.

Grasping for conversation, she looked at the many stairs yet to take, and spoke louder than she meant.

"So...if you are not the terrible beast who tears out hearts of maidens, are you the guardian of all these lands? A being of magic? Trapped here or choose to be?"

She did not stop between each question, rambling her theories while he was the unmovable statue walking beside her, hot under her palm. Though he was silent as she tortured them with her mumblings, he was a vast, comforting enigma.

"Must I stay here?"

It was her last question, untied to any of the others, and he paused their amble in the middle of a stairwell.

"You do not need to stay, no."

"I am not...required?"

"None who come here are."

"But...."

"You wonder why I brought you here, then? So I ask you, where would you have gone as you fled your life? To the past? The future? Another village, without friend or family?"

Her tongue tied itself in the face of his own questions, and she tried not to stutter a response. "I...only wished to be gone from the...the otherness. The malignant thing that grew around me, squeezing my soul, starving me and my sister. It felt like I must give into it, whatever it was, and it would have exacted a price I was unwilling to pay."

"You speak vaguely."

"It appears all I can do!" she suddenly burst, pulling away and holding her hands to her forehead. "All day I have been thinking, wandering alone, forming plans and words to throw at you, in hopes something would crack through the magic here, but I find as each hour goes, more slips away."

"Words do?"

"Yes! And no. The stories. The tales. They break in my mind as I think them, and I cannot help but believe that if I could only recall them, I would understand properly on the magic here, even though it is far greater than any story could say."

"Magic does not surprise you, then. It has not disappeared completely?"

"I...no?"

"You seem uncertain."

"I am here. It seems there is still something unknowable in the world. So, yes, there is magic, or else I would not be in an impossible castle. You would not exist. So magic has not gone. Has it?"

"Some say it will, someday." The Gargoyle slowly re-started them again. "Some soothsayers would predict a time when this would all be dust. I am inclined to believe it." He pointed to another room, a massive dining hall, where the windows had tumbled in and crushed the oak table in the center of it.

"It is only there is no one to keep this place tidy," she said, realizing belatedly that only magic could hold a castle of such size against the face of a mountain. "That is...I mean—"

"Do not try to reason your way through this," he said. "It is not meant to be matched with rational thought."

"Oh." Her shoulders ached. "Then I fear I will be of little use."

"You are here. And you still are asking questions. That is good."

"But...without the old stories in my head...without considering the true logic... It is one thing to behold little bits of wonder and magic, and even to meet one who wields it with ease. And some of it is a hidden kind of power, too. Both good and evil. But never have I seen it like it is here, so all-powerful and beyond comprehension."

"I believe that was the point," he said, and opened a set of doors near to their right.

It was a mouth, a tentative opening to what would be the vein of the mountain. She could not know, though, for she had no idea how deep or tall it all went. All sparkled with an unearthly white, from ceiling to floor, and under their feet was a thick powder that seemed to be ground from precious stones that crunched underneath.

"It is a cave of wonders," she said, and her voice sounded muted and dead in the great space, for it was not only filled with stone and crystal and veins of gold and bronze but also gnarled trees of ebony and bone-white bark, with leaves cut from emerald and amber. In the green leaves nestled apples, burnished with silver, and in the ochre trees dripped clusters of ruby berries that glittered along the edges.

"They said a goddess planted them," said Gargulec, as he reached up to pluck an apple. "Some said the fruit was forbidden forever. Others...did not believe."

"What did you believe?" she asked, taking the fruit as he offered it. It smelled sugary and tart, and did not weigh as much as she expected.

"What does it matter?" he said. "But I do not recommend you tempt any ire, in case the goddess still lives."

"Gods and goddesses were supposed to be immune to death, usually," Zaklina said, and pocketed the apple for later. "I think."

"Is there no belief in that, either?" he wondered. "It sounds as if much has changed."

"When was the last you wandered among others?"

"I learn of the world by those who visit me."

"Then you have been likely given quite a slanted view, if your company is so limited."

He bowed his head slightly in admission, and she felt vindicated in his acceptance of her notions. She trailed a hand along the cherry trees. The leaves were rounded and seemed sanded to softness, but the berries bit her fingertips. When she pulled her hand away, she thought she'd somehow crushed one, but the air suddenly filled with the iron and copper of blood.

The Gargoyle came to her side, and pressed his handkerchief to her palm again. "Perhaps you should keep it," he said, and his tone sounded almost amused.

"I'm clumsy, is what you mean."

"You are more curious than most, that is true," he acknowledged, and moved on so he did not see how the observation made her flinch. She followed him slowly, dabbing at the blood, wondering how much a body could lose in one day before falling over. As she walked behind, his scent overrode that of bleeding, and the urgings she felt from the old dream came at her full force. Tangy, woodsy and powerful; it was a sensual smell – heady and nearly sexual. Her unblemished hand found her throat, and her heart fluttered. Unwilling to face what her reaction meant, she paused, only to realize he had already done so, and was gazing up at the mound of crystal, which stretched from ceiling to floor.

"What is it?" she came to his side and looked up at the rock.

"The builders of the castle say it is the Veil, but I have never seen any being on the other side. Perhaps it is just a name."

"Perhaps it is the basis for all the magic keeping the castle together," she mused.

"Then it is doing a terrible job."

"Maybe it just needs a modern stonemason."

They both chuckled softly together at her idea, for the work needed on the crumbling castle was more than enough work for a hundred masons for a hundred years.

Suddenly, a shudder went through his stone-like body, and he turned to face her. "I am still surprised you are here, shocked you stand so near me, and are not afraid, nor have begged to leave after the loneliness of the day. Once—long ago, I thought I would be so fortunate to—." He stumbled to a stop as the revealing sentence nearly choked him.

She traced the fine threads in the embroidered cuff of her dress, and then tentatively stroked the velvet of his. She marveled how the softness of the cloth was like his palm, and slowly, she drew the limp hand to her, turned it over, and ran her fingers along the broad span of it. He turned immobile as she touched him and twined their hands carefully. As much as Zaklina wanted to push him to reveal more of his mind, to finish his sentence, she found the questions barred from leaving her mouth, as if her lips had swollen and her tongue too fat to move. She swallowed hard, and tried to think of something else to ask, something that would not pressure the magically charged air around them. As soon as she'd changed the vein of her thoughts, her gums seemed to shrink back to her teeth, and saliva flooded her jaw. She could speak. She could change the subject.

"Do you believe it best to follow the questions of your own mind, or to follow the whims of the masses?" she asked, locking her more inquisitive thoughts away as best she might.

"I suppose it depends," he said slowly.

"Does it?" she asked, thinking of Mrs. Staryski and Marek, of Milena and Ludoslaw. "I do not think so. I think following your own logic and mind is the only safeguard against a world of uncertainties."

His breathing pulled from the deepest depths of his chest. "I will not refute such logic."

Zaklina turned, surprised. "You do not think it odd I come to such a rational conclusion?"

The Gargoyle looked puzzled. "Well, it is strange. It is certainly not the traditional musings of a woman, to be so straightforward."

"You've no idea," Zaklina muttered, thinking of all the thoughts that often crowded her mind, and the trouble they brought when she dared to speak them aloud even among mere men and goodwives, let alone in a castle filled with a curse and a hex in every dusty corner.

"But I promise you this," the Gargoyle plucked the cherries without slicing his fingers, and offered them. They were as cold as ice, and smelled pink. "I will never lie to you. I will always tell you the truth."

"People have long thought the truth to be ugly."

When she glanced back at him, he was so still she thought he had indeed turned back into stone, and the thought chilled her more than the iced berries in her palm. But his eyes were still liquid, and they met hers.

"You did indeed leave your village in time," he said, and he spoke the words so slowly it was if they were dragged from the deepest recesses of his chest. She wondered if the magic stifled him as well, and if she could grasp at the whisps of memory allowed and piece together the answers to the riddles.

If she figured it out, would her stories be returned to her?

Would the magic be so kind?

The walk up the stairs was in dusk, with purple haze where the sun had been, and early starlight the color of glass. She clung to the rippled fabric of his sleeve, gripping the edge of his cuff so that her fingertips curled under it, and her nails skimmed the strange flesh-and-rock combination of his body.

"Who have you left behind?" he asked, a conversational tone in his low, scratchy voice.

She looked away, stunned at his acuteness. Did he know of Milena, then? Or of further back, of Narcyz? What did the books say? Sometimes the magic offered a way of seeing. A ball of obsidian or scrying with oil and water. Was he testing her own honesty? Anxious at being caught out, lest he realize she did not quite fit, she fumbled for a change of topic but the only one bubbling up she could not voice.

Finally she managed, "I...would rather not..."

"I understand. Sometimes it is less painful to forget. The numbness is better than anything else, is it not?"

"Is that how you have survived?"

His utter silence, save for the soft tread of his leather soles on stone, made her ashamed. She should not pry so much. She scrambled again. "There are those left behind, to be sure. But I am glad I am able to...be here, though. With you."

There was a sigh like the wind from him. "I worry that when I wake tomorrow it will have all been a dream."

"I have felt that way myself, ever since seeing you, only to realize you are more than a dream." Then, incredulously, she found herself saying, "If you worry I will disappear, do not leave me tonight. If you should wake in the evening, I will be there, solidly, beside you."

He jerked under her palm. "I would not harm your reputation, not even for my own peace of mind."

"What reputation? There are none here but us."

She swore she could feel him acquiesce, and tried to press her case, knowing she would not fear the night in this crumbling castle if she could wake and see his shape nearby, as ungainly as it was. "Besides, I am sure you are a gentleman. You are the most solid thing here..." she glanced around. "Here, where I am uncertain of the magic in the walls and the air. Where there is magic at all! Please..."

"I can deny you nothing," he said slowly. "But I cannot do this. I must instead ask something of you."

"I beg more time, please," she said at once, wanting more answers, as uncouth as they would be when she eventually asked. "We have only just met."

"I will not ask for marriage again in the same day. No. You have chosen to stay, but the danger is not over," he said, and his words rumbled and caught in her ears as he stopped outside her gem-studded door. "It will not be safe for seven nights, and it all rests upon you."

"What does?"

"The breaking of a long-forged cycle. The death of the flowers. The end of an era. All it takes is one, and you are here."

She wanted to contradict him, to tell him flat that she was not some silly maid who did as she was blindly bid. But then she would have to tell him she was no virgin, and she felt quite sure all the stories required it.

"Will it help? You—this place? Will it fix the magic? Guarantee my sister's safety?" She meant acceptance of his proposal more than anything else, and he understood, but only shook his head slowly.

"We can try. I must leave you now, and your door will be barred. It-the lock-cannot keep out everything, though. Whatever happens, do not cry out. Do not call for me, for I will hear it and be unable to come, and it will drive me to madness. Do not make a sound."

"Will all be well? Will I see you in the morning?" She turned and grasped both his hands in hers, squeezing and memorizing the solidness of his bulk. "Can you promise?"

"I can promise nothing in this, Zaklina. It is your own mind that will save all."

The sound of a bar going through the door made her shudder. She would have much preferred Gargulec's company than the emptiness of the huge room and massive hearth. The glass tub had been long emptied, and it sat drying near the largest fire. The heat pouring out of the fireplace scorched the ends of her hair, and made her skin tighten.

Though it was not so very late, she found herself aching for bed, and the one in her quarters was nothing like the old lumpy one of her attic in the city, or the straw-tick she had left in Marek's kitchen. She turned her thoughts from Milena. The food had to be back, the people sated, the babe close to leaving her sister's womb, where Zaklina would not be to create strife and knock wills with old Mrs. Staryski. She had to believe all was well, because to think of Milena in worse condition was impossible.

She sank into the luxurious down and feathers. Whenever she moved, the quilts and pillows gave off the scent of cedar and rose, and sometimes a juicier spice that reminded her of citrus. It still felt odd and lonely, for she had never slept in a bed so fine or so large. It was as if there was room to spare, room meant for the Gargoyle. She imagined him taking up the other side of the bed, all hard and heat, and was halfway to please herself before she stopped.

It seemed unreasonable to think of him as a man—a male being—who could pleasure her, and she knew the anxiety of the entire situation made her dwell fondly on the one figure she'd met in years who did not rot or cast her aside as a foolish woman. She would not deny she found him attractive, and that his essence seemed to call to her. Tied her to him… Zaklina gave in to the daydream, into the fantasy that he might love her, care for her.

Want her.

Had it only been morning when they'd sat to eat, and he had asked her to marry him?

Yes, she'd said she didn't know, that it was too much to ask. Because she still had so many questions. Much of that was true. But there was more. After Narcyz, she had promised herself never to love again—not like that. To shield herself from the chance to be hurt once more. And though she didn't think the Gargoyle would ever hurt her, she couldn't trust him thoroughly. It mattered little that she was compelled to him, that her body responded to his.

How could she believe he would not cause her heart to crack?

Just thinking of it all made her chest crash. Recalling her loneliness and the desolation and crippling sorrow made her breath come short again and this time it caught with pain. She must not think of this—she had managed to keep it all at bay when she cared for Milena and battled the fields of Miódshire. She was safe here. Gargulec had promised that at least, and she clung to it. In truth, now, she preferred his castle and his company to any others she knew, as fuzzy as some of it was in her memory now.

She was safe, there, at least, from her heart being torn, as long as she took care with it and was not rash or hopeful.

There were many ways to rip out a heart.

Slipping into uncomfortable sleep, she did not know how long she slumbered, only that when she woke, it was dark, and a noise had startled her. Had a whole day passed? Was it only an hour later?

The sound came again.

She sat up, looking around the empty rooms. The fires still blazed, the door unopened, and through the golden keyhole wafted the black fog of Miódshire, snaking in jagged, ethereal vines across the patterned marble, and straight to the hearth, where it began to swirl and take shape.

Zaklina thought it was a maid at first, like a ghost of a long-ago girl who once used the rooms in a kinder time when the castle was freshly cut and mortared. But as the head pulled itself outward, a slow taffy-stretch of elongated nose and chin, a jaw of flat teeth, and trailing ribbons, spiked ears and glowing eyes, she felt her mouth open.

She closed it before she could even gasp.

The Night Mare swung to face her, all bleached bone and grey rags on the body of a hag. With a lurch, the creature limped toward her, skeletal hooves raised. From the trailing garment, bumps humped and grew, and at first Zaklina was certain it was only rats. But as the mare came closer, the bumpiness lifted higher, until demons burned through the faded cloth. Zaklina covered her mouth, just in case, but in truth she was so frozen she did not think her voice would work if she wished to scream.

Each of the demons was decay personified. One oozed with burst yellow pustules, and another was all knobs and warts. More were dripping with green-and-blood bile, or popping orange globules with every step. One was only fire made of arms and legs, with a skull of a dragon for a head, and the smallest was a strange animal-creature that looked to be dying of mange. She could smell them, too, and was glad she had not eaten a solid meal so she could not lose it on the fine bedding.

They came to her, reaching and groaning, cracking and scraping.

She wanted to call. To whimper at least. To cry. Surely if she shouted for him, the Gargoyle would come to aid her? He did not mean for her to endure this horror alone – could he? All the courage Zaklina had stored throughout the long day and terrifying ordeals bled out of her, and she felt as if her skin was made of dried corn husks, brittle and ready to turn to powder.

The demons reached for her, and at the first touch of a claw on her ankle, she jerked away, scrabbling silently up her bedding and grasping the closest carved post with both arms. She wanted to keep her eyes squeezed shut, but the not knowing was almost worse. When she peeked an eyelid open, she wished at once she'd been braver to keep them closed as the vision of all the demons crawling up her bedding, oozing and burning it up as they came, with the Night Mare waiting at the foot nearly made her cry.

But no.

She had promised. She could save the Gargoyle, just as he had saved her.

At the next tickle of a yellowed nail on her calf, she did not cry out, and did not flinch. The crooked fingers and searing limbs of the different demons slithered up her knees and calves, before grasping her hips and yanking her clothing from her limbs. She said nothing. When she was nude and blistering from the fire demon dragging his teeth on her flesh, she lay limply, waiting for their torturous touch.

The Night Mare loomed over her, growing in height. The stench of the moldy robes, which seemed to have spent a year in a privy hole, made her want to cough and choke, but she did not, biting the sides of her tongue until the blood bubbled out of the corners of her mouth.

In a minute, the demons were gone, and the mare stood over the bed, taking all the space. A rasping whisper grew, and Zaklina tried desperately to recall the lore of the dread Mari Llewyd. Or was it the Brenin Llewyd?

But the grinning horse skull said nothing, did nothing except collapse into a pile of dust on the floor. Behind the cloud of ash, the demons dragged a rope made of slimed vines and prickly briars, with the berries crushed and dripping on the polished marble of the floor, staining the gold veins and sinking into the porous cracks in the pristine rock.

In an instant, they wrapped her, binding her toes and fingers, stringing it between the soft flesh of her thighs and dragging up the crease of her buttocks. The thorns tore open her flesh. One sat at the corner of her left eye, so she was afraid to blink. Every breath, even as tight and short as they were, pushed against the tightness of her bindings, bringing a fresh torture and prickles of needles.

When would it be over?

When would they tire of this game and simply finish it?

Did they want to only make her scream?

Make her go mad?

Zaklina thought perhaps she would indeed go insane if it continued. There was very little skin left for them to bind, but they seemed intent to cover every inch of her with the vines. She thought she might want the Night Mare back instead, to stare at her with empty sockets of hatred.

Could they just end it? Kill her. Be done with this unknown—

—the demons wrenched her from the bed, and her head whacked the edge of it as they went, pulling her by her feet. As they dragged her to the large hearth, she was shocked to see a massive cauldron rise in the middle, steaming and bursting with liquid now stirred by the mare, who had returned though Zaklina was certain she had been dragged through the ashes of it.

The demons giggled and gurgled, cackling as they darted and danced about her, reveling in her sacrifice.

The mare turned, the goo of the pot dribbling on the floor and wherever it landed, it bore holes in the tiles. Zaklina's eyes grew wider as the skull dipped down and near touched her nose.

"We are going to boil you and eat you," the Night Mare said, in a voice like chalk and grey mushrooms. "And we will devour even your bones." The voice grew deeper with each word, and the yelping of the little demons went higher, until all she could hear was the yips and screeching of their joy. Her heart beat the drum of her pulse in her ears, and tears fell onto the destroyed floor. The heat of the hearth began to crisp the wetness of the vines, making them dry and tighter.

Zaklina wondered if perhaps giving in to Mrs. Staryski would have been an easier fate, after all. If she had only been a more amenable woman, perhaps Narcyz would still love her. She would never have had to leave for Miódshire, and never had to cross wits or challenge the centuries old stories of the village. Milena would not be starving, and she would not have had to sacrifice herself.

Would the cauldron kill her at once?

Or would she boil slow, with the skin peeling from her sinew in chunks, until she was nothing but a living skeleton, clattering bones and blood?

Would the Gargoyle still want to marry her, then?

The thought cracked into her just as the sun shot a jet of cold white light into the room.

In that instant, there was a clatter, like the sound of a dainty silver spoon falling on a carved wooden floor. Zaklina's eyes, still wet from her silent tears, blinked, and then fluttered again.

She could...breathe.

She could move her toes and fingers, her knees and elbows. Sitting up, she was astounded to see the room untouched, as if the night's horrors never happened and the damaged erased. And though she still laid on the floor in front of the hearth naked, the burns and blemishes of the night were gone. Except for one. She winced as she touched her face, finding the scrape by her eye from the thorns.

The hearth was banked, but mostly cool, the blaze of moments ago a memory or a dream, or some lost, broken magic of the night.

Inhaling again, and pushing back the terror and fear, she shivered and stood, looking about for her damaged nightgown.

A knock at the door made her jerk, her heart leaping against her ribcage and crashing to her core. Her voice seemed stuck at the back of her throat, and she attempted to clear it. The knock came again, more urgently and twice as long.

"Zaklina? Are you undamaged? Are you...there?"

The Gargoyle sounded worried—perhaps there was even a note of fear in his voice. She turned in two circles, looking for something—anything— and grabbed the sheet of the bed to wrap around her in a fashion as she stumbled to the door. She laid her head against the rough carved gold.

"Is it barred?" she asked, her voice a croak and crack. "Am I locked in?"

"No. With daylight the door will open. You have not tried it? May I...are you well?" Hesitancy crept into his tone, and she grasped the handle, her hand shaking with a new tremor.

"Am I..." she paused to clear her throat again. It was as if the screams she had held in glued her gums to her mouth and indeed, she felt the blood from her bitten tongue clot between her back teeth.

He dove into her pause, as if trying to guess her question before she asked it, and thereby answering in a riddle. "There is no requirement. You are not bound by me, or this castle. I saved you from the meadow, yes, but you are not obligated to do more than this. If you wish it, you may depart. The danger of the meadow is not so far as to reach here – not yet. You will find the road cleared for travel, though I cannot say what you will find on it."

He seemed resigned, as if expecting her one night to be enough to send her scurrying back to what she had left behind. And perhaps, if she had a husband or children, she might have gone at once. And even her love of her sister made her consider his offer.

She thought of the woods, of the leer of Mrs. Staryski, and the unspoken, unseen danger meddling in the cobbled streets and in the yellowed grass of Miódshire. But she also thought of Gargulec, and found enough strength to open the door.

His eyes widened. Even in his unfamiliar face, she read the surprise—disgust?—as he spun on both heels at once, almost tripping himself.

"My pardon, please," he rumbled, sounding gruffer than before. "I did not realize you—I did not know that afterwards, as the others were so quick to—I am sorry to have arrived so early. I was only...anxious."

"I am glad you came," she said, her voice now a whisper and a snap. "It was all I could do not to call for you last night."

His shoulders hunched forward. "Then...am I to hope you will join me this morning?"

"I've only to dress," she said. "But don't leave."

"I'll wait, and shall not move."

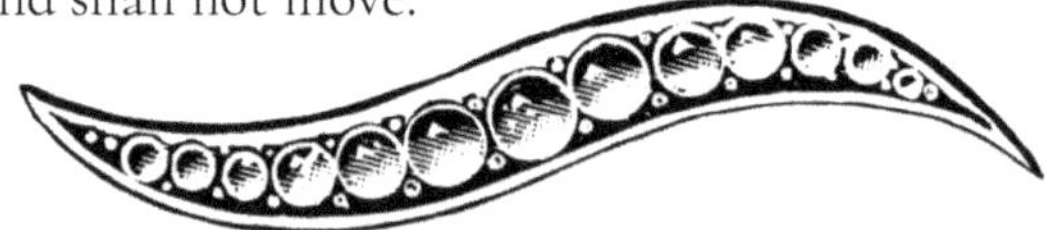

They broke the morning fast in the same garden, which already felt like a refuge. Zaklina stared up at the blinding sun by shading her face with a long slick leaf, still amazed at the way it seemed to be touchable, yet feeling the vastness of the cosmos around it.

"Some say the sun is a man, who rides his chariot each day, driven by wild horses. Others say it is a woman who drives her own chariot with giant cats. And still others would call the sun a god in its own right."

Zaklina put down the leaf and turned to her first cup of tea. She shot the Gargoyle an arched look and said without thinking, "And others say the chariot is pulled by dragons, or that there is no chariot at all, but a goddess who eats the adoration of kings." She paused, the teacup halfway to her mouth, and met his eyes. He, too, was looking at her with something like surprise on his cheeks.

"I...I didn't think I would remember that."

"I must confess, it surprises me."

"That I know myths and history?"

"No—as you said. That you remembered. The remembering...usually the only thing any have remembered is their homes, their families. Their own beloved. It is part of...it is the...hmmm." He shook his head as if to clear it, and dove in for a large chunk of white cake studded with flecks of green and pink petals baked inside.

She watched him swallow the whole thing in two bites, then took a piece for herself, assuming it to taste well enough. "There is a curse, then? That is what you're trying to say?"

"Yes. That. Your memories are restricted here, and my ability to...nudge things along, give helpful advice or even explain what has happened in the past. It is as if you are supposed to muddle yourself through each and every trouble, and I am to watch, helpless, bound by a code of silence I have never...It is apparently part of many hexes and spells all jumbled together. They defy the logic and even the history of existence."

"I will continue to ask the questions, then."

"It is a good thing you are not an easy woman," he said.

She held in the tremor flickering through her as he said the words, so offhanded and without malice. It reminded her of her differences. It was a way to say she was...unlovable.

"Then I suppose we must muddle together." Zaklina offered a small smile instead. She served him another large piece of cake before taking a bite of hers, careful to move her lips around the glass tines of the fork. Today's cutlery spun with vines of copper in blue and green swirls. The cake tasted of strawberries and mint, with a bit of rosewater, too. She thought it would pair well with orange slices, but when she went to peel one, she discovered the inside was frosted with blue fuzz, eaten by mold and mildew.

She dropped it with a huff of shock, coldness pouring into her bones even as the sunlight blazed with determination above. The orange rolled and bumped under the foliage, disappearing inside the densest part and plopping into one of the small pools half-hidden by birds-of-paradise and an unnamed flower in the shape of a pineapple, but white and red swirled.

Zaklina stood, forgetting her linen and rushing to the water with her fork. Under the crystal of the water's surface, she spied the orange lolling, hidden for a moment by the undulating lazy swish of one of the spotted koi. She closed an eye and aimed down, the too-sharp fork poised to stab the orange's exposed flesh, where the pith came off in ragged clumps.

"Stop." Gargulec was beside her, silent as moonlight, but stronger than any man as he paused her arm in midair, clasping his wide thumb into the tender flesh on the underside of her wrist. "It's too late."

And indeed, as he spoke, the orange's poison already drifted out, strange waif-like tendrils that first were white and blue, but then turned to silver, then black, choking the pure waters and decaying the edges of the small pond. A moment later, three plump fishes rose to the surface, belly up and already rotted clean through, so decayed that they were beyond stench.

Zaklina pulled away from the destroyed water, appalled at the damage. "It is ruined!"

"Yes."

"Forever?"

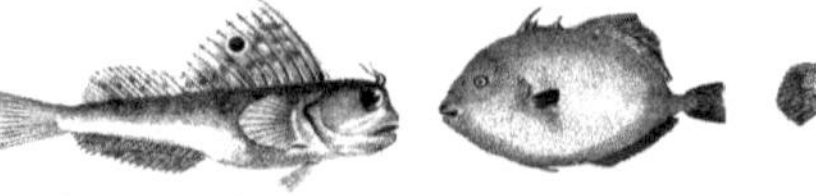

He gazed at the ash-and-cloud still water, and said nothing.

Zaklina felt her heart clench, burrowing inside her ribs and throbbing with sorrow. Would she only bring woes to this place, too?

"I don't believe I like this particular part of the magic," she said. She hunched small and breathless in the stillness of the garden, for even the sound of leaves rubbing together had paused. She looked up at the grim countenance of her host and lifted a hand. He took it, and helped her to her feet, briefly putting an arm about her waist to steady her. When he let go, she found herself wishing he hadn't.

They sat back down at the table, gingerly and without touching another orange. Finally, Zaklina inhaled and took up her teacup, now filled with cold brew. "I did not think…I did not expect to find something rotten here at the table."

"Surprises show up anywhere," he said, looking forlornly at the oranges. "But those were my favorites, so I suppose it is a trade of some kind."

"A trade?"

He looked at her fully. "You are still here. I suppose there must be some allowances for success, to be met with something that must be taken away."

"It seems unfairly advantaged to the magical side," she said, frustrated. "It is almost as if…"

He waited, slowly eating the second piece of cake. She repoured them tea, then cleared her throat, feeling as if by speaking she was inviting more of the decay into the castle instead of banishing it.

"I was reminded of…of Miódshire."

"We must assume that is the point. It is trying to remind you of home."

She shook her head. "But then why choose something so awful? Why remind me of the terrors I left? It only makes me cleave more to…to this castle." Zaklina stuffed the other part of her thoughts down, wishing she could finish, for all it would make her seem a wanton woman. Cleave to you…to your own self. She wished to say such tender thoughts to him, with such desperation it seemed unnatural.

Her lengthy silence made him clear his throat, and then he asked, as if trying to circle their conversation, an echo of his earlier question, "Who, then? Who is it in your mind, who pulls you back to your old life, so you will leave this place, who the castle wishes to make you remember? For all you say you are unusual, surely you have some who mourn you?"

Zaklina concentrated on the delicate crystal tweezers, balancing a pale pink sugar cube between it before it dropped into her tea without spilling. She yearned to tell him all, but could not for the life of her remember why she should not. Was it...her old wedding vows? No—the stories, they called for something else. There was something else wrong with her, something that would have him shoving her out of the castle. But...the memory quickly shattered again, destroying her mental grasp. She turned to the old memories instead, which shone like cloudy diamonds in her mind, unblemished by fractures in her mind.

"Our—my sister Milena and I—our parents died years ago. And...she is married now, to a man who does not care for me as his kin."

"No other family? So small, then. Families used to be quite large."

"Some are," she agreed. "And we've cousins and uncles, aunts and great-aunts, all living in the city where I...where I was, too, before I came to care for Milena."

"What of these others, then? Will they miss you?"

"No. They do not wish to know of my...of my predicament. Whatever it may be. The women run much of the small pieces of the world, for all men like to believe they hold all the power. But the women...they hold the power of the home and of social strings, hidden from view, but sometimes stronger for it. My aunts and cousins...they think little of me."

He seemed surprised. "The women don't like you?"

"I'm not an easy woman," she reminded him, eyeing a dark plum before deciding against trying any more fruit for the day. "And the things I...I did not live quietly as I was supposed to do. I spoke up. Argued. Debated. Drove away... Well, it is not so surprising. In fact, it was my own doing that—." She stopped, feeling as if she was sliced from stomach to throat, and choked on the complete story. "Well, men and women both seem to have troubles with anyone who is different. Who doesn't...follow the thoughts of others without question."

The Gargoyle settled into the chair for a moment, the dark fabric of his clothing melting into the shadows of the cushion. He straightened and stood fluidly, hesitated only briefly, and offered her his hand.

She took it at once. "You must go?"

"Not yet," he said, sounding almost merry. "You have decided to stay another day. It is more than I could have hoped for—and so I will be able to give you many hours this morn. I've another place to show you."

They stepped away from the table, and Zaklina worked very hard not to turn and look back once more at the ruined little pond. She shuddered, pushing away the thought of rot and decay, and the black teeth of Mrs. Staryski's spittle-filled mouth. Their footsteps sounded tiny in the hushed walks between the vignettes of plants and trees, but the rustle of her gown seemed scratchy and overloud. She wondered what made her senses so sharp and tense, and then realized she had shoved the night's terrors away, too, and yet it bubbled tightly and hotly under her skin.

"Last night—"

"I know." He cut her off swiftly, harshly. "That is, I know enough. Do not speak of it, for it will only make it worse."

"How so?" She could not think any way the night could be filled with more horror.

"If I know the details, I will worry more than I do. It is already terrible enough, to stay away, knowing unthinkable acts of...that you are..." He threaded her arm tighter around his elbow and pressed her closer, briefly.

In a flash, she spoke again without thinking. "Well, then, as we go, you might tell me of yourself. Have you left anyone?" As the thought tripped out, she realized there was a crack in the magic after all. It would give way to words, if she did not hold back. If she did not think overmuch.

His long mouth went down. "I have no one left. They're all gone. And all dead."

"I'm sorry!" What a fool she was! "Of course they are. I shouldn't have asked. But...surely I'm not the only person to stumble on these gates in the years—decades? Centuries? You have hinted at others. There have been other women."

"Girls," he nodded as they began to descend the unending flights of stairs. "Perhaps one every hundred years."

"Girls then," she encouraged, patting the fine, soft cloth of his sleeve. "You say none of them wished to stay."

He gave a rumble that passed for his laugh, bitter and sad. "No."

"Did you ask any of them to marry you?" she pressed, needing to know.

"I did." He paused on a landing to half-turn and meet her gaze squarely. The answer pained her more than she expected, though it only confirmed what she'd suspected.

He did not love her.

She was not special to him.

He asked for marriage of any maid, perhaps, as a requirement of the magic that bound him to this place and form, or for his own plans and plot. It only reconfirmed what she believed to be true about herself: that she was unlovable, that something was wrong with her.

That she should guard her heart.

For if even such a creature did not love her, who or what could?

"I see," she put quietly, and pulled her arm from his, feeling a band curl around her ribcage and slither knives into her core. Then again, he did not know the worst of it. Didn't the magic in all the stories ask for a maiden? She could recall such a thing now, and she grasped at it before it withered away from her mind.

And she owed him that much of the truth, if she could spit it out.

"I must tell you," she admitted suddenly, looking up to hold his gaze. "I am not a girl, and not a virgin. I'm a woman. I was married."

There. She'd gotten it past her stiff lips, and it felt as if she was ripping apart her gut to say so. It broke something. Changed something. Switched a story, unwound a thread.

None of the stories accounted for someone like Zaklina. She'd long ago become less than worthy, something she sensed suddenly, acutely, in the new frigidness of the very air.

Utter shock and surprise rang across his wide face. Funny how she could read him now, the way she would anyone else. Had that happened over breakfast, or when she'd opened her door after her night of horror?

"Widowed?" His voice sounded strangled.

She shook her head again. "No."

"Then he lives?"

"He does."

"You should return to him."

His determination was no laughing matter, but she tried to laugh all the same, a hard, stiff bark. "Oh no I shouldn't. He does not want me. Remember? I am not an easy woman."

He took a step toward her and faltered. "He cast you off? His own wife?"

She glanced at her left hand, where the ring had once spun, a fine circle of silver. It had been her one constant, and when that was ripped away, she'd never found her footing again. Not until this castle. Not until the

Gargoyle had shared his small confidences. Until she realized she was the mistress of the whole space should she want the position.

"In my time, especially in the cities, a man or woman may leave their spouse whenever they like," she explained. "The marriage is completely ended, as though it never happened."

He seemed dumbfounded, but before he could speak, she spun to walk down the stairs unaided. She was unwilling to hear any claims he'd feel required to make: that she was beautiful, that her man should never have left her.

He would be wrong to say such things.

This time they went lower and deeper into the bowels of the castle. The stones darkened with wetness and slime. Blue-black and lime lichen and moss fizzed along the lower rocks, hiding their jagged edges.

"Do you recall the stories?" she asked him, as the light dimmed to a pale pearl and the disrepair of walls and rooms became more pronounced. "Are you allowed to remember?"

"Remember what?"

"The tall tales and fantasies. The folktales and lore. Everyone grows up with them, everyone has some."

They paused on the edge of a large crack in the stairs. Zaklina leaned over it, and noted the darkness was complete. How far down did it go? They were already reaching the belly of the mountain, and she could not imagine such a place did not, could not have dungeons. She shivered at the thought of how terrifying they'd be, stifled with outrageous layers of stone and mortar...

The Gargoyle took one gigantic stride and crossed the crack, and then held back a hand for her to leap across to him. Zaklina eyed the depth. It would be rude if she denied him her company after begging for it. She wanted to close her eyes to make the jump, but that felt worse.

She took the offered palm and was at once weightless as his strength swung her over in half a moment. It was as if she was truly flying, and when her feet touched the slick rock, she slipped and caught the fine heel of her slipper just in time and did not make an ungraceful fool of herself.

"The stories are distorted here," the Gargoyle finally answered, once they were on their way again, her hand clenched on the fabric of his inner elbow. "They are meant to be, so the castle can welcome anyone, at any time. That is what I have deduced anyway, and there are some truths to this existence. All my own memories—and the stories tied to them—are fractured and half-forgotten. I recall only the barest shadows of my past, and they are muddled with time and pain. My existence, this castle, is bound to the land, the people, and their tall tales. That I do know. And if their stories turn me into a monster...then that, too, is a truth." His voice dropped and cracked with sorrow the more he spoke, and he stuttered to silence.

"Truth is not truth if there is more than one version of it," Zaklina retorted, feeling protective of him, the swell of empathy surprising her. He was a monster. A creature who some said tore the hearts out of maidens, which was certainly not true...

Then again.

"But...people make up their own truths," she finished slowly.

He bowed his head, and stopped them once again at a crevasse in the stairs. "They do."

"How can something actually be true, then, if all come up with their own idea of it? If every person's narrative is unique to them, their life, their experiences, there is no such thing as truth."

"Ahh, but that is why we turn to stories," he said. "For no matter the language, or the details, many of them speak a constant human truth."

Zaklina's heart thudded thrice, hard and quick, and she caught her breath. "And...if many people believe an untrue thing?"

"That, my dear, is how rumors start."

"And what? Become fact?" she stared up at his face, surprised to see the echo of a man's features overlayed within the gargoyle's stone-carved lines. Had the night's fears made it possible to see him more as he was—or once had been? "So, then what are you, and how do you fit in? Perhaps you are Truth personified."

"'People have long thought the real truth to be ugly'," he quoted her. The corner of his long mouth twitched, as if he was considering a smile. She wondered if his jaw was full of overlarge teeth, or a great black maw of only stone-flavored darkness, and thought it better not to know.

"Regardless if truth is ugly, it is better than false words creating much trouble," she reasoned. "I have always asked too many questions to get to the heart of reality, which has not brought me any favors. But the truth is what saves us. Everyone says that, too. Truth is what we should love..." Heat splintered out of her gut and frosted her skin, prickling its way up to her cheeks. What had she just implied?

He cleared his throat, deep in his chest, and gestured to the overlarge break in the stairs. "This was not here the last time I ventured. We do not need to continue."

"We've come this far," she said. "Can you cross it?"

"I can. It is your comfort that gives me pause."

She pulled in her lower lip, then shook her head against any fear. "You may carry me over."

His eyes widened. "Carry you?"

"It's not as if you have not done so before," she said, flushing harder against the memory.

"But that time...it was different when I took you from the meadow. It is a different kind of...permission."

She lifted her chin and waited. Having now decided, she wanted it. She wanted his nearness, even in an offering of chivalry. He let out a great gust of grumbling air, which bounced and echoed down the twisting stairs.

"Very well." Was it hidden eagerness in his voice, or resignation?

When he put both hands on her waist, the initial coolness of them seeped through the layers of cotton and silk and satin before turning warm. She placed her palms over the backs of his and nodded once. With a great inhale, he bounded, the deep bellow of his chest rumbling against his throat and into her. Intertwined so, they leapt across the expanse, leaving small pebbles to fall below and offer back a tiny crackling and popping as they scurried and tripped into the black below.

He let her go the minute it was possible, but Zaklina felt boldness creep inside her blood. It was golden and bright, liquid copper and bronze. It felt like...hope? Home? She refused to let herself lay claim to a word to go with the emotion and instead clasped his hand in hers, twisting their fingers together in a gesture more familiar than the more formal arm-in-arm. His tightened around hers, first ice, then heat. She was sure he'd pull away, but when he didn't, she let out the breath she'd held since he'd taken his leap.

As they continued down, he seemed disinclined to continue their conversation, and she grasped for another topic, finding it difficult to make the proper discussion. It was as if the castle liked to bar the typical mundane topics the same way it broke the lines of stories, random and without warning. Maybe that was the point. The only ideas to be easily discussed were the tricky topics just when one didn't want to do it. The ones proper company discouraged—the very things Zaklina was always skirting in public, as they seemed so obvious yet were never allowed in a drawing room or even in a tavern.

She wondered if Marek had resigned himself to the low and muddy tavern in Miódshire, drowning his shame in beers with Ludoslaw and the others who had failed to keep her safe. Would they make another story—a rumor of the woman who left? Or would they think she had been stolen by the beast of Mrs. Staryski's tale? She had a brief vision of the menfolk—long guns and pitchforks, and sharp sticks for the younger boys—trekking through the cold and dripping black trees, crunching through frost, huddled around fires made of evergreen, eyes shot with white and blood, all looking for her. Zaklina tossed away the thought. None would waste much time chasing her, not knowing where to go or where to start. And besides, would Marek leave Milena so near her time, especially now that Zaklina had disappeared? Who would feed her and the growing babe?

"Here we are," Gargulec paused, and she pulled herself out of her mind in order to take in a wall made entire of wood.

The Gargoyle released her palm and placed both of his on the wooden slats of the wall and pushed. His shoulders rolled through the thick blue-grey of his coat, and the wall cracked and groaned. It was not a wall of wood, but a set of immense double doors.

As he opened them, she was washed with pink light tinged with orange and white, and the scent of salt poured through the air.

It was a chamber chopped and sliced from the depths of the mountain's roots, hewn into perfect angular edges and sharp points. The end of the space was too far to see, for it stretched as a massive hallway, with a flat roof high above that pushed into a hazy salmon glow at the end of her vision. Every inhale felt heavy with sea air, sodden with the salt, for it was all salt. Everything from the walls to the floor to the soaring arches that sank to hard, square alcoves were carved from salt, as if they were walking through an artery of the hills which had once been solid salt and instead some great force had turned it into a hall of pinky blush veined with white. Even the seats inside the shallow alcoves were nothing but slabs of salt. Everything seemed to glow from within, though Zaklina could not fathom how candlelight might live behind the walls. She took a deep breath and the salt in the air fell on her tongue and coated her teeth.

"It is...a wonder," she managed to say, and fought the urge to spit the excessive saliva that filled her lower jaw. "A grand place, one of greatness. Someone must have wanted to carve themselves a sacred hall in the heart of the mountain."

"We are not at the mountain's heart," the Gargoyle said at once, then shook himself. "Pardon. I...I did not want you to think I would ever take you there. Here, you should rest. It was a long way down."

He led her to one of the alcoves and bade her sit. She was surprised that the salt, while rough and grainy under her fingers, did not chill her. It was as if the salt lived. Maybe it did. Maybe salt lived until it was cut away. Zaklina brought one of the tiny grains that easily clung to her skirts to her lip and licked it away. It tasted of salt, but salt tinged with froth and water, and aged with mud and coated in vanilla.

The Gargoyle stood over her, watching, and she felt her cheeks heat under his gaze. She shifted and laid a palm on the place next to her. "Would you like to rest as well, my Lord?"

The offer was a test, and both of them knew it. Would he willingly place himself so near, so intimately, in a seat normally taken by a lover or spouse? There were none to see them, but that seemed to never be the trouble. Zaklina held her breath to keep the salty air from saturating her lungs but also with a deflated hope. He had already admitted she was not special, so why did she push him to behave as if it were so? She knew the answer to that, too, though she thought to keep the idea buried as it'd do her no good to come to the surface. She'd already experienced heartbreak once before and was not inclined to do it again if she could help it.

Gargulec remained standing and turned toward the great wooden doors. On this side, they were crusted over with white crystals, glittering points of clear salt leaking into the very fiber of the door.

"I will get you something restorative. I should not have asked you to walk so far, so long, after such a difficult night."

"Do you have servants who travel this far?" Zaklina found herself wondering how their morning breakfast was made and served, and who washed the dishes. Was there invisible staff, or a rotund chef hidden in a castle kitchen? Or was it all just magic—the very same which filled her glass bathtub and lit the fire in the hearth?

She bottled up the questions and decided not to beg him as it would only betray her own growing attachment to him, even as he so bluntly had told her of his lack of it for her. "I will take whatever is available, and gladly if it's not too much trouble."

He spun and nearly fled the room. If he had been wearing the long traveling cape, it would have once again looked like wings with the speed of his departure.

Alone in the massive hall of salt, Zaklina leaned against the wall of her alcove. If she had magical powers herself, she might see what she could carve from the soft material. How many bodies had it taken to create such a space, and with such precision it hurt her eyes. Could slaves be trusted to engineer perfection? Or was this another space built by the desires of a god or goddess? Was there some clue or hint to the nature of the mountain itself, or the castle that clung, crumbling, to it? Zaklina tried to think back, beyond the common stories, to the ones that were lost and mostly forbidden except for scholars who wore black kid gloves and could read the ancient languages?

When she was married yet to Narcyz, and when he had stopped coming to her table or bed...back when she still believed it to be the nature of his business and not his repulsion of her brain and his preference for the quiet mind and lovely limbs of another, she had snuck into the lower tombs of the city. It was there that the greatest stories were kept, studied for any hints of leftover magic that could be squeezed from the earth, for some literary men believed it was still possible to discover the last of the world's secrets without trying to do anything but learn the tales of the old ways and uncover how the people of other cultures and lost civilizations had spoken to gods and made pacts with demons and devils. Zaklina had kept a cloak and hood over her head and stuck to the deepest pockets of the caves and rustled among the more worn scrolls, hoping to find something in a language she could read.

It was not a hunt for power or magic she sought, but an understanding of the world. Answers to her questions about what made fog rise or cats scream, or at the very least the truth behind all the stories. The root of all the folktales and the beginning of the lore. It had to start somewhere. Stories did not just spring up out of the ground or burst from a soft big flower, no matter how fanciful one might embellish a tale. She'd found one parchment at last, one with crunchy corners and a crumbling middle with ink that looked purple, but was actually blackened blood mixed with the feces of a crocodile. It began not with a story of the beginning, but of the realities of birth and life, a woman's way, the best ways to ensnare a man's affections, from a love spell woven with anise seeds and a tea heavily infused with white and gold strawberries. From there wove a tale Zaklina had never heard whispered before, one of birth again and death linked, the sun and the moon, and the great goddesses of the sky and sea, each needing the other but hating it, and the cycle of blood and earth linking them together—and how humanity connected it all, and the deep fault that sat, dormant and diseased, within each man and woman that lead to a disconnection with the truth of life itself. It was difficult to read, as if the words were unwilling to offer themselves up, and she did not get a chance to learn the names of the goddesses or the magic binding them together before someone had spied the crimson ribbon of her dress below the cloak and she'd been pulled out by arm and hair and tossed to the streets.

That had been the last day Narcyz had looked at her with anything close to affection. Someone must have told him of her brazen attempt to learn, to break with tradition and to push the boundaries. She argued that no official rule existed barring women from the caves of knowledge, that it was only that most women were too busy with children to have time to care. It had been the wrong thing to use, for it only reminded her husband of her failure in that, too.

The first night she'd realized Narcyz was not going to come home at all, she'd gone to search for him and to beg forgiveness, even if the words tasted rancid. Not knowing if he was at the docks or in the forest with the woodcutters, overseeing the building of his ships, she looked for him in both places, not watching the sun or the cast of shadows. On her way home from the woodcutting glen, she'd stopped to pick the frost plums to make a tart to entice Narcyz back to her table, if not her bed.

It was a plan born from foolishness, as she'd forgotten the panthers that stalked the chestnut trees and slunk through the beech forests at dusk. The yowling growls came from above in the branches, and then closer, behind her, and she'd only had the thorny branches of the plum vines to whip about her in defense, tearing apart her hands with the fat thorns as she stared at pairs of yellow eyes and dripping teeth as the animals approached from multiple corners. She'd screamed, once, and it had made them pause just long enough for the last of the woodcutters to come to her aid and swing their axes, shouting and putting the panthers on the run.

But their eyes...their teeth...

It was not unlike that of the demons of the night, who had also come to rip her, tear her, eat her...

And who might come again...and again...

"Zaklina."

A massive hand, thick and carved of living stone gripped her forearm, shaking it. "Zaklina! Wake up."

She woke with a cry, her face wet. Ridiculous woman! It was only a dream, memories that could not be undone. She lifted her hands to her cheeks to wipe away the tears, only to find her palms smeared with blood.

"Again?" she gasped, smudging her skin further, rubbing out the liquid as it pushed from under her eyelids.

"Allow me," the Gargoyle balanced a small glass tray on one arm and scrubbed at her face with the old grey cloth of his. "The fabric is part of the castle, made to absorb all." He finished quickly and then offered the tray. She took it and picked up the bone china to gulp the pale red tea before she lost her wits at the appearance of blood once again. Her hand shook as she put the teacup back, noticing the glass of the tray was etched with a scene that seemed to be made from her dreams and fragments of folktales she'd known by feel if not by word—seven houses each embedded with seven emblems of lost power from stories so old they had been forgotten: a tied reed, a stone crown, a horned cap, a four-pointed star.

"You are fatigued. I should get you back to your room, and you might get some sleep," the Gargoyle took the finished tea tray and set it to the side. It made a strange crackling as the glass scraped on the salt table. "I didn't think...I have never had..."

He turned to the side and offered his arm formally. Zaklina sniffed, hoping she was not swallowing blood, and stood. She brushed crumbs of salt from her backside discretely, and wondered if salt discolored silk and satin. "You have never had to worry on a woman like me?" she finished for Gargulec as they exited through the great wooden doors. "You have never had such a delicate woman? I assure you, I am not so weak."

"It is the opposite," he said. "It is that you are the strongest. No woman has ever stayed this long. I admit I do not know what to do next."

Zaklina suppressed the bloom of a smile and banished the tendrils of her daydream away as best she might.

His arm tightened under hers and he glanced down. "You're trembling. Was it a nightmare?"

"Ha!" she laughed shortly, but swallowed the second half of it, for it would only be sarcasm, and he had been nothing but kind. She tempered her voice. "It was no 'night mare,' for I have seen one of those and it was nothing like."

"I should not have brought you so far," he repeated. "I did not think. Forgive me."

She nodded but kept her silence. She spun in her mind, afraid of her fear of the coming evening, and that even the memories themselves might make her speak out of turn. Even though the Gargoyle was not her husband, would he turn from her if she was too forthright?

Then again, he had not cast her aside after learning she was no maid. Perhaps he might keep her near if only for the conversation on philosophy and history, lore and possibilities.

He peered down at her further through the gloom of the stairwell. "Will you be alright?"

"You will leave me once we return to my room? I would not prefer to go if that is the case."

"Is it not to your liking?"

"It's not that. The room is lovely. I just...I'd rather be with you."

"You don't need to stay in my company all night," he said, quite likely innocently misunderstanding her veiled request. They paused at the large crevasse. Zaklina peered down into it. Was it wider than before, and in such a short time? The Gargoyle seemed to hesitate for the same reason, but there was nothing for it. They had to leap.

"Hold on and do not let go," he said, his voice suddenly low and fierce.

She gripped his shoulders, finding strange relief to have a reason to bury her eyes and nose into the thick grey ruff of his neck, a beard that served as something more on him. As she inhaled the pine and wild scent of his clothes, he jumped.

And then they fell.

The whoosh of air took hers.

Zaklina might have screamed but could not.

All was silence around them as they dropped, and even the Gargoyle made no sound. For one moment, she thought he had turned to rock and she was anchored to him and falling to her end.

He reached. Long arms curled and caught, wide fingers latching onto purchase. And they hung over the abyss, with yawning darkness yanking at their feet and eating at their sight with the pale watery grey high above.

"What—what happened?" she asked, her voice raw and raspy.

"It is the castle, the power within it, that built it," he said, sounding muffled and grim. "It is attempting to beat us."

"What do you—"

"I must get you back. And up. There may be no time for you to rest, let alone eat. I am sorry, Zaklina."

He began to crawl up, scaling the wall but without speed for if he brought his body too close to the black rock it would scrape Zaklina's back. She gasped softly when she bumped into it and the slow curdling drip of blood began to snake down the center of her spine. The dress was certain to be ruined now.

At her gasp, he froze. "I should have thought. This is untenable and we cannot continue."

"Will help come?" It seemed a frivolous question to ask, and Zaklina felt a fool the moment she did. "Or perhaps there is a ledge you can leave me on, and you might go up yourself to find aid. Or a rope ladder?"

"I would not leave you here alone, and we have little time left," he said. "You must climb about and hold my neck from the back."

It was an undignified scramble, but she accomplished it with only a few tears to the silk and one or two more scrapes. If the Gargoyle was injured or frustrated with her slowness, he said little, a gentleman even in a difficult situation.

"We must hurry now. Hold on tightly."

In the new position, they moved much faster, and Zaklina tried not to choke him as she gripped his neck by holding onto her elbows with both hands. She ignored the black hole below, and instead enjoyed the nearness of the Gargoyle's body and the roll of his back and the muscles of his arms and the large rounded ones of his shoulders. He moved faster with each passing moment, and Zaklina wondered if the castle drew the exit farther away on purpose.

"What happens if I am not in my room when it is night?" she asked. "Would it be so very awful if you were with me? Perhaps you could keep the demons away."

His movement stuttered. "It is forbidden."

"Why? Because you are male and I am female? I have spent my entire life attempting to do as I wish without regard to tradition, even if I did it quietly and without fuss. It did not always serve me well, but then again, we are no longer in the world of the typical. Perhaps allowances could be made for properness."

"You are...not an easy woman," he said, and she winced at the familiar accusation. It made her tongue freeze while defiance grew deep in the recesses of her ribs. At last Gargulec's biceps hooked onto the final ledge, and the stairway soared above them.

The rest of the journey up was covered in a blanket of stifled silence, reminding Zaklina of parlors and wide scratchy collars, starched ringlets under tiny hats and the careful dance of conversation about weather. Hers was the silence brought by a woman who tried to know her place and it chafed at her, reminding her of what she had lost and what she could never accomplish.

Her knees and thighs ached and clenched with pain by the time they arrived at her gem-studded door. Would there be time for the hot water bath before she met him for dinner? He had mentioned dinner, hadn't he?

"What time might I see you for the evening meal?" she asked him, as he relinquished her arm.

"It is too close to dusk," he said. "I must go. I do not dare to be near, to hear...it would ruin it all."

"Then, instead of dinner, might you...would you come..." She caught herself before she might offer something even more brazen than before. It was only that he was like a protector, a savior, for all his monstrous appearance. He was a guardian of some sort, was he not? But then she reminded herself not to beg for any favor or comfort.

She was a fool.

For of course, the Gargoyle did not love her.

"Never mind. I should not ask." Shaking her head at her own folly, she turned to the handle, but before she could enter, his hand covered hers.

"I do not...I did not understand. Not at first," he said from behind. "How could I? What girl...woman...would possibly wish for, let alone suggest..." Words failed him completely, and she turned to face him once more.

"Well, you asked for my hand in marriage," she said. "I should think, even without my answer, that has opened some avenues to explore."

His eyes, black and chocolate, grey and stormy even in the half-light of the setting sun behind them, widened with shock.

"You have said I am an uneasy sort of woman," Zaklina reminded him. "With that comes unusual ideas, too. Perhaps you might wish to…oh… reconsider your request?"

"I am afraid it is too late for that."

"Then—come in, please," she said, finally stating her original request aloud. "We still have time, and perhaps, if we are lucky, the castle will have rewarded our escape with a meal."

It was an offer no gentlewoman would give, unmarried, married or set aside. To have a man—even if he were not fully such—in a woman's private rooms went against all the rules of every societal propriety across many continents. Zaklina wondered if they were still on the one of her birth.

She opened the door and the scent of foodstuffs filled her nostrils. The Gargoyle glanced about, uncertain maybe of the magic's strength or what was allowed. But without another protest, he followed mutely into the glittering, polished marble sitting room of Zaklina's front parlor.

Instead of a glass tub filled with aquamarine water and bubbling soap, there was a brass table on legs of glass, covered with golden domes. Steam wafted like pale, uneven fog from under several, and two wine goblets of cut green and blue stone were filled to the brim of wine the color of water.

He sat gingerly in one of the chairs, the bulk of him making the cushions sigh and sag a little more than necessary. Suddenly, the Gargoyle looked tired and uncomfortable, and Zaklina's nerves twitched and twanged. Somehow, having him in her own rooms, steps from the great canopied bedroom, was the most intimate thing they had done together thus far.

"I apologize for my forthrightness," she said, sitting across from him and lifting off the golden covers. "I should not have asked even for this. It was forward of me to force you to come in, though now that you are here you might as well eat."

"Ask anything of me, and you shall have it," he said once more, but he glanced at the door with unease.

"I will not ask it of you in the future," she promised. "If we are to share anything private, I should wait for it to be on your offer."

He actually barked a laugh. "What I would offer would repulse you."

They stared at one another across the table, and then she busied herself with the meal, putting sliced white meat and even whiter sauce on the silver plates, with slivers of purple potatoes and dark red lettuces. She did not know what a gargoyle might eat at dinner, even one who looked more and more like a man.

She squinted slightly at him across the table. Was he indeed less the Gargoyle and more human? Or was she only becoming comfortable with his physiognomy?

"I don't know if any offer of yours would be truly repulsive," she said, handing him the plate. "I would personally ask you to stay the night. Take me in your arms so I might sleep protected."

She could tell she had surprised him further and she wondered at her boldness, for it was blunt, even for someone who wished to disregard the rules at the best of times. It was as if...Zaklina grasped at her daydream, where the symbols and the memories, and even the etched glass tray in the salt hallway seared into her mind but did not come together. It was as if she...

"I would never believe it." The Gargoyle broke into her musing. "That you would wish for it."

"It was silly to say," she murmured, picking up a gold fork. "Forgive me."

"There is nothing to forgive. I would have offered you the same, except I never dreamed you'd prefer such a choice. I would not want to run the risk of you leaving the castle out of fear and disgust," he said ruefully.

Her head jerked up and she met his gaze. Shock tripped through her blood. So he did indeed want to be near her? Of his own accord? Something like hope simmered through her fiber, but she shook it off. There was no reason to hope for anything more than this small piece of...of comfort he was willing to give.

He dashed the glimmer of hope in the next instant anyway.

"It does not matter in this instance what I want, and it is the one thing I cannot offer you even if it truly was the wish of both our hearts. The evenings are not mine, and you must continue on, as it all rests on you. Your will. Your strength."

He stood, having inhaled his food over-quickly. Bowing low, he reached to touch her cheek with two fingers, briefly and without lust.

"Have courage," he said, his voice tinged with pleading and hope mixed together, and then he turned and departed her rooms as if the demons of the underworld were after him. Behind him, the locks on the door clicked together.

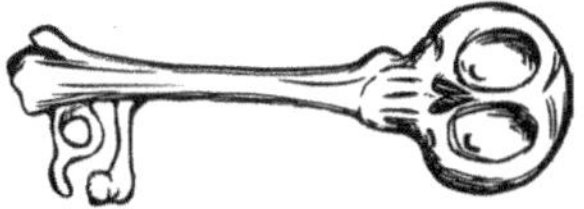

Zaklina ran her hands through the drapery and along the carved walls of her room. In some places behind the tapestries, the wood gave way to stone—grey stone mottled with silver and purple, or black as pitch. Whenever she touched the stone itself, it quivered under her fingers, buzzing with anger or malice. Visions of Miódshire filled her mind, hard broken memories that stitched themselves back together out of order.

Zaklina, arriving lost and alone, to face the questioning eyes of the village. Milena, arriving with Marek as newly, happily married, folded into old Mrs. Staryski's narrow—no, buxom—bosom. Milena frail and starving, then round with child, and Zaklina burning her hands black on the stove as she slaved for the children she taught. No, the children she would never have. Or for Narcyz, as he dozed at her table and left her bed. Wait! It was Narcyz, in bed with Milena, not Marek, kissing her sister and leaving purple-red bruises on her back...

Zaklina released the castle wall, her hands sticky with a pale yellow slime. She shook her head of the visions. Narcyz was gone. He had never come with her to Miódshire.

It had to be the castle once again, pouring human hate and the mind of Miódshire itself, with its grasp on the minds of all its people. It was the dying castle thinking to lure her back to what she had left. Zaklina wondered if the stones always offered up such terrible thoughts to all the young women who had come to stay. But if so, why had they all left? Did they think the awfulness of their pasts to be a much better choice than the uncertainties of a crumbling castle? Or did all the others have a much happier place to return to if they departed?

She must ask the Gargoyle his thoughts. Zaklina closed her eyes against the day, reveling in his nearness and touch while trying to forget the terror of their fall and the closeness of death. Why was she not more rattled? Was it trust that he would save her, no matter their trials? Was it a lack of emotion on her part – had she blocked her feelings so entirely after all the heartbreak and roughness of her life? She would speak to him about the castle and its deep crevasses, and about his strength that had pulled them out of it. He was part man, part monster, of this she was certain, though she could not tell if he lived in the castle under duress or by choice, or if he was the last remnant of magic left in the world. Maybe that was what he guarded. Zaklina worried that he might be failing such a duty.

She sank onto the silken bedding. Today the bed was draped in a red so deep it looked like an old scab, patterned with golden threads tangled in tiny embroidery. Looking closer, Zaklina noticed the pattern was not so random, and instead wove wolves and fish tangled together, climbing mountains or swimming beneath skinny gilt waves. Some of the wolves and fish were part human, and others were not. In the center of the quilt was sewn a massive mountain with a waterfall cleaving it in half. At the bottom rose a woman from the frozen waves, her arms reaching up as if she was Aphrodite cresting from below the sea.

Zaklina gently traced the woman's face. It was beautiful, even in the starkness of the embroidery, and she imagined it would be the type of maiden princess normally captured in castles and befriending monsters, taming them with their beauty and kindness. Zaklina only had her wits and her practicality, her lack of fainting and the ability to cook and tell stories – and even that had been stolen from her. She was little more than a worn out woman, long past her prime, long ago unable to win hearts or turn heads.

Pushing away the thoughts of her unworthiness, she sank onto the embroidered coverlet, facing the door and the keyhole in hopes that she might be warned of any incoming black fog or Night Mare creatures and demons. Perhaps the castle would give her a night of reprieve. She was so very tired...

Zaklina woke to the fireplace hissing, white smoke curling from wet wood. She sat up, confused in the murky darkness of the great suite of rooms, and wondered if the chimney had fallen in, allowing for weather to somehow worm its way into her hearth. It took her a moment to shake off sleep to remember that her room was so high it was above the clouds and no rain could pour down.

The bed jiggled.

Zaklina swallowed a scream, remembering at the very last second she must not make a sound. She would not torture the Gargoyle with a single noise—she did not know what he endured each night either. And he had warned her...

The bed shifted again.

She scrambled her feet under her dress, for she had not bathed nor undressed before drifting to sleep. How long had she slumbered? An hour? Five?

A deep sloshing sound ripped around her, and Zaklina realized she was soaking wet, just like the fireplace. In the dim white moonlight, which wafted down from the now-dark hearth, Zaklina looked toward the door and held her breath.

But it was not the door.

The movement came from behind.

Carefully, with deep-rooted terror, Zaklina twisted her head over her shoulder. She'd learned now that it was always better to see what she faced, and get the unknown over with...

It was an arm, wet ink against the paler black of the room, pulling itself out of the center of her bed. Long and gnarled, it found purchase on a part of the mattress and heaved. Another arm followed, and then shoulders and a bowed skeletal head. It raised itself on a neck made of bone and enormous ebony eyes met Zaklina's.

The eyes twinkled, but with a light that sucked all certainty from the air. The head tossed up, and long hair flung over the back. The lithe body slithered behind the arms, squelching and slopping onto the bedding, as if there was a hole of water in the center of the mattress, and this monster had found an opening.

Zaklina backed herself off the bed, hoping the creature was recovering from its appearance. The eyes followed her. Long fingers clicked together with a snapping sound like that of a crayfish, and the fireplace re-lit. It was a sickly light, extra smoky and smothering and smelled of wet and rotting pine needles and last year's old leaves left to decay in a puddle.

There was just enough glow from the fire, though, for Zaklina to see a long tail made of seaweed and kelp, fish scales and rough nobs disappeared and split, turning into legs of the purest white. The creature slipped off the bed, long hair trailing to the floor, and smiled at Zaklina again with the smile of a predatory female, one hunting for a man to ensnare or a child to trick.

"Do you know what I am?" the woman asked.

Zaklina shook her head, backing up further until her buttocks hit the door. The jewels in it pressed into the soft flesh of her waist and the curve of her shoulder blades.

"I am both sought and feared. I am beauty and death. I lure, I trick, I beguile. I am these things because they exist in the hearts of all men and women. But most of all, I drown."

Zaklina new the mermaid then. The port city where she'd lived first as a child, then as a wife, and then again as a governess brought sailors and captains from around the world. Yet no matter the color of their hair or the tones of their skin, they all told the same tales, which she had gathered into her mind as she walked the seaside markets for quinces or when she'd taken the children she'd taught for long strolls along the quay. No matter the language, she could tell what the sailors spoke of and what they feared. Even those immigrants who came from the mountains and hills of towns buried in the valleys spoke of this creature, for she lived in the streams and waterfalls, the ponds and the lakes.

It was the rusalka, the wila, the selkie. Nexie. Nyavka. Siren. Mermaid was the kindest word used, and even that was spoken with reverence and dread mixed with distress and panic. None wished to really see one, for no tale ever ended happily if the mermaid was in it.

She remembered that much.

Zaklina watched the woman curl her seaweed hair around her body, and churn it so tightly it became dripping foam, which trailed behind the creature as her long limbs rose to reach for Zaklina's. The coldness of her fingers spread faster than her actual flesh. Zaklina's teeth set to clacking of their own accord.

"I know what you think. I drown in water, yes, that is true, for men and women fear what they do not understand. And many do not understand how to swim. But it goes deeper than that, doesn't it?" Her eyes gleamed in the blue and white of the night and sparkled in the sick green of the hearth. "A person can drown in other things. Sorrow and guilt, ignorance and willful blindness. I can make one drown in any of these, too."

The edges of the mermaid's seaweed hair undulated like snakes, as if the ends were alive and could hiss in the gloom. Their edges poked at Zaklina's bare toes, the delicate lick of careful tongues, before they curled around her ankles and calves, brushing past the backs of her knees and leaving a trail of itching salt and the rasp of sand. Soon enough the weeds choked her, pulling tight against the softness of her neck and stuffing into the shell of her ear.

If she had wanted to scream against her bonds then, she could not, for the mermaid's weapon laid against her vocal cords and would have stuffed themselves into her mouth if she had opened it.

Had the Gargoyle known of these tricks? Is that why he warned her not to make a sound?

Soon she could only see, for the seaweed had dulled all her senses except her eyes, which were left bare, as if the mermaid wished her to watch her own doom.

"There are some who say I eat the soft flesh of maidens," the mermaid said. Now her voice was a lusty, throaty growl as she neared, tracing her long forefinger along Zaklina's weed-wrapped hip and shoulder. The scaled creature sniffed deeply, the thin arched nose widening slightly as she did.

Suddenly she backed away, her pale face twisted in disgust and nausea.

"You are not expected."

For the first time in her life, Zaklina was relieved to hear it. She would have sobbed with the relief if she could have done so silently.

The mermaid's disgust turned to swift anger, and she lashed out, slicing through the seaweed and leaving five gouges across Zaklina's belly with her shell-nails.

"I am always promised a maid!" Her voice was broken now, cracked and rough along the sides. The seaweed on Zaklina's body began to tighten, as if it were drying out. But in their drying, the strands became hardened and unbendable. In their unyielding curls, Zaklina's lungs could not expand, and there was less room for her breath to move from mouth or nose. She felt her eyes bulge out at the implication.

She would not be cooked over a fire hearth this night, then, but instead suffocated and squeezed to death? She did not know which demise she preferred and did not think she would have a choice anyway.

The bit of air allowed her diminished as the mermaid stalked in front of her vision, gesturing with her skinny arms above and below, muttering in a language of long lost words, so ancient even Zaklina, if she had retained her memory, would not have been able to place.

With the sting of salt in her throat and nostrils, Zaklina felt the last of her air puff out and then be lost in the tight rubbery bonds of her latest nightmare, though a nightmare at least meant one would wake. Her eyes darted to the walls, before she recalled the windows did not clearly show the sun's rising or setting. Her vision went grey along the edges, quickly moving to a pin point of faded blue and the gritted pointy teeth of an angry mermaid.

Just as her vision paled to milk,
a beam of light, champagne and tinged
with silvery gold, shot through the
slot on her gilded doorway. It was bright enough
when it hit to make her squint, even through the haze of her fading. The mermaid shrieked, a sound that started high and disappeared to a note so incredible it ceased being heard, and yet it seared into Zaklina's brain like a hot poker of cherry metal.

The bonds of seaweed melted away, tugged back by the mermaid, who suddenly sloshed into a massive puddle of water on the floor.

The hearth burst into flames and cracked with extra vigor.

Zaklina sank to the floor, gasping for grateful air and gripping at her stomach, where the five strips of blood trickled red and maroon. The crustiness of the seaweed left crumbs of white everywhere on her body, and a strange soapy slickness on her limbs.

"Zaklina?"

She tried to pull sound up, but the salt had eaten away at it.

"Are you well?" Gargulec sounded resigned and hopeful at the same time, a strange and unnatural combination in any tone of voice, made worse by the gruff roughness of his. "Have you... Did you wish to go back home today?"

She wondered if the magic required him to ask such a question each morning, just as it likely had forced him to ask her to wed. Then again, how many girls had stayed more than one night? Would he soon be as uncertain as she was in this labyrinth of living, malignant stone?

Struggling to her feet, sodden, she grabbed for the handle in half-blindness, for the salt had even crusted on her eyelashes and weighed them down. Grasping the heavy golden knob she twisted, and thought it seemed heavier this morning than the last. Surely it was just her weakness from two nights without sleep and lack of air itself.

"You may leave without chase or malice," the Gargoyle continued, his voice now leaden. "I will not stop you, and the castle will show you the way out. Though…I cannot leave again to save you, no matter what you encounter. The trail back to your village will take a week, so—"

She twisted harder. The hinges flaked gold on the ground before giving way. They screamed and ground against one another, but the movement was enough to stop his assumptions. Instead he put his weight against the frame and pushed so it opened. Zaklina noticed the edges of the door were dusty with old salt, puckered and eaten away at the gilt.

"I wish to stay," she croaked, her voice scratchy with slime and leftover stale breath. "I do not plan to seek my sister or Miódshire or my lost life by the sea. Do not ask me to leave."

The Gargoyle stood at the threshold, his carved cheeks scrunched in confusion, and his eyes gleamed with a different light in the dark depths. "I thought, given your silence…"

"It was only the evening trials. I could not speak fast enough," she said. "I am sorry."

Relief and shock raced across his face as he gazed down at her. She clutched her sodden clothes about her hips, holding in a shudder from the sudden chill of the hallway, and then covered her chest so the white chemise would not give away the darkness of her nipples.

"Forgive me," he finally said. "I did not remember."

"How many?" she asked, unable to stop, and damning herself for the question anyway. Why could she not learn to stop? "How many girls have stayed more than a night?"

"Two," he said, and turned away, his shoulders still blocking the early morning sun from the narrow window across from her door. "You will wish to dress? May I wait for you in your garden?"

She thought of the decayed fruit and destroyed pond of the previous morning and wished she could ask for another location. Yet Zaklina did not think she should press the castle. It seemed a fickle thing—friend and magical one hour and filled with evil meant to push her and kill her the next. Why ask for too much? She already asked too many things.

"Will you be alright?" His concern seemed genuine.

"Would you wait here?" she asked instead, daring herself to continue to break the expectations around her. Why not? If she was not going to be given the threads of stories and fables to guide her, she may as well continue to do as she pleased and wanted instead of following all the rules.

After all, Zaklina was named for it.

The Gargoyle's eyes widened. The whites of them were so pure they seemed almost blue. She tightened her arms about the wet and bloody garments and shivered again as the silence stretched.

She did not want to wait for his refusal, nor hear another rejection, and she let go of the handle, so the door slowly closed between them.

As the door caught the latch, the bulk of him slammed into it so it would not shut. He breathed unevenly, a broken, cracked sound out of his barrel lungs.

"You truly want me to come into your room again? It is still...not proper."

"Nor is spending a night the way I have the past two."

Without another protest, he followed her mutely into her quarters. The stone walls that were not gilded with metal or wood seemed to echo his own flesh. She wondered if he was carved of the same rock. Could rock live? Zaklina tried to think of any story that said so and could only come up with cracked memories of emerald mountains, and she was sure that was wrong.

"Sit down on the bedding," she instructed. "I won't take long."

Before she could question herself any more, she ducked behind the long brocade screens, unsurprised to find a rack of gowns there for her choosing. They were the same from the previous day, except now there was another, of all green velvet, long-sleeved and warm.

"You were still trembling," he said heavily, his voice bouncing off the overly tall ceiling. "I am worried for you. This is too much to ask. And I cannot help."

"You are very kind," she told him, finding speech easier when she did not have to look at him. Bashfulness seemed less strangling. "Last night... what I wanted... It is forward of me to...you said yourself there are rules. I will follow them."

"I am sorry you must overcome these trials. They are unknown to me, though I fear they must be terrible as no maid stays to explain...Let me try to atone. Ask anything of me. If it is in my power, you shall have it."

She shook her head at his dramatic overtures and stripped the last of the wet garments from her icy limbs. Inspecting her belly, she saw the damage of the mermaid's claws had healed, leaving only lines of shimmery white scars.

"I don't know this castle, nor most of those rules," she said through the screen. "What will you offer for my nights?"

He chortled, a strange chocolatey sound. "I would offer you what you asked, if I could. I would give you all..." He stopped, and his voice chopped in half.

Zaklina knew she should not ask for her wish, to have him near each night to stave off the demons and horrors, for he had made it clear she could not have it. What astounded her was that she found she could not make up something trivial instead.

In the new quiet, the sound of the green velvet snaking over her limbs sounded raspy and scratchy, even as the fabric itself was fine and soft.

"Well," she said, feeling unnaturally brisk and defiant after her second night of sleeplessness. She'd say it anyway. "You said you could not, but I would ask you to hold me in the evenings." Zaklina slipped on soft kid shoes embroidered with pine trees and turned the corner of the screen. He still sat on the very end of the bed, as if afraid he would break it. "If not that, then give me your days. As many hours as you can. I should not like to be alone, and I don't think you like it, either. We are not lovers, but we can at least be friends."

She could tell she'd surprised him yet again with her request, and it pained her for she wondered if by asking it, she asked him to do something he did not wish to do.

His head jerked up and she met his wide eyes. "I would that I could offer you all of what you wish, even the secrets you won't share."

Hope simmered through her fiber again, but she shook it off. Of course, the Gargoyle could not stop the nature of her stay at the fortress-castle and knowing he would protect her with his arms if he could...that had to be enough.

He stood from the bed as she approached, and once again offered his arm. They walked across the slick marble of the rooms to the open door and out into the hallway stairs. She wondered if she could find her way around more of the building given time.

And then she wondered how much time a woman was given in such a place before she was told to depart or fled in despair.

As they walked together, he cleared his throat and asked again, "You truly wish to spend your nights in such a way? With me? Even though it is something I cannot give?"

"I do," she said.

After the longest moment, she felt him wince and shift carefully and then, stiffly, he unwound his arm from hers. The loss of contact left her feeling chilly again. Her damp hair made the back of her neck clammy. But then, very slowly, he slid an arm around her waist, though he remained poised and tense.

"Very good," she said, recognizing his offering for what it was and was suddenly warm for the first time since the mermaid had pulled itself out of her bedding. She slipped her own arm around about his hips. "Shall we?"

They walked, so entwined, toward the door of the garden. The walkway seemed to be shorter, as if the time quickened with their nearness. As they entered the garden, Zaklina was surprised to see how much taller the trees were, and how lush the massive waxy, shiny leaves grew. Some of the flowers opened as they walked the path, which was now studded with mica stones and quartz sliced in half amid moss and grass. The carpets were still there, but moved aside, and the nook for eating was furnished with a low table and velvet cushions of various deep colors in green, blue and blood red.

The Gargoyle stared at the couch nestled between lush vines, his brow drawn into a crease.

"Is it not to your liking?" she asked, as if she had some choice in the layout. "We do not need to stay."

"You need to eat," he said, releasing her and gesturing to the pillows. "It looks comfortable enough, I suppose."

He said so with a question at the end, and Zaklina hid her smile as she tucked her legs under the short table. The settings on that morning were plates made of silver. The goblets gleamed, cut from raw emeralds, etched with symbols and script that wound in a spiral from top to bottom. They looked like the color of an algae covered lake, and Zaklina could not look at them without shivering from the night's threat.

The Gargoyle slowly folded next to her, his body jerky and his form unwieldy in such a position.

"You prefer a chair," she said, watching him shift among the pillows.

"I do, but only out of habit. It is only...I have not seen this table before. It is...intimate. Are you comfortable?"

She arched an eyebrow and nodded, thinking him truly obtuse if he did not understand her earlier flirting for what it was.

When he settled, he reached to the center of the table and began to serve them both from the soup tureen. It was an odd choice for breakfast: a stew made of clams and mussels in a clear and yellow swirled sauce. Whole hunks of white fish floated in it. When she took the first bite, she expected nausea or the taste of old fish, for it seemed the castle was determined to cling to the mermaid's memory. Instead, it was meaty, and garlic flavored every bite. The spice of it filled her bones, as did the buttery potatoes. Finally, she was hot again through and through.

They did not speak as she ate quickly, just stopping herself from an unbecoming slurp at the end. The Gargoyle ate, too, though he speared the pieces of seafood with a silver knife, filed so long and thin, just like a filleting knife...

Zaklina paused with a chunk of whitefish at the end of her spoon.

It couldn't be...could it?

Her spoon clattered as she gripped the stem of the goblet and then poured water down her throat, lest she be sick all over the breakfast...she had thought there was a cake under one of the smaller silver domes...

"Are you well?" the Gargoyle asked as she gulped.

"Where..." She swallowed so hard it was as if the water turned to earth in her throat. It hurt to force it down. "Where do you think the castle gets its food? This...seafood?"

The Gargoyle inspected the bits of fish on the end of his knife, his eyes squinting at it. "Well...there are gardens. Other ones. Not like this, which is for beauty's sake alone. There are more with beds of vegetables, others filled with fruit trees..."

"But meat?"

He put down the fish and it splashed into his bowl. "You have me at a loss. I only eat like this when there is a...a guest at the castle. Other times, I do not. I don't need it."

Zaklina stared into the soup, watching the white flesh bob. One piece was not completely cleaned, and grey-green scales clung to one side of it.

It shouldn't be...

But maybe that was the point. If a girl—a maiden—escaped a night alive, she was granted the same offering that the demons wished. It would make it come full circle. Were there tales of god-eating? Stories of devouring the flesh of one's enemies for strength? Would the powers of those who hunted her in turn be hers? She could not remember, of course. The only real piece of any story that had clung to her mind since her arrival was only about the maidens at the middle of each. The maids who saved the beasts and turned the hyenas into men, who tricked the evil so they could save the prince. She turned from the food in an attempt to stop the swirling stories inside her brain. She was certain there was a story of a mermaid who was just that as well—a maid. She had to remember it was not the same. She was not the same.

"Gargulec?" she asked.

"Mm." He was back to inspecting the fish, looking puzzled.

"Did you love the girls that came here? The ones who left?"

"I did not love them all. Only two."

There, proof enough to stop her head from spinning.

He did not love her, at least. She was no maid.

Even though she knew he must have loved the other girls, and that he'd asked them all to wed, it did not stop the cut his words slashed into her heart. Zaklina clenched her hands around the emerald goblet, reminding herself that she was unlovable and should not expect devotion from any male—be he creature or man or a mix of both. Reminding herself that she was a fool, she pressed on, looking for another way they could speak that was not about magic or stories or the castle and its terror-filled nights.

"You know the pain of loss then?"

He nodded, and lifted the cover of the little plate, revealing a cake made of white fondant and covered in tiny lily pads of sugar.

"I do as well," she confessed. "And in that, perhaps we are the same. For I have loved and lost too."

He seemed unnerved with the emotional conversation, serving her a slice of the cake, which was a pale green in the center. Crumbs fell into her empty water goblet as he carried the cake on the serving fork. When there was nothing left to do, he finally twisted to face her.

"The man who cast you aside," he said at last.

"Him," she agreed. "The one I loved."

"Do you love him still?" There was heavy curiosity in the question.

She shrugged. "I love him only in the way one mourns the past," she explained baldly. "The love has been replaced with sorrow and sadness. For he showed me truly how being a difficult woman is a curse in its own right.

"You see, though I am not covered in the skin of a beast, or made of stone, I am shunned in my world. For any ambition, for the stigma of being a woman, for the disgrace of being cast aside. My husband and I... Our marriage was supposed to be a love match, and I loved him purely. But then, soon into our union, he stopped smiling at me. And he stopped eating at my table. He stopped...touching me. I thought perhaps he was ill. Then I wondered if somehow I had stopped enticing him, that I repulsed him. And perhaps it was that. He did not like that I remembered the stories. That I could spin a tale and keep people entranced and liked to search for more of the myths to feed my mind. He was right to be angry, for I did not know my place. I questioned too much, too often. I just...I did not expect him to find another woman."

"He chose a different woman?" The rage in the Gargoyle's voice made her smile a little.

"You say it with indignity, but you have not been around a woman in... how long? A hundred years? Likely more if Mrs. Staryski's stories are true in some part," she said. "You forget that there are countless other women who are meek, who are exceedingly beautiful. I am neither. And you said yourself that I am not an easy woman."

"But..." he spluttered, and then fell silent.

In the quiet, Zaklina picked up the emerald goblet, forgetting it was empty save the bits of cake crumbs. Her thumb rubbed the ridges of the cup's exterior, and she peered closer, surprised she could understand the words. She'd expected something fancy or ancient, like Latin or old Greek. Instead, beside the delicate carving of a beautiful woman, it read *co ma wisieć, nie utonie. What is supposed to hang, won't drown...*

Finally, he rejoined. "But I said such a thing knowing that you were... mine."

His ownership made her ache in all the forbidden places. Did he mean he had trapped her? That he wanted her? The heat between them became the point of her reality, hovering with possibility. *What is supposed to hang won't drown. What is meant to be...* Did she dare reach to touch his knee? It would be an act so intimate that it could spur him to sweep her up or dash away in embarrassment.

The choice fled when he stood and offered her his hand so she could flounder her way out of the luxurious pillows.

"Today, I will take you to a place I have admired many times when I went to do business with the masters who once lived in these parts. It is not so very far as yesterday's trek, but if you wish to rest—"

"No!" Zaklina wrapped herself around his arm. "Please don't let me be alone longer than I must. I already dread the night and it will be better if we are busy, so I forget, even for a little while." She leaned into him as she spoke. His scent was wild and musk and manly all at once. It was overwhelming in the way only a woman understood, and she wondered if the others—the girls he'd loved—had been frightened of the richness of him, the sorrow in him.

Had they not seen the virility of his body and his mind, and past the skin of his form?

Would she have done so, had she come to this place before sadness had marked her?

They walked straight across the castle instead of taking stairs up or down. Zaklina had not opened every door, as there were always too many to count. She was quite surprised when the Gargoyle opened the door across from her garden to show a yawning great hall, so long that there was no ending to be seen.

"How is this possible? Were we not on the edge of the castle's walls? I thought this door would open to ramparts and the sky," she said, gazing up at the ceiling. It was painted, and the details were so far away they were fuzzy, but she could see the gilded edges of massive creatures with wide flippers and wings, terrible eyes and long claws. Their faces were not angry, though, and she found strange comfort in gazing up.

"They are the gods and goddesses of creation," he said, matching her. "I often come in here when I am...particularly weighed with woes. They seem to rain down contentment."

"They look fearsome."

"Creation of all kinds is indeed something to fear," he said. "For one never knows what is created will become. Something small can grow to be too large. A single sentence can become a stiff decree. A question can unravel a kingdom."

"There are so many of them," she said, letting her eyes wander. They were painted in lurid colors long faded, as if dust had plastered itself upwards. There was a golden-yellow mother with long arms and legs and covered in pentacles, a sun with the face of a man, and a serpent covered in the colors of a rainbow. Several had shining beams shooting from their heads or hands. Women wore headdresses of feathers or held spheres. Some were nude, with overlarge hips and stomachs, sagging breasts and teats that suckled gods the color of a murky sea or glinting with silver stars. Many wielded scrolls while others waved strange weapons. Four rode in chariots pulled by different creatures and chased by others.

"They seem unending."

"They are the roots of all stories, offering advice and condemnation, a map for religion or the blood of royalty, or so it was once said. Their days have long passed, and all that remains is myth and lore, and even that is disappearing in favor of easy lies and half-truths."

"There are those who would say stories are not truths. They are only an allegory," she said.

"Is that what you believe?" he asked, as they paced the hall.

"No," she said. She paused to gaze a for a time at a woman who roared silently, her body bloated and stomach filled with spilling waters. It looked primeval but also powerful, and it oddly made Zaklina's own womb ache, but she ignored it, used to its emptiness. She turned to the Gargoyle. "I believe there is a grain of truth in every tale, and though the meaning is often lost to time, and the tale itself can be twisted for a greedy purpose, the truth inside still exists. And therefore, each story is both allegory and truth combined. It may be what makes them so powerful...and the loss of them so great." Tears suddenly stabbed the edges of her eyes. She missed the stories. If one could not escape in the fantasy of long-told tales, or find the secret lesson buried in them for guidance, how did one live?

Unwilling to seem weak, she cleared her throat and squinted down the long hallway. "Is this what you wished to show me? This hall of pictures?"

"No. It is only a scenic way there."

"Where is it, then, if not down or up? Surely heart of the mountain, perhaps?" she asked.

He stopped cold, so quick she stumbled and would have tripped over the velvet skirt had she not grabbed his wrist. Turning her to face him, he put his crackled stone hands on her shoulders and squeezed so hard she was certain she could hear her bones bend.

"Never go there!" he said fiercely. "Do not seek it!"

The tendrils of a horrible tale slipped into her mind. "Is it severed heads then? Kept as trophies?"

He looked appalled. "No! Why would you think..." His eyes widened. "A story? It has found its way to you?"

"No." She frowned, hoping more would come to her. She focused on the vision of the ghastly, hanging heads. "I mean, perhaps. It is a tale of loss and defiance. Beheadings and broken promises. The husband is a beast? Or is it...the villagers come to save her. Her brothers? She is saved from the one who would enslave her. Kill her...saved by those who have sought her and come to rescue her..." Zaklina's forehead hurt. She was likely just tired. "It's there, but jumbled."

"That is more than I would have ever hoped for," he said, and his voice was almost merry. "That is more than has ever happened before."

"But what is there, then? Why can I not seek the mountain's center?" she asked, unable—unwilling—to be deterred, even if pressing would garner no answers.

"It is a place of heat and horror. Of endless depths and darkest black. Fire and ice. It is where...it is where it is said that demons come from, those that have roamed the world. Most of them have returned over time, weak, hungry, forgotten. Only a few remain. They're the most insidious of all, for they are the ones who can change form. Those who have not come back best know how to prey on humanity. They are the tellers of twisted tales and untruths. The ones who use stories in a different way, for their own means. The ones who eat the innocent."

Zaklina was both pleased and appalled. It was the most the Gargoyle had spoken at once on the topic, and she wondered if his voice loosened the longer she lived with him. Would her very presence weaken the hold on his secrets?

"This one is now my favorite," he paused again and stared up. "It is very old, but I remember enough. She is a goddess of more than the world. She reminds me of you."

Zaklina cocked her head. The woman rode a wild-maned lion, her breast bared and full, the virility of her sex radiating even in the ancient lines of the paint. She held one shining eight-pointed star in one palm, and a sword in another. Behind her trailed a line of unclothed men carrying offerings of grain and wheat, or leading sheep and goats.

"I do not think that is like me at all," she said, a flush crawling up her chest. "She is clearly much beloved and worshiped. We have established I am not. I have never been such an object of desire."

"She is unafraid of what men think," he said. "She is contradictory, that is true, but in that she is unpredictable. This is good, for in breaking with tradition, she holds power beyond any other."

"Such make her an outcast, if she clings to the untraditional." Zaklina was unable to stop the bitterness from her tone, and she shook her head. "You are too kind."

They drew up to a great door carved with long lines of symbols. She recognized some, but others looked like nothing more than squiggles of curves or harshly drawn animals. The Gargoyle leaned into the door and it cracked down the middle, unevenly and leaving jagged edges. She walked through and immediately shielded her eyes with both hands, gasping at the whiteness of the clouds all around, and the narrow beams of sunlight shooting through it. Everything seemed to sing with brightness, and she was certain she had forgotten the sun's strength. How could everything be so dazzling even on a cloudy day?

"Here, this will help."

The Gargoyle's hands covered hers, so she could remove her palms. Though his fingers were smooth and cool as polished stone, they were warm at the same time, leaving a strange tingling in their wake as he gently tied fabric across her eyes.

Zaklina blinked. Her lashes caught on a fine black meshed netting, which knotted at the back of her head, acting as a shield yet transparent enough to see through. It felt like cloth made of air. The Gargoyle did not wear one, though he squinted fiercely into the light.

"Do you need one, too?" she asked, hoping she had not taken his.

He looked puzzled and put a hand over his brow. "I do not. I haven't after all this time. But it does seem brighter today than ever before. Can you see it all, now?"

Zaklina wiggled the cloth and then looked about, gulping quietly when she realized they were indeed on an outdoor rampart, with the castle walls slick and black, soaring impossibly high above. Below, the forest was a bumpy, spiked green, stretching so far it curved around the corner of the horizon. She had been certain the brightness was caused by the sunlight, but the Gargoyle was correct. There was no real sun, only clouds and beams. Instead, it was the glowing beams of the swords and the piles of silver pouring out of black holes cut into the mountain's face that created the extra unnatural glare.

"It is an old forge. A silver-smithing one, where the best blades were said to be melted and poured. They were the swords of heroes which were often woven with spells and copper, threads of blue and the last dust of diamonds." The Gargoyle wandered around with some fondness, touching the tools with familiar movements.

She watched him through her black veil for a moment, surprised at his ease. It was the first time she had ever seen him look so contented.

"Did you work here? Long...before?" It seemed unkind to mention his appearance, but he did not seem to mind. Instead, he picked up a crucible and a matching plate of iron, where triangles cut deep into the ore and his mouth curled with memory.

"No. But I would frequent it, speak often to the smiths, and purchase silver-tipped arrows." He set down the plate. "There was once a seam of gold in the mountain, too, and a forge to match it, but it was stripped bare long ago, and now they only serve as doorways."

He pointed down the rampart, where the mountain stretched as the back wall, and where huge open caves screamed a blackness so rich it seemed to pour out.

"Doors? To the heart of the mountain?"

The Gargoyle nodded. "When people seek one thing so much, they will always unleash something terrible, whether it is a demon or a troll, or the worst nature of oneself. Obsession is like that."

"It is why...well, it is why many of the old stories warned against such excess." Zaklina inhaled. "And likely why this forge is no longer in use, too. One doesn't want to steal all the silver."

The Gargoyle stared into one of the caverns, where silver spilled out in gobs, half-melted, mixed with mica and citrine. "This forge went quiet because the heroes died. And then I too, was unable to wield my arrows. Granted, I did not like to use the silver as often. Besides, the remedy for them was gone when the gold dried up. It is why..." He sighed, a great gust of wind. "It is part of why this castle festers, I think. Too many silver arrows were left in the world...and the demons knew how to use them."

A sharp sound cracked below, far off in the trees, but loud enough to carry and echo across the great distance.

Zaklina spun, her hands clutching the cold stone of the ramparts, and the breeze of the metal caves at her back. The stench of ammoniac and the tang of iron tainted the faint wind, and she shuddered, the hair on her arms rising.

He came to stand behind her, blocking the rancid air and bracing his own arms around hers, so she was encased in the shell of his body. She wanted to lean back into him, and melt her bones to his, but instead they stared out as another snap ripped the air.

Trees moved of their own accord far off, so very far she knew it must be leagues and uncountable miles, but the castle's great height afforded far sight. The pines boiled, as if a battle raged below in the roots. A cloud of dark birds swirled, circling above the thrashing boughs, and their voices rose as a babble and a call as their wings glinted with deep green and dripped feathers that fluttered back down.

"Crows. Or ravens. I cannot remember which to avoid."

"Neither," he said, the cavern of his chest rumbling into her shoulders. "They both serve a purpose. But those...they are certain to be crows, for I have an inkling of what is on the wood paths these days."

"What are they doing? Waiting?" She could not finish the thought. Waiting for death? Carnage? Did not crows peck at melting eyeball jelly and scavenge dried skin from bones?

"They are eating bees."

"Bees?"

"Only crows eat bees," he said, as if that explained it all. And maybe it did, but nothing came to her in the silence after the trees went still. No old story trickled through the fissures of her mind. Instead, there was only the quiet, which somehow seemed more ominous.

"Is it good or bad that the crows are here, eating?" she asked. Her voice sounded timid in the great space, bouncing off the silver and absorbed in the dark, empty gold mines.

"If a crow eats a bee, it will never return to the hive. The queen has lost another." Not for the first time did Gargulec speak in riddles, though this one seemed to have more weight in it than usual. Zaklina wanted to curse the difficulties of such a magical place, that could hold back words and erase memories. Still, his words made her pause and stare out over the land. The crows faded back into the trees, hidden and waiting. For what? Another swarm? A bear to disrupt a honey alcove? Her musing wandered to the fate of the bees, for they sometimes reminded her of a village of people, under the rule of royalty. How many subjects can a queen bee lose before she fails? And where does she go when she does? How does she eat with none to feed her or bring her treasure?

"Beyond the trees, farther than we can see, is your Miódshire. Do you wish to go back, or continue facing the nights and trials? And facing me?"

Zaklina gave up pretending. She turned and curled into the Gargoyle's body, burying her forehead into the curve of his chest. The strange warring of cool stone and warmth of him fizzled in the pit of her stomach. For a moment, his arm tightened about her, squeezing her into him briefly before he tore himself away. His absence made her shiver, both from loss and chill, so she wrapped her arms tightly around her stomach and looked up at him. She could not help but wonder if her warmth and her nearness revolted him too, in the way her previous husband had turned away from her, unable to be aroused and unable to enjoy her arms. The notion that the Gargoyle might be unwilling to be near her cut her lungs and brought tension into her shoulders.

"I do not mind facing you."

"And suppose I asked you again to wed me?"

"You said the magic assumes I will choose home, will choose the easy way... the comfort of returning to what my existence was before. Perhaps the other girls preferred it, and the castle reminds them of what they left behind. Love and happiness and good food. But the only memories I have of Miódshire is decay. I have no desire to return. But to stay here and wed you? A marriage without love? You do not even wish to hold me."

He stood, unmoving, and his eyes darkened. She continued, unafraid of his anger, slashing her own self-worth.

"And why should you? I am no beauty, no innocent maid, and besides, you love the other girls. The innocent ones who left. I'm nothing like them. Shall we return?"

She turned from him and from the shining silver, and walked to the great oak doors, though she felt the fool when she had to pause her grand departure while waiting for him to approach and reopen them to the great painted hallway.

They walked in silence, the dusty carpets gobbling up their footsteps and letting small geysers shoot up around the pads of their shoes. This time, she did not take his arm, for she feared any kindness from him would only make her heart ache more. As they went, he glanced over tentatively, as if embarrassed.

"You think I do not wish to be...close to you?" he finally asked.

"Well," she shrugged, rearranging her skirts. "You did fly away from me. A woman might think from such a reaction that she was...repulsive."

He started to bark a laugh, a deep roll that ended with him chortling so much so that he had to pause walking. She watched, unable to join him, unable to see the joke. When he cleared his throat, he finally managed to squeeze out, "Repulsive?"

Pressing her mouth together, she continued onward. He trailed her, but they did not gaze up in wonder at the gods and goddesses above them, who likely rendered judgement on them anyway. Zaklina only remembered that her private garden was on the other side when she reached the end and flung open the far door. The garden's greenness had reached outside of the garden itself. Vibrant vines snaked between the door jam, and tiny white flowers dotted the moss creeping around the frame.

She paused at the threshold of the great hall, uncertain if he would wish to have tea with her, or if now was when they parted ways. Why had he laughed? Was it such a jest? She had not meant it so. She closed her eyes and wished, once, and desperately, that she might be brave enough one day to believe she might be worth something. That she might find joy again.

The Gargoyle was suddenly behind her, moving as silent as a mouse. "Repulsive?" he said harshly into her ear. "You think you are repulsive? Then what do you call me?"

She twisted, the heavy velvet a weight around her ankles. Without pausing to consider the motives, she touched the long straight line of his mouth, along the shape of a man just below the surface on his skin, where it wavered, fleeting.

"Perhaps regal. Handsome in your own right. But not for me."

He only stared at her, unmoving as rock, and she sighed and left him, going into her garden, where she could smell a floral tea already brewing, pungent and stronger than any blossom.

He did not join her.

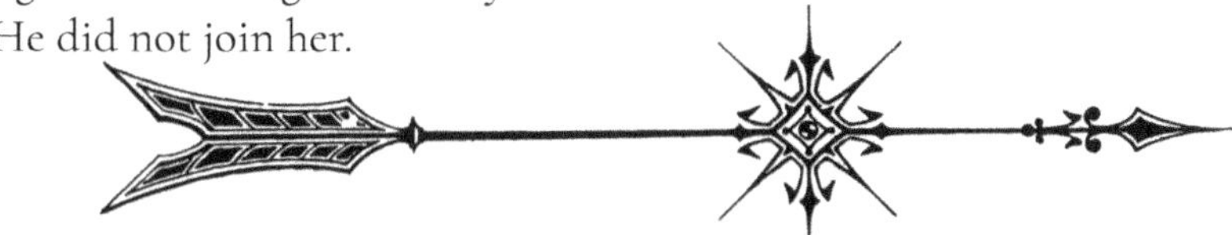

The day stretched before her, for they had not spent the whole of it together. Zaklina took her time with tea, drinking it in minute sips and pouring the entire pot out cup by cup. Left alone with her thoughts, she tried to recall and recite any of the tales she used to tell Milena, and then had hoarded for her own children who had never come. She had enjoyed gifting them to the ears of those she taught, for all it brought her trouble.

The magic here stifled with tantalizing, unspoken teases. She was on the cusp of something whole one moment, yet still it remained just as elusive as before between bites of her tea cake. It was like the castle itself eddied about her. A current pulled on the edges of her eyes. There was a story she could remember, she was sure. Something simple.

Always about a beast.

Or was it a golden crab? A dog. A pigeon.

Something about a mountain. Four mountains.

The four corners of the Earth...

What was it about stories and tales that people did not like? Why were they called myth and not truths, even as the deepest truths of humankind were buried within them? Why were the old fairytales considered false, and the words of those who twisted facts the true sentences? Suppose it was the other way around, but everyone was afraid to say so? What was the old turn of phrase, one spoken by a mother near forgotten? *Kiedy wejdziesz między wrony musisz krakać tak jak one. When you're among crows, you must caw like them.*

Well, she had seen crows earlier, and was not sure she wished to dance with them. She thought instead she should feel sorry for the bees they ate.

With the tea gone, the crusty bits of the little cakes all that remained, Zaklina stood and glanced around the lush bushes, intricate designs of carpet and moss, and exotic flowers. The ruined pond stank now of old oil and bloated fish, seaweed left to rot in the sun and of stagnant water. The plants around it crusted with mildew and spidery, translucent mushrooms. Some of the leaves dripped bits of brown into the water, adding to the decay.

But the rest of the garden was as pristine as before, and even more full than the first day. Some of the herbs overflowed their borders. The flowering oregano spilled out in sprawling clumps, and the long necks of lavender stems bowed over the edges of a stone pot. In one corner, the mint—chocolate and lemon, spear and pennyroyal—tangled together and ran white shoots anywhere and everywhere. It was wild, but it was free in the wildness, and Zaklina was torn between admiring it and thinking of Milena's garden and the tiny beetles that spilled from the vines there.

When she exited the garden, she was not interested in returning to her room, knowing the sun would set soon enough and leave it in pale shadows and whatever horrors waited her. The Gargoyle was nowhere to be found, and she did not think she should shout in the castle. Suppose the walls devoured her words and kept him from her? Before he returned to lock her into her room, there would still be time to explore a bit.

And a small, bubbling, defiant part of her wondered what truly would happen if she was not so available. Suppose she did not submit to the key and wait for the night to come in her bedroom? Was it possible to avoid it all? Was it possible to hide?

She went down toward the lower caves and crumbling rooms and halls instead of up to her rooms, keeping her right hand always on the right wall, as if it served the same purpose as Ariadne's thread. Each narrow slit of a window offered a view of the sinking sun, which was first gold, then orange, and then red before fading into a purple bulge at the edge of the earth. Zaklina felt the urge to return to her bedroom, if only because it was where she had spent the previous nights and she did not know what the castle did at night.

Did it break further?

Heal?

Come up with devious plans?

One of the doorways to her left was open, as many often were. It always offered glimpses of great banquet halls gone to seed, or rooms of armor that had crashed to pieces and rusted long ago. But this was different, for it was warm.

Warmth seemed to be hard to find in the clammy castle of dripping black walls and flaky dust. Zaklina drifted toward the heat as if it filled her belly with fresh milk. As she neared, the steam hit her nose and filled her mouth with a roundness that was full and hollow at the same time. She found she could hardly form a word, and if she had wanted to call for the Gargoyle now, the moment had already passed.

But the warmth...the warmth was so delightful.

Slipping inside, Zaklina closed her eyes. It was dim and dark, and smelled like wet cedar and packed earth like the old bathhouses, the ones of her childhood. Before she had married Narcyz, she and Milena had of course entered their family house many times. For births and deaths, for womanhood and healing. It was a place of the old ways and yet never aged, for the traditions inside the privacy of the space went back thousands of years, in the guise of many faiths and stories and worship.

It was a woman's place, yet it was always overseen by a man.

Zaklina glanced into the corners of the room, where light was swallowed by grey and brown shadows. The steam gushed from a hot stone—one of many against the far wall—and in the shape of it, she saw the outline of the genii, the Juno, the domovyk, the fountainhead. A surge of hope rang through her, hard as brass and just as supple under heat. Was the castle offering this slice of respite? Was it showing her the root of the magic? Would she be able to barter for peace with the spirit who oversaw all?

"Hello grandfather," she said, remembering a bit more of the old tales far easier than the new. Surely some sort of gift was needed, of that she was certain. She had only the crumbs of her tea under her fingernails and the velvet of her dress to offer. Yet she would not do this by half measures, not when she felt so close to escaping a night of horror. "I have nothing worthy of my recent meal, but I have the clothes of my very back."

There was no sound or movement in the corner, and Zaklina paused, her fingers on the hem of the gown. Was there something of a rooster? Or blood? A hot stone. An offering, a sprinkling, a swathe of it, to keep the evil spirits at bay...

She couldn't recall well enough, and it was no matter as she had no chicken or even a knife to kill it. Stripping off the heavy velvet, the steam curdled around her skin and wilted into the cotton of her petticoats and chemise. It all clung limply to her limbs, a melted mess that left her feeling more bedraggled by the second. Bundling up the soft gown, she carefully placed it at the edge of the corner where she'd seen the shape of the bathhouse spirit last and stood back, her fingers twisted together so tightly that her knuckles shone.

For a long moment, there was only steam, glorious and dripping, a fog draping itself everywhere. She inhaled, letting the slow heaviness of the water-soaked air cake the lining of her lungs and fill her belly.

An arm, long and shaggy, pulled the velvet into the corner shadows. Ripping and chewing filled the room, which felt close and low with each long minute. She did not care to think further, only looked with longing at the benches along the ends of each wall, where sleep for an entire night might overwhelm her. What she would do, for a full night...

The chewing and chomping paused, and a screech, high and grating, a sound of iron on iron and shovels scratching clay. It shredded the air and cut through the warmth with ice.

"There is no bread." A voice hissed, deep and soft at the same time. "There is no salt."

"I have none!" Zaklina said, desperation leaking into her eyes and tongue, making her sound weak, even to her own ears. "I did not know."

"There is no white cloth, and no milk. No flesh. No blood." A short pause filled a breathless gap, and the fog gathered and took the form of a great bearded giant, with blazing eyes that pierced the dimness of the bathhouse room. "We will take yours instead."

Before Zaklina could remind herself not to make a sound from that second onward, she was silenced by the slick steam coating her throat. She could not scream if she tried.

Besides, it did not matter.

She had not escaped it, after all.

Tiny men danced through the steam, swirling it around her so she was blinded by warm whiteness. Their eyes glowed red, and their beards trailed the floor, though they were all arms and legs, naked and sexless. Banniks, so many of them, under the direction of the greatest one in the corner, the Pyvsyan'sa, who stood and touched the ceiling at the crown of his head. They all held sticks of pine, sharpened to points, and waved them with delight, reminding her of the child army of Miódshire and Edek's lost eye. As they moved closer, the whisps of fog covered her eyes, though it was not thick enough to stop the drag of the weapons against her, cutting through the weeping, dripping fabric of her undergarments, shredding them first before scraping into her skin.

"We will eat you raw, your flesh our bread, your blood our rightful drink." The voice was one and many at the same time. A whisper and a chuckle, a boom and a command. It didn't match, it didn't seem right. But the roof of her mouth was full of tongue, fuzzy and thick. It was closing her up from the inside, while slicing her from the outside.

The tiny spears poked. They stabbed. Through the stays and the linen. The sticks seared and slid, somehow finding flesh beneath clothing, until she knew the old wounds from the mermaid's claws bled, dripping down her belly, across the bump of her hips, and trailing into the creases of her legs. She backed up as she could, and still could not find the door...

And then it was there, a great heavy thing, designed to keep a woman in and the menfolk out. It was the door of womanhood, childbirth and bed fever. The daylight itself was kept at bay with a thick panel of oak, sewn with symbols of hearth and home, hexed and blessed alike. A deep Perthro and elegant Tet, a graceful Nǔ and the cycles of the moon. It was all there, as she stared up and put her hand to the latch. It blocked her way completely, as unmoving as the rocks themselves. She pounded her fist, and thought to call out, remembering only at the last that her voice was lost and the Gargoyle had begged her to never make a sound at night.

For him, she could bear it. For him, she would survive it. She had to...

And then all thought was lost, as the small demons were upon her, their spindle arms squeezing tightly, their sticks clenched between jagged teeth. Dragging her down, down, pinning her to the rough bench on the edge of the room. It was soaked in old slick sweat, oil and something darker.

The blood of lives spent and given, begun and ended. The steam coiled around her, and the little demons piled above her, ripping at her, tearing the chemise. She tried to sit up, to fling the demons from her, but more were always on the edges, until they overwhelmed her once more, until she was bare, stripped to the waist, her skin like a solid milk amid the foaming of the mist.

The tendrils of it spun around her ankles and wrists, wrapped like a heavy arm around her bones until she could not move, her breath short and tight. The steam parted as the demons danced on her limbs and the greatest of them all, the domovyk, stood over her with a great branch, sliced from a tree and sharpened so carefully the end of it shone.

She arched her chest up, away, uncaring of her plain nudity, twisting desperately and scraping herself against the nails and sticks of the smaller old bathhouse demons and not caring for anything but escape. There had to be an escape. A stop. An end!

The end came with the sun, but how could the sun enter this space? Where were windows, sunlight, morning?

There would be no morning!

The domovyk raised the tree, the end so tightly carved that it looked like a needle. Zaklina opened her mouth, about to scream at last, but the steam poured in, freezing her tongue.

The slice into the center of her ribcage was a maelstrom of white and ice, blue and melting heat. It was pain and pleasure, wound together and bound by unnatural rules of impossible terror. The ends of the wound festered and curled, turning red and then black in an instant, charred and burned like ash and oak.

"We will take your stomach and liver, and eat your humors and drink your blood. And the heart...that is ours and we shall savor it, too."

Zaklina watched her organs lift out in tapered fingers, still connected by tissue and vessels, dripping with blood and stared at hungrily by all the eyes. Teeth gnashed about her, a clattering and clacking by the hundreds. Her liver a large heavy weight lifted with reverence, her kidney a slippery bean, and lastly her heart, still thrumming and beating, a strange bulbous oval, pale and bumpy. She wanted to touch it, but also clawed away from it, could not bear to see it, to understand how she could live while they ripped out her very insides. Could a woman be devoured so? Could they truly eat her alive? And would she still be aware of it?

The demons danced and chortled. They licked their teeth, and their long white tongues trailed out, longer and longer, and...

She'd lost.

She was going to die.

And as the pain sunk into her bones and tore through her sinews, as the demons chortled and lapped her blood from the floor and the bench, and ran their long nails through the deep trenches of her spleen, she thought of the Gargoyle and the castle.

She had failed...

She always failed.

The mist spun, brighter and brighter, and the pain rose up with it, stark and wild, a feral thing that swirled inside her limbs and poured across her skin. The demons scrabbled against her flesh, tearing it as they writhed, screeching against the brightness, lunging into one another.

"Give it to us! Give us all! It is ours! Bone and bread, blood and water!"

They flew to her, just as a great bang and a heavy iron scream sliced the mist. A block of palest champagne chased the steam and fog, and with it went the demons, all of them, washing away from her as they melted.

At last she could gasp, move, shift. Zaklina immediately clutched her stomach, prepared to scoop her organs back inside the open cavity, her heart beating so horrifyingly fast it took a moment for her to realize it was still safe inside the cage of her ribs, hiding behind the sponges of her lungs. She started and stared down at her stomach, healed and only blemished with faint lines, the color of long-dead coals. It was impossible.

It was magic.

It was—

"Zaklina. You are here? It's—"

"Morning." Relief poured into her, the exact temperature of a bath she would love to slide into, carrying away the impossible ache of ripped flesh and sharp knives. It was morning. It had to be. And he'd come for her, even if she was not in her own room. That meant almost more than morning.

He'd come looking...

She swung her legs off the bench, afraid to stand or move too fast. Would she re-open? Would her heart fall out?

Gargulec entered, blocking the light for a moment as he loomed. In the farthest corner, Zaklina was certain she saw the long arms of the great domowyk, once again forming, but then the light splintered around the Gargoyle's shoulders and the shadow fled, leaving her in a mossy, drippy bathhouse, still feeling the pinch of tearing inside her gut. She clutched her arms around her middle.

"They…they cut me open," she said, her voice sounding full and oddly fluid. "They took out my liver and spleen. My heart… But it didn't last. It's like a dream. Was it a dream?"

He towered over her, frowning around the room, and then found her eyes. "It was sadly not a dream. But such magic does not – cannot – last the night."

"But if it was real…they cut me open and I lived," she said, tracing the pale scars of her stomach. She wondered if they would ever fade, and then realized with a jolt it would not matter. She would have no husband or man to see.

"You did not offer anything yourself. They cannot keep what you do not freely offer," he said, and then he inhaled and took a step back. "You are still bare." He spun on a heel and she suddenly realized her breasts were left for his eyes, her stomach a plain below them. He had seen her… Warmth filled her bones and made her knees quiver.

Embarrassment? Disgust?

Or something else entirely? She crossed her arms across her nipples, and considered the ruins of the velvet dress.

"I'm so sorry, but I have nothing to cover myself."

He did not wait a moment longer, unfastening the great cloak and sweeping it toward her, keeping his entire face averted until she covered herself. It had the look of wet rock, and she somehow excepted it to weigh a great amount, but instead it was feathery, almost like real wings, and folded itself around her in thick swathes of fabric. She wound it about her shoulders, clutching it closed at neck and navel, before stepping up to him.

"Might we walk to my room?"

"Of course. Where else would I take you in such a state?" he asked quickly, looking anywhere but down at her. "Can you walk easily enough?"

"I think so." She took the first steps out of the wretched bathhouse room, happy to remove herself from the cursed space and the memories harbored in its corners and in the last droplets of stubborn steam.

But as she moved, the cloak wound around her ankles and bunched between her thighs, yanking until she was sure another step would have it falling open. She did not think the Gargoyle would wish to see her naked twice in a morning.

At her pause, he turned and bent in one movement, as if able to read her worries, sweeping her up into the cradle of his arms. She could not wrap her own around his shoulders for fear of leaving the garment to gape open to her pelvis, but the strength of his body hugged her to his chest, and she did not see how she would fall out, anyway.

"Are you comfortable?" he wondered, as he took massive strides up the stairwells. "Is there any pain from the night?"

"There never really is," she told him truthfully, knowing he must mean the marks and terrors given to her flesh. There was another toll, though, which made her suck in her breath as they entered her private rooms. It was the scars on her mind, branded with the vivid detail of each night's demons and their many horrific visages. It was the knowledge that untold nightmares awaited her in coming evenings, and there was only one way to escape it – one she feared was quickly becoming less an escape and more an impossibility.

She would be untruthful if she believed she would ever want to return to Milena, to the stifling rumors of Miódshire and Mrs. Staryski's stories. The Gargoyle had hinted that the road back was long, and she had no interest in trekking for a week in the dark forests stretching from the castle's walls. How had the other young maids done so? Had they returned home, or were they just as lost in the woods as she was amid the nights of terror?

Had she been wrong to think sacrificing herself to this beast of the stories would be the correct answer?

It was too late to wonder now.

She truly did not want to go.

And she did not begrudge her fate. At least, not during the day.

The sitting room held a bathtub again, though it was not made of glass now, but of a milky pale jade, thin swirls and whorls embedded within the silky surface. The water within was a brighter blue-green, and the thick scent of jasmine and eucalyptus hung in the air.

"I shall leave you," he said, his voice rumbling from his overlarge chest into her own. "You will wish to rest and clean yourself."

She was indeed exhausted, likely due to the loss of blood if not the loss of sleep, but the tub was deep, and she feared loneliness almost as much as she worried about the nights.

"Please stay," she said softly, turning her face to bury it in the hollow of his shoulder. His solidness, for all its carved edges, was still human enough, his presence a reminder that even in the deepest hour of the night, she was not truly alone in the great castle walls. If she could only be with him, sit with him, feel his body next to hers, maybe she would be less nervous about it all. He'd make it all feel as if she belonged and all would be well. He always did.

He put her down, silent as stone, and gazed at her, searching her eyes and cheeks, as if thinking she jested, or that she was insane. Zaklina knew she didn't look the part of the innocent princess, wrapped in his cloak and drenched with leftover steam and bits of dried blood.

But she wasn't a simple, easy maid. She had been married.

She knew about the world, about loss, and a wedding bed. She had lived with another and spent years working her hands to chapped cracks, and served others for long hours. She knew she was unlike any girl in the old stories. She knew all this, and yet was drawn to this strange person who had somehow tied himself with her.

She ached for his words, for his nearness, in a way that could only be explained as necessity.

"Would you? Stay?" she asked again, quieter, shrinking into herself. Would he be angered at her forwardness? There was no way to know. He stood before her, head bent and eyes closed. She took the last three steps between them and placed a hand in the middle of his chest, and his eyes opened, steady and straight.

He inhaled slowly. "I would do whatever I can for you."

"Because it is your duty?"

"Because I wish it."

"I do not wish to be alone."

He let out his breath and nodded slowly, once. Behind him, the great hearth burst into a crackling, happy flame, merry and orange. Turning, he gave her his back so she could slip out of his cloak and into the warm tub, with its spicy scent and deep middle. She sank low and the rim of the tub afforded her some modesty, though she thought perhaps they were past some level of privacy. How much was she pushing his sense of old chivalry? His manners reminded her of the kings and knights in the fairy tales and fables. He was unlike the rough coarseness of the villagers, nor even was his way the threadbare manners of the men in the city.

There was a slight scrape near the fire, and when she turned her neck, she saw him settling carefully into one of the small spindle-legged chairs.

It sagged under his weight, though did not seem in serious threat of breaking. He sat as if it would, and she debated sending him back to her bedroom and the great strength of her mattress, but there were a host of problems with that request, not least of which it would nullify why she had asked him to stay in the first place. She craved company, a voice, a mind, and he had it all.

Still, she could not help feeling as though she was stealing. Perhaps he would not choose to be in such a compromising situation.

"I have asked too much of you, once again," she said. The water in the tub lapped along the jade, making a soft splash as she drew up her legs. "You are not comfortable in my rooms."

He shifted a fraction. The chair squeaked, and he froze and met her gaze, then looked away. "It's only the chair. It was not built for this." His arm swept slowly up his body.

She looked down at her own. In the course of three nights, she'd gained a number of pale and puckered scars, memories and talismans of her trials. Would he overlook such ugliness if they wed?

The thought of a wedding—and its conclusion at the end of the ceremony—made her pause with shock. She had not really considered...

She tried to breathe through her nerves, wondering if she should pose the question her mind begged, that her history and her very nature would demand she ask.

"Are you like a man..." Zaklina swallowed the very end of the question, already shocked the words left her lips. She bunched her hands over her stomach, as if shielding the soft flesh from another blow, even if it was only his derision. She expected him to stand and depart, even if making a kind excuse.

His whole body reacted, reflexively jerking toward her and then straightening away, an odd reflex and one that made him look more like a gargoyle than a man.

"Are all the women of your village so brazen?" he wondered hoarsely.

"Some more than others," she admitted. The sentences came easier now, as if a clamp on her thoughts had been released. "And I am likely the worst of it. But I think it a fair question, given you asked me to marry you. A woman should know her marriage bed."

He froze, his dark eyes glittering, the firelight behind him dancing on the edges of his carved cheekbone. "What are you saying?"

"I am only asking a logistical question," she said, meeting his gaze and ignoring the tremors of anticipation running through him. She reminded herself that he did not love her, that he might only need marriage to break a spell. That once he released himself from it all, he would cast her aside as well. That he would have a thousand beautiful women if he were a man in truth. That she did not want to love, for she could not bear the pain of it.

He was quiet for so long she thought he had decided not to answer her raw and inappropriate anatomy question. She remembered, then, that the girls in all the stories would never ask such a thing.

She had perhaps broken another unknown rule. Would the castle send rocks tumbling? Would more rooms crumble to dust? Would it deliver ever more evil at night?

Then, rusty and gruff, he answered. "I am as a man, though perhaps... not as... My proportions are greater, and thus..." His voice was thick with mortification, but he did not stop looking directly at her. She suddenly felt, finally, she had found someone who would not judge her and her uneasy ways. Her heart lurched, as if it meant to leap out of her chest once more, and she worried that if it did, it would this time be of her own perilous choosing.

He did not leave her all the hours as she rested her limbs in the warm jade bathtub. The water never cooled and her skin did not shrivel and she sent a thought of gratitude to whatever kindly magic had been enlisted to help. She laid her head back on the generous curl of the tub's edge, which fit her neck gently. He grew less rigid in the gilded chair, and the fire crackled in any wide silence between their discussions.

He asked her of her life in the city, her time as a governess, her work as a seamstress. She spoke too of Milena and even Marek, of the grouchy Gnegon and Aldona, and the shriveling gardens and lack of food. She plied him with questions about the castle, the magic within it, and he answered as well he could, often throwing up his hands in a limp gesture of failure when the words stuck in his throat.

"I am forbidden of speaking such things," he would say, and then she would attempt to find another way to draw out information, probing into any possible cracks in the magic that bound his tongue.

"If so much depends on me—whether I survive the nights or...agreeing to your request—then why are the rules so difficult?"

"All the magic of the castle is focused both on seeing to your needs and repelling you. It is tied to humankind," he said, then waited, as if expecting his mouth to be glued shut again. When it did not, his shoulders relaxed a bit more.

"Why do you suppose you cannot talk of so much of your castle and your world? It is not because you do not know, is it?" she asked, running her fingers along the curve of the tub.

"I know much of what I do thanks to the years spent here alone, with little to do but explore, for the castle has changed much with time. And before it all became ash and dust, yes, this place was filled with life and no corner was empty. But it seems I cannot tell you such stories. And in this, they are as lost to you as they are to me."

"And you...are you truly made of stone?" The question was intensely personal, but Zaklina felt they had crossed another threshold with their candid chatting, and besides, it was less a question of magic and rules.

"Yes. And no. I am mortal enough that I can be killed, I suppose. But I am old, Zaklina. Older than all the stories you know, older than gods and goddesses, and yet I depend entirely upon your people to exist. We have spoken of stories, and how the seeds of them are the truest truths. But if they are stamped out...all will crumble, even me. Without the deepest, basest truths, no matter how beautiful or ugly it be...humanity is lost. I am the last of it, and all my arrows are spent. The only ones remaining are with the strongest of the demons, and I do not think they will ever depart now that they are so powerful."

She frowned, finding no rejoinder to his situation, and felt any words of sympathy would be paltry and small in the face of his massive existence. It made her itchy. If only she could help him. He asked for marriage as if it might heal some great loss, and yet it was the one thing she felt would be an unkindness, for she did not, could not, love him. He had made it clear he thought her uneasy, and that he had asked other maids. Even loved some of them. What was she to that? And what was a marriage without at least affection?

Zaklina felt warmth spread from her shoulders to her pelvis, and she pressed her legs together, unwilling to admit to the last.

Affection? Yes, surely, for he was the only other person in the castle. Why would she not crave his company and his voice? While he was carved, and his body and face more like a stone mason's dream, she could sense and shape of a man, flitting beneath the surface.

But love?

Shaking her head, she sat up, crossing her hands onto her shoulders.

"Shall we eat?"

"You are hungry. Of course." The Gargoyle made to stand, then realized if he did so he'd see directly into the translucent green-blue of the water and paused, flustered. "I will close my eyes until you are ready for me to reopen them."

He abruptly squeezed them shut, and suddenly looked intensely peaceful. Zaklina stared at the change in the line of his mouth, the hollowed caves under his cheekbones, and the tilt of his chin. A man of stone. That was what he truly was. Not a gargoyle or a monster, a beast or a terror of the night. She liked looking at him like this, and would have reached to trace the line of his jaw if she thought he might allow it.

But instead, Zaklina pulled herself out of the bath and picked up the thick linen put to the side, curling it around her hips and over her breasts until she was swathed in white.

"You may look," she said, then squinted at her words. She made it sound like an enticement!

He did not seem to take it as such, or at least, did not react as if she had made overtures. His eyes opened, but he did not move, leaving her to move to the bedroom and behind the screen, where she was surprised to see an entirely new set of gowns and dresses laid out. They were each so different, she could not choose alone.

"Gargulec?" she called.

He cleared his throat, a sound more like chocolate than a cough, before raising his voice to respond. "Is anything wrong?"

"No, of course not. I was only wondering what we might do today. After we eat."

"You...wish to spend the day together?"

"Yes."

"Even after yesterday? After I..."

And their last conversation flooded back, a torrent of emotions stronger given the night's terrible hours.

She had been upset. Frustrated. Both at him and herself.

At his disbelief of his own merits, and his inability to offer any to her. And under it all thrummed the feeling—an inkling, a knowing—that his stilted words meant she was nothing but a fleeting distraction. For all he seemed ever more amazed she survived and stayed one more night...and yet he did not think her worthy of a compliment.

And then he wondered why she did not accept his proposal!

"Tomorrow is gone. We must not look backwards at it," she said firmly, unwilling to waste daylight hours dwelling in sorrow. "Where will we go?"

"There is a place of beauty made by the hands of men and women. It does not seem to be in danger of destruction – perhaps because it is filled with objects, and people still speak of them with reverence."

She tried to guess at the room, picturing a great carved hall. She asked if it was filled with books or maps, boxes of coins or even swords and shields. The Gargoyle denied each thing, and she gave up by the time they reach her garden. They ate persimmons and limes from plates made of fine near transparent china. Each had been broken and mended with gold, which spidered like veins or rivers across each dish. Their goblets were fluid cones of silver, but Zaklina did not see a message inscribed on hers.

"Try this," the Gargoyle said, pouring a pale red wine into the cup. "It is rare to see a vintage, and this one is old."

She brought the wine to her lips and paused. He was just about to take a sip when he noticed her hesitation.

"Do you think it will taste poorly, given the age of it?" he wondered, peering down into the goblet.

"It just seems unusual. Generous, even."

He stared at her, then the bottle. "You believe it poisoned."

"You don't?"

"There has never been a reason before for such a thing."

"But now I am here. And I am staying. The nights do not make me depart, and I'm not enticed to leave. It's breaking the cycle, and in that...I am a threat." She looked down into the wine. "It seems my uneasy ways are a threat no matter where I go. It is perhaps why I am unlovable."

A bubble floated to the top of the ruby liquid, and when it burst, a thousand tiny flies shot into the air. Zaklina dropped the goblet as if it burned her fingers. It shattered the white plates along their golden lines, and stained the pale mint of the table linen.

Gargulec sprang to his feet, a movement more creature than man, the move stunning in its power and fearful in its strength. He pressed his chest outward, and let out a roar just like the one from Zaklina's dreams—a sound of dismay and frustration, loss and might—and all the louder for its nearness. She did not cover her ears, only closing her eyes as the table rattled above her knees.

When he finished, she opened her eyes slowly to discover the wine had disappeared into the ether, leaving a pristine linen. The plate had mended. And the bottle of spirits had disappeared, replaced by a pitcher of only water, clear and sparkling in its cold pureness.

"Not poison," she said calmly, as he slowly sat down. "Just tainted."

"I do not want to know the ploy of the magic this time," he growled, pouring the water into new glass cups. "But it is enough that you must sacrifice yourself at night. It was too much, too far. I do not wield much of my own power, but sometimes...sometimes I am heard. Especially when I am asking for justice."

They did not spend much time over the table after that, the coziness broken, and when they departed, he took them up through a small door, and they continued to climb a narrowing staircase. It was soon so tight that she wondered if he would fit all the way through, but he kept telling her to go forward and was always only a step behind her. The stairs became slivers of stone, slippery and slick with interlaid mica and polished quartz. The walls of stone became pale sand, but were smooth and like satin.

"It is almost as though this place wishes to be left alone!" she said, wheezing slightly as she continued the careful climb up.

"We are in one of the highest spires, a mile beyond your own rooms, and much higher than the clouds," he said, his voice as even as always. "But you're not wrong. The makers of this space did not want the room to be easily found, or easily looted."

"A treasure room!" she said, and was a little annoyed with herself for sounding like a giddy courtesan with the promise of glimpsing the fine family jewels.

"There is some of that," the Gargoyle amended. "But not in the way you might think."

The winding stairs finally stopped abruptly at a golden door that filled the entire end of the climb. The gold was only overlay and in many places it had flaked off to reveal the bark behind it, which bled a slow white liquid, so the door looked to be weeping.

"Is the tree encased in gold still alive?" Zaklina asked, reaching out a finger to the drop of milky dew slowly trailing down the carvings.

"Stop!" The Gargoyle grabbed her hand just before she touched it. His grasp was tight, still cool and then warm, the oddness of it now familiar to her. He began to release her, but she interlaced their fingers. Inside his, her hand looked less worn and rough and instead dainty and slim.

"Is this poison, too?" she asked, offering him a small half-smile in jest.

His shoulders went up and down as he glanced between the door and her face. Then he turned so he could gaze at the carvings without letting go of her palm.

"It is," he said. "Can you understand what is carved on this door?"

Zaklina peered at the shimmery gold, which laid over the bumps and curves of symbols. They seemed to come alive and wiggle as she stared, so she blinked often. It helped a bit. As she looked, she saw the shape of circles and lines, two sets put side by side, and differing only slightly by where the circles sat and how many there were.

"I see geometry," she said. "But I see nothing written to read."

"But you see the two trees? The trees of life?"

"They aren't very much like trees," she said, noticing now the carvings on the exterior of the two main images. "And around them all are little tiny apples. Does it mean...is it to do with the one story...the one of the... oh, it's very famous. I can't recall it! A man? Woman. An apple."

"And a snake in a tree," the Gargoyle finished. "I remember that much myself, for it is one of the stories told most often, even though it has been re-crafted and the words used within it have often changed throughout time, and still do. Its age makes it hard to disappear, so I can recall enough. Some say the snake came from the tree of life. But given it was fruit that would harm, others say it was an apple from the tree of death that the snake offered."

"And this door?"

"It is a last stand to protect what lies beyond, though it has been many eons since it has mattered. The door is carved from the bark of the tree, and the small apples a reminder of its poisonous fruit. The sap itself is dangerous. Everything about the tree is so."

"So how does one enter, then?"

"With pain."

At that, the Gargoyle took his other massive hand and pushed. The loud immediate sound of sizzling matched his grunt.

As the door groaned open on wooden hinges, Zaklina looked to him first before the wonders within the sunshine washed room, grabbing his injured hand and pulling it toward her.

His entire palm, from fingertips to wrist, was covered in large blisters, fat and bulbous. They were a pale grey-white against the dark grey of his skin, and as she watched, they burst and peeled, leaking onto the floor.

"Does it hurt very much?" she asked, aghast. "I would not have chosen to come here if I had known you'd be in pain."

He stared down at her with an unreadable expression, one mixed with surprise and wonder, anguish and something far more guarded. It was a disconcerting gaze, so she busied herself with her underskirt.

"Let me use some of this to mop up or bandage it," she said. "That might help. If I had a rose or so, I might wrench some oil from the petals and make an ointment, but—"

"It will heal," he said calmly. "It will be healed before we depart. But you are kind to worry over it."

"Over you," she said, the correction automatic. Then embarrassment flooded her cheeks and the warm went all the way past her ears and up into her hairline. How flushed was she now? He was getting more adept at making her blush, that was certain.

"Well, do you want to see this? I assure you, it is worth the climb and my temporary injury," he said, gesturing at the room. Zaklina turned around, and her mouth dropped.

It was a greathall carved entirely of a golden-hued wood, matched and fitted together so it looked to be made all of one great hollowed out tree. The color was further heightened by the many windows on all three sides, which were the height of six men and narrow as a sword. But there were so many it was as if the sun lived in the room, dancing on the floor and soaring through the ceiling.

But the might of the room was not matched by the beauty of the items on dozens of simple pedestals. The ones closest to Zaklina were made of gold and silver, inset with massive diamonds of every hue, sparkling with masses of gems and pearls. Some were tall and spiked, and looked to be what an ice queen might don. Others were squat and heavy, with velvet in the middle, surrounded by a moat of jewels. They were all too much, their grandeur haughty in their very expense, and yet one could certainly not stop looking.

Zaklina wandered from one to the next, marveling and oddly appalled. The Gargoyle walked a few paces behind her, his hands clasped behind his back. He had not put the cloak back on, having left it in her bedroom, and he seemed far less imposing, and more man-like without the swirl of fabric around him.

"They are all very..." She refused to touch any of them, but she paused in front of one with a thin band of whitest ermine around the edge. "Heavy?"

"I would call these gaudy in the kindest term," the Gargoyle said. "But they are the most recent ones. They are what people think of when they think of crowns and the power they wield. They were not always so."

As they continued down the rows, the shapes changed; some simpler and more conical, with only bands of inlaid gold in the form of curls or vipers. Soon, the gold and silver gave way to copper and iron, before it left off finery entirely, and the pedestals held crowns of preserved leaves and wood, woven together in multiple strands.

"I recognize the laurel," she said, stopping in front of a crown of long, glossy, dark green leaves. "And the next is made from mulberry, for I know the fruit. But I do not know the rest, or their significance."

"They are all made of different Trees of Life," he said, then pointed at the next half dozen and beyond. "Fir and almond, fig, tamarisk, acacia and ash. And others, lesser known but older still—baobab and palm. They are all part of the old ways, the oldest belief. Their branches and leaves used to be filled with the strength of the earth, the meaning of why life exists in the first place."

"Virtues," Zaklina said softly, stopping in front of the pale twisted circle made of the tamarisk. "And virtues kept are a way of living."

"Do you believe virtues and morals are the exact same thing?" he asked, coming beside her. The movement made the fronds of the crown stir slightly before settling.

"They are only words," she said. "They are ideals, something greater than a category, don't you think? It is difficult to put morals and virtues into words that span their full understanding."

She walked to the next, which was covered in pale pinky-white blooms. "I have never seen an almond tree in bloom."

"This one is different in that it is not quite the tree of life, but a tree of heaven. Divine grace and hidden truth. Resilience and vigilance."

"It sounds very much like your tree," she said, allowing a tease to touch her tone. "Perhaps you should wear this crown of flowers."

"No, it would be you, not me. It is meant for the woman, for some say the almond tree is a symbol of feminine beauty as well. And—" He stopped himself, swallowing the rest of his sentence.

"And? Is it a tree of fertility, then?" She did not know why she jested with him so much. Perhaps it was a sort of hysteria, leftover from the night's terrors, and seeing how her heart could be removed though she still lived.

"It is a tree of virginity," he said.

The word hit her hard, and the small grin fell from her lips. She did not feel like teasing any more. "Not for me, then."

She walked away, leaving him gazing at the fragrant crown, his forehead slashed by a deep frown down the center.

Well, should she be surprised? Of course feminine beauty and virginity would be prized virtues. That had not changed in thousands of years, and it was certainly still true in her experience.

"Here is another of blossoms," she said, stopping at one of the last crowns, the most simple by far, with only one large true-pink bloom. "I suppose this one is for the virgin, too?"

He joined her, and, to her surprise, took up the crown in his hands. The damaged palm had already healed as promised, the peeled blisters shadows against his skin.

"It is a peach tree," he said. "I would use this wood for my arrows, long ago, as it repels demons, and whether silver or gold, I did not want to send evil into the world even when I shot silver arrows to cancel a gold's overzealousness. Peach is a sacred fruit to some, and auspicious to others. It is joy and immortality, and yes, feminine charms. It is not for the virgin, though, but the opposite."

Zaklina took a step back. The hidden message may as well have been slapped into her physically, and she thought he meant to tell her how she failed to live up to his preferences. Surely the others—the ones he had loved—they would have all been pure. She balled her fists.

"I don't wish this crown, either, for I'm not a woman who sells her body. It is what it is! How many times must I reminded by you—this place—that I am no virgin maid?"

He flashed her a bemused glance while still cradling the crown gently in both palms. "It has been untold years, but that will not erase the fact that I am not, either."

The admission sent her mind reeling. Were there once others just like him? Men and women, carved in strange likenesses and living together, marrying, and finding love? Sharing a bed?

Was he just looking for companionship as this last place of magic refuge crumbled around him?

What was the Gargoyle? *Who was he?*

He left her in her rooms, and the door locked as always, and there was enough time to snatch moments of sleep before she woke, hungry. There was a small table by the giant hearth, and a plate heaped with cheeses and pate, melons, and red, brown and yellow raisins.

She was glad of the comfort of the space, which seemed familiar even as the dreary last sunlight dripped from the walls and settled into the gray and green gloom. The night crept in slowly, but the fire did not yet go out, so she stood in front of it, her muscles aching with how tightly she clenched them. There did not seem to be a purpose in going to bed.

This time she was expecting it and knew by the moment of stillness that the night was fully formed, for her torture would only begin when the sun was gone and the moon a full witness to her terror.

But instead of a black mist or a sheen of water, it was the fire itself that changed. It went from yellow to orange, and then to fully red, the color of new blood, freshly spilled. The reminder of the night before made Zaklina shiver despite the roaring of the flames, and she took a step toward the heat just as a figure detached itself from the redness and approached.

It was only a young woman, new into adulthood, with black hair reaching the edges of her heels and covered in pliant white leather decorated with large mother-of-pearl shells. Pierced bone and smaller shells jingled as she moved.

In her eyes blazed a fire of newly-released, womanly emotion. Instead of reaching for Zaklina, she simply sat in front of the fire and raised her smallest finger.

From it slowly dripped a trickle of blood, the same color as the flames behind her.

"It is a splinter," she said, looking at nothing. Zaklina did not know if the young woman could see her, or if she was only the precursor of something bigger. She seemed harmless, and there was nothing terrible to behold. She did not even have teeth filed to points.

"I was cutting a maple tree for an apron," the woman continued vaguely, looking at the slow ooze of the blood. "But it will not stop flowing."

After a long moment of staring at the bleeding, as it made a sticky river down forearm and pooling in the crook of her elbow, the young woman stuck her pinky finger into her mouth and began to suck.

The gentle slurping was a small sound, but it soon filled the whole of the space, and Zaklina wanted to run and bury her head in pillows, though she was certain it would not stop the echo. As the blood was licked, more came, and it would not stop.

The hours ticked by, each longer than the last, until Zaklina was quite certain the night was near finished. As each minute passed, she became more worried and yet hopeful until her insides spun in a deadly cycle of fear and relief. It made her faint, and Zaklina would have fallen asleep for the waiting, but she seemed unable to tear her eyes from the sight. How much could one small splinter bleed? And why would it not end?

And then, the young woman pulled the finger out, frowned at it, and bit.

The crunch and grind of sinew and fat mixed with the snap of bone brought bile to Zaklina's mouth, where it piled and soured in the edges of her jaw. She wanted to cry out, but now silence was part of her nights just like the terror. So instead she gripped the edge of her chair, appalled and mute as the woman became less human and more a monster. From the finger, the bloodied teeth moved to the hand, and then the other. Blood poured from the wounds, and yet she still munched and devoured her own body, mindless and without a thought, moving as if she did not notice pain or care that she ate herself.

Zaklina stood, the chair crashing behind her. The young woman did not flinch, for she had moved to her feet and legs, always chewing, the bones and gristle of her knee squeaky between her back molars. Her mouth grew until Zaklina could see the mashed bits of plump flesh and yellow fat speckled between the girl's teeth. As she began to eat her entire body, Zaklina gave up waiting.

This was the horror then. This sight of self-ingestion, the unforgettable sounds of a person eating human flesh—this alone would drive her mad.

She flung her body against the furthest wall, away from the massive pool of fire-red blood on the floor, her eyes still stuck.

Now she understood. It was clear.

This would not be a night of demons of the usual sort.

The young woman was nothing but a head now, with long hair trailing behind the skull like a stream. And finally, her eyes fixed on Zaklina.

"Oh. Just let me rest a bit after such a meal!" The head's eyes closed tight and a light snore bounced around the room.

Zaklina wanted to ask how long she had, and how many minutes did such a creature need to rest? She glanced around, trying to see how soon the sun might find her, and fearful to take her eyes off the head so it could not roll over and pounce. She looked for a weapon, but the only thing left was the plate on the table, now empty of fruit and nuts. She could throw it, but if she missed...or if it was not enough...

"Ah!" The head's eyes opened, and immediately found Zaklina in the room, rolling slightly as if able to scent her body. "Time to eat again."

There was no time to grab the plate.

No way to strategize as the head began to launch itself by rolling hard, covering the ground in awkward little jumps and rolls. Zaklina dodged out of the way, but the head only twisted and reversed. Soon enough it became nothing but a chase and match of wits. Zaklina tried to climb the bed, but the creature just clamped onto the furniture and began to chomp its way up or pull the bedclothes off, bringing Zaklina with them.

Her skirts tangled between her ankles, her chest felt squeezed, and sweat poured between her shoulder blades and under her breasts. There was no time to catch her breath, no time to stop moving and no reprieve from the chase. Soon enough her feet were bloodied, blisters torn open along her heels and between her toes, leaving sticky footprints across the marble. The floor became a trap in itself, slippery with the blood and the fluid, so that she must skirt these as well or risk sliding, which would give the creature-head all the moments it would need to pounce. She could not afford to—

And then half of her left foot lost purchase, skidding her leg from under her, and Zaklina went down, hard, hearing the pulp of her knee shatter, blinded by the shock and pain of it. It was over, then, dull teeth sunk into her calf, and she was sure she would be dead long before the creature ate her up, so the pain might be hot and fast, but over soon enough. She thought of the Gargoyle again, and wondered if he might miss her. And then she wondered why she thought of him at all... It was as if she was tied to him. As if her very essence screamed for him, though she would never—could never—call out...

Her entire leg muscle was ripped from the bone, and unlike the night before in the bath house, this time Zaklina could feel every pull and snap of her vessels. She must think of something else. Must remember...her sister.

Her mother...

What had their mother always said...?

Serce nie sługa...the heart knows no master...

She was certain that her very heart pumped her lifeblood out through the wound in her leg. She felt the thump and spurt of it with every other second. And she was sure she'd feel the crunch of the bone, the grind of the gristle of her ligaments, chewed up by the ravenous head. Would she die before the creature ate her, or would she—

"Zaklina? Are you awake?"

She gasped and shot up from the floor, glancing about wildly for the long black hair of that bloody head, but there was nothing on the slick marbles. Only a few stray drops of dried blood, now the color of orangey rust, marked the night's battle.

She scrabbled for purchase on the floor, ripping back her skirt which stuck with the stickiness of wet blood, only to find a jagged pale scar along her calf. It looked to be ages old, like an injury from a childhood wound, long bound and knitted. The pain seared through her once again before dropping away, so sudden it left her gasping.

"Zaklina, my dearest?"

The Gargoyle sounded both inquisitive and worried at the same time, as if he had grown used to expecting her answer, but still believed it possible she would choose to leave him. And perhaps, if she had been a different sort of woman, she might have done.

Zaklina only knew he had offered an endearment.

"I'm here," she said. She tried to stand, but found the leg lacking.

Limping as she went, she gripped the backs of chairs, hoping the spindly designs could hold her weight, until she could lean against the door and gulp air. The gems cut into the great wooden door seemed sharper than usual, and she hissed when the edge of a diamond drew a line of red down the side of her hand.

"I can come back when you are ready to eat?" he asked, sounding even more uncertain.

"You should come in now," she said. "I need your help."

She was able to pull away from the door as he opened it, but the movement left her staggering to the side. He grabbed her, moving unnervingly fast, catching her elbow, and holding her up with ease.

"I'm inelegant and not graceful at all," she said, tremors running down into her ankle. "It's a wonder you wish to keep me here."

"You are inordinately unkind to yourself," he said, depositing her in the nearest chair. "And you need to rest a bit. You are injured?"

Zaklina thought of all the scars crisscrossing her body. Would they be considered injuries or proof of her bravery?

And were they not the same thing?

"I was," she said. "As I am each night."

His dark, carved shoulders slumped as he kneeled in front of her. "I suppose I should not dare to keep asking if you will stay. I should stop hoping I might convince you to choose me, to share this solitude. It is too much to ask of any maid."

She still did not want to go back to the yellow and flowered meadow, with its sickly scent and Mrs. Staryski's ever-changing notions and webs of stories and facts, interwoven until it was impossible to tell where the fable began and the reality lived.

She leaned forward instead, daring herself to be forward so her hands might say what her throat could not, even as she berated herself for this softness. She had already reminded herself—and him—of her unsuitability and her undesirableness. For all he said he loved the others, though, she could not help but feel that had he but given her a chance...

Perhaps he had asked her for marriage out of affection and not some strange, unknown duty...

It was only she was quite certain her love would never be enough to hold anyone, not even a man made of stone.

Her hands found his. "I must keep reminding you. I am no maid."

He bowed his head, then brought her fingers to his lips. The coolness of them was not unbearable, and she stood, pulling him up so they were locked, handfasted so tightly that she felt the length of his thick thighs caressing hers, even though his height mismatched her own. She tried not to breathe so he would not stir and settled into the embrace, imagining she had agreed, and they were wed, that her life would be as it was, though with more, with him—with intimacy, with devotion, with affection and lovemaking. The visions filled her body until she felt she would puddle with imagined sensations in the grey of the morning light. And through it all, she knew she was a fool for entertaining the dreams.

After a long moment, he pulled back as he always did. Though she still strengthened her hold on his hands, they slipped away.

He turned to the fireplace, his arms locked behind his waist. "You should dress. I will wait, if you wish."

She stood alone in the center of the room, hugging her elbows near, closing her eyes against the sorrow.

His rejection of her body was chokingly painful, deeply cutting.

Perhaps she did care for him.

Perhaps, if she let herself, she might love him.

She already knew she craved his company above anyone she knew, but she also knew loving him was dangerous, for it only led to refusals.

"Zaklina." Her name was a rumble. "Look at me."

She did not wish it, but opened her eyes anyway, finding his whole face as he turned back to her. Everything there reminded her of their days together in the castle, exchanging stories, preferred foods, debating old philosophy and morals. She looked at him knowing that she understood him and who he was. She saw the man under the layer of monster. She knew he was more than he seemed. He was more real than anything she had known before.

She would indeed love him if she thought there was a chance of stealing his heart.

"I see you," she said.

He was quiet for a moment longer. "Do not think I let you go of my own accord," he told her, his voice so quiet it seemed to whisper along the tiles.

"No? Does the magic pull you away?" The tart sarcasm in her voice was ill-concealed.

His eyes darkened as he winced. "No. I only..." he sighed, as if forcing himself to be as forward. "I do not wish to...frighten you."

"How so?" She inched her way back to his side, spreading the length of her body along his hip, curling her arm around his stomach, simply to see if he would stop her and push her off.

Expecting it.

Instead, he settled deeper into the embrace, putting his own arm around her, too. "You know what I mean. You said you were wed once before. Do you truly need an explanation?" he said, suddenly irritable, but innately she understood it was not at her but his own bashfulness. Was there a chance...a small, uncertain chance...that he desired her truthfully? That he was trying to shield her from his own lust?

The idea took hold and she pressed her face into his shoulder, breathing in the wild scent of earth and stone, moss and smoke.

After a long moment of silence broken only by breath, he shook his great head and picked her up. In eleven strides, he was in the bedchamber, putting her in the center with tenderness, and climbing onto it so he could see her leg for himself, as if the medical care would be enough to stop further romance. But she'd broken through, she was certain of it. Zaklina sat up, stopping his inspection of the newest scar, and buried her forehead into the softness of the thick beard about his neck that served as something more on him. He sighed, but it was a sound of contentment, and his fingers stroked her hair, her spine, and finally, carefully, the curve of her bottom. When he did, he pulled back his palm fast, burned, uncertain.

She grabbed his hand, stilling his retreat. "I do not mind your touch. I... want...If you asked me..." Her offer hung, frank and outlandish. Perhaps it was the castle itself, playing a game, unleashing such wantonness.

Or perhaps she was giving up, after many nights of pain, and only sought a reprieve.

"What kind of..." He paused, swallowed. "You yearn for me as I am?"

She nodded into his neck. He inhaled, the sound low and loud and wide in the room.

"I am not frightened. I know what desire feels like, or at least the ghost of it. This is something...more." The truth of her statement weighed them both down, tying them to the sheets, willingly and with surprise. She could not believe she had spoken aloud. And he seemed shocked.

He turned to her, still kneeling on the bed, the position one so simply human it was easy to forget he was more. "Now it is my turn to disbelieve."

Acting on impulse, on buried passion, she leaned into him and kissed him, featherlight and sudden, before he could shy away. The leanness of his lips was what she expected, the softness of them less so. His eyes were closed, and before he could open them, she took another kiss, lingering, wondering, and then he took her into his arms, pressing her body against his, so that their mouths melted together. His reaction soared into her, tempered only by the fact that he did not love her.

Passion and lust were one thing.

Love was something she only knew one-sided, and had never expected —would never—for herself.

"You'd give me yourself?" he asked, as if deeply bewildered, breaking their kiss. His eyes were cloudy. "You'd take me fully, all of me?"

"I would," she reaffirmed, meeting his gaze straight. "And I expect I'd find it beyond pleasurable." The idea of his weight over her and his length within her was enough to send a shiver of wishing and wanting into her bones. She pushed into him, wondering what he might look like without his layers of fabric. Hoping he would like to see her, and would find her attractive. That he would consume her, taste her, worship her.

"You ask this of me. Now?"

"I will ask this of you always," she said.

He offered a soft sound. "I will always say yes."

"Because of the magic?"

"Because I desire you. Magic has nothing to do with it."

Did he mean it? He had no reason to lie on this, no reason to mislead, for he had no need to love her to marry her. Did he tell her the truth of his heart? How she wanted to believe! And she could not believe they spoke of such things with such ease, as if a spell had been wrenched apart. Or perhaps Zaklina had broken too many of the usual rules of story, allowing for unusual conversations that fit nowhere else.

"If this is all you will offer me of yourself... If this is to be our lives, sequestered in this castle, let us take this comfort. Let it be our beginning," she told him. "And I will be yours."

"I will not deny that I ache for you," he said, very slowly and with faint desperation. "That I have yearned for you since the first time in the meadow." The deep rumble of his voice in the cavern of his chest bubbled through her own.

Something that had been tight unfurled inside of her.

"You want me? Knowing my faults, that I am not anything fancy? That I am...an uneasy woman?" She had to ask, to hear it.

He pulled her tighter. "Your disbelief is misplaced. Why should I not? I know you, your mind and your secrets. Yet I am here."

"You are here."

He leaned down to kiss her again, airy and quick, before he glanced down at the ruin of her clothes and the old blood curdling on the fabric.

"You should get out of this."

"I will need help," she admitted, trying to find her breath after their explosion of kissing. "It's only...I don't know how long the leg will take to heal fully, and I don't wish to fall on the floor while I dress."

He frowned, but the situation only offered a single solution, scandalous as it seemed.

"I will help you, though I do not trust myself to act with honor," he said, a statement perhaps the most honest he had ever offered, one laced with passion and rawness. "It would be best if you could at least put on the small layers."

"I will do what I can," she said, shuffling off the bedclothes and behind the screens. She had not noticed, but they were embroidered, blue upon blue, with images of nude women bathing, and satyrs all watching from behind thick groves of trees. It was an erotic scene to be sure, and Zaklina thought perhaps they were new.

She stripped off the layers, wishing for a morning bath but having no way to ask. There was only the milky pitcher of icy water and a washcloth. Sponging herself off as best she could, she winced as she brushed the fabric along her calf. It had healed quickly, the wound as magical as the creature that wrought it, but the remaining pain was something new, and still enough to make her stiff and slow.

Once she put on the chemise and fine-boned corset, which was trimmed with cream ribbon and the tiniest layer of lace along the edge, she glanced around the edge of the screen. The Gargoyle sat on the end of the bed, his shoulders and head bent over his hands, which he clasped between his knees. It was a posture of supplication, an offering of a prayer, and she desperately wished she could ask him what he wished so much. She had offered him her body, her most sacred gift, for all it was not an untouched one, but how could she offer more when there was no hope of a return of his affection? She endured the nights to break the worst of the magic of the castle, or so she had come to believe. She did not ask to leave. What more could she give?

"Gargulec? I am ready for your aid," she said gently, loathe to upset him from his thoughts. But he stood quickly at her voice, turning to her with an openness new to his visage, and it struck her as quite handsome indeed.

He came about the edge with small steps, as if waiting for her change her mind.

"Which do you wish?" he asked, gesturing to the small rack of gowns. Today they were mostly brocade and embossed fabrics, some with cloth of gold. They seemed too rich for the likes of Zaklina, and she could not pick because of it.

"You choose, please," she said, her eyes stuck on him as he loomed in the smaller womanly space. His very coloring seemed out of place, but the masculinity of his nearness was only heightened because of it.

She swallowed hard, and waved her hand vaguely at the dresses in an echo of his own movement. "They are very fine, and I am afraid I'm out of my element."

He turned and frowned at the different options, picking up one from the end. It was not the most dramatic. No jewels crusted the hem or the ends of sleeves, but it was not the plainest, either. It was one of blue—midnight and cerulean and the palest sky, with gold leaf pressed into the pattern of the underskirt.

"This will look very fine on you," he said with certainty. "Most things would, my Zaklina, but for today, this will do well."

"Where will we go this morning?"

"Where stories are made for posterity."

The answer was cryptic at the very least, but she knew not to press, and besides, the surprise would make it better. The Gargoyle helped her step into the skirts, holding her forearm so she did not tip over, and then put up the buttons and silk ties along the back himself, though it took quite a long time given the thickness of his fingers. When he was finished, he bent and whispered a kiss on her exposed shoulder, leaving a delicious shiver behind. After she swept up her hair with pins, he supported her so she could step into her shoes. And though she limped on the way to breakfast, the slice of white-hot pain numbed with each step. She hoped it would heal even faster once they ate.

The garden had overgrown itself even more, and the destroyed pond was nearly choked with new growth, big sprawls of swamp flowers that gave off the scent of marigolds, and several of the palms and trees crowded overhead. The Gargoyle stared about, his arm securely about her waist, but wonder trebling through his whole body.

"I have not seen something this lush in ages," he said.

"There has been very little crumbling of castle walls, too," Zaklina said, her eyes crinkling up at him. "Perhaps my days and nights are working. With time, all may be healed?"

He turned to look down at her, and he gave something like a smile in return, though there was sadness behind it. "It is a lovely thought, and yes, your tenacity matters. It has stayed the worst of it."

"But?" Her heart sank.

"It will not be enough, not in the years to come. Not like this." He said the words with as much tenderness as the gravel of his voice allowed, but she was expecting it, anyway. She would not ever be enough. She still thought he might wish to find a more worthy woman. A maid with a stronger character. One who would not ask for love before marriage, whose purity would break through most of the stories and perhaps save so much more.

"Zaklina," he said, pulling her out of her spiraling thoughts. His finger found her jaw, pulling her face up to meet his. "It is more than anyone has offered since it all started to go wrong. It is beyond what I had hoped...do not despair. I have hope yet. You are still here."

She inhaled, swallowing the tears clawing their way up her throat, and kissed his palm. There was nothing else to do but accept his words and latch onto his hope.

After they ate a meal of kumquats and berries, churned butter spread on long thin loaves of springy bread, and drank hot chocolate from golden cups, he led her back out of the garden. The sun shot through the windows opposite the garden doorway, though the clouds boiled far below.

"It is a fair way down," he said, pausing at the stairs. "If I may?"

She started to nod, but he swept her up into his arms before she could finish. He took a right turn at the next landing, taking a new stair and new route which offered a wider passage and thicker stairs. There were small crevasses sprinkled through the rock, and his boots thumped and clicked on the stone. Below her thighs and above her waist, the hardness of his limbs nestled in the curves of her flesh, creating the illusion of a perfect fit. The Gargoyle moved with purpose, without changing the pattern of his breath, and she marveled at his strength.

They went deeper and lower, reminding her of her first travel up the great stairs when she had first arrived. When he opened up one of the doors they were indeed on one of the higher ramparts, connected to long walls with wet grey paths of mottled blocks and cobblestone. It was the first time she did not have to squint at the surroundings as the clouds were once again overhead. She wondered if all the time she had been at the castle that the sun had yet to break through the churning fog. Below them, the dark trees, silent under a layer of fine snow and a dusting of frost lay unmoving except for the lazy circling of a dozen crows near enough that she could see their shapes.

She wiggled a bit. He grunted and put her down. The leg was only a bit sore, and she walked slowly to the edge of the wall. The stone came up to her waist, and she leaned over it, gazing into the distance. If she had any sense of the world, she might half-close her eyes and believe she could see Miódshire still, but instead only the gloom of the trees was really all she could view.

The Gargoyle joined her, but kept himself apart, as if entry to a place below the sunshine meant their earlier intimacy was forfeit. She stepped up and wound her arm about his.

"How many day's journey is it back?" she asked.

He went stiff, his arm further rock-like. His answer sounded strangled. "A week or so if one were to walk the footpaths. Less as the crow flies – as I brought you."

She thought of Marek then, and the fire in Ludoslaw's eyes, and the strange push and pull of Mrs. Staryski's boldness and ripeness. She wondered if the harvest had changed for the better, or if the flowers wilted finally in the field, or if Milena had birthed her baby. She wondered if her sacrifice—if that was one might call it—had tamed the malevolence of the meadow. Or was it not the meadow, but something else? Something more insidious? She only knew it was not her Gargoyle who caused anything. He was something greater, and older, than the rumors of Mrs. Staryski's hills, and something far more pure.

"These paths through the woods. You have said you don't know what I would find. Would they be safe?"

"I...would not be able to come to your aid when you called, and you would surely do, for in the forest the horrors do not stop at daybreak." He became harder yet. "There are the panthers and other wild cats who hunt. There is starvation and cold. There is worse if you are even more unlucky."

A murder of crows shot up from the woods, an arrow of black, only to scream and plummet back down. It was closer to the castle than the last time she saw a disturbance, but still not so close that she could see what trembled in the trees below.

"I can take you to the lowest door," he said, his voice dragging, like the covering of clay on a coffin. "But I cannot go with you."

"You came when I called you in the meadow," she said, looking for a chink in the magical rules. "Is it like the nights, then? I cannot call you for rescue except the once. And now it is impossible for you to come to my aid again?"

He bowed his head over the rocks. "I only know the nights are not mine, and I cannot come again, no matter how you might beg. It would destroy me, to hear you call and be unable to answer, and it would help give the demons all the power they need to kill you. And yet... Come. I will take you to gather something warm for the nights, for at least I can give you some small comfort."

He turned so swiftly she only caught the very hem of his cloak, grasping it with a hard thumb, her chest collapsing inward at the realization.

"No!"

He stopped short, his fists curling into claws, clenched so tight the lines of his skin split white against the dark.

"You speak of departing," he said. "You need not beg for a freedom that is always yours. And I...there are some words of pleading I cannot say though I wish to do so."

"I do not want to go!" she cried, grabbing handfuls of his cloak. It was of the softest cotton, shot with wool and silk, woven together in a warm and lovely undulating pattern that looked like water and sky mixed together to form stone. "I only wonder sometimes, what has happened since I left. If my sister has birthed her child. If they have forgotten me, or if the menfolk hunt me in vengeance for their honor. Would they come to kill you or destroy me for pushing against their stories? Are they driven to silence me, for now they know I could re-write the old rumors knitting together their village, for my knowledge threatens their world? I do not know, and the not knowing brings questions. I cannot help them, they always come... But please—do not send me away!"

He thawed slowly, first in his arms and shoulders, and the minute straightening of his shoulders and neck, the tendons smoothing through the back of his hands. When he finally turned, it was to a low crackle, like rocks struck with lightning and now brittle with heat long left to simmer in the depths.

His eyes were black but liquid. She met them straight, a sharp prickle in the very center of her ribs. He had thought she meant to leave him, and all because she was too obtuse to see how he would misunderstand her musings. For all their morning declarations of desire, it was still new and fresh, and she should have known he felt it so fragile it might be false.

"I do not plan to go. Not now, nor ever," she said, as solemn as she might, a vow that could only be strengthened by blood, and Zaklina was sure she had offered enough.

He closed his eyes, and yet did not seem to be able to move beyond that.

"I did not mean to cause you worry," she said, searching for something to say that would calm him. Did his heart race like hers at the thought of separation? Did he think she had not meant her words of affection not an hour prior?

"You don't want to go back?" The pain lacing his voice was like an axe to her gut.

She had a vision, suddenly, of a great slice through her center, near cleaving her in half, and her heart beating in the cold of an empty hearth. Taking the three steps between them, she reached across the last of the inches and gripped his waist.

"No! I will lose you if I go away. I will stay here happily if it means we are together," she said vehemently. "I have no wish to go wandering the forest to my death."

The tension quivered and then eased out of his body completely, and he sighed. His head dropped heavily. "Thank the stars." His voice was thick, and she didn't dare press for devotion from him in turn.

Nor did she expect it.

Instead, his arm wrapped around her hip, hooking her closer against his body. Her bosom fit into the cave of his chest, and her hips sat between the low cradle of his. It was far more delightful than she expected, and she closed her eyes against the warmth and the sensations.

"I thought for a moment I dreamed our morning, that my mind had given in to my hope entirely," he said, hoarse and broken, and bleaker than he had yet to sound.

She did not know if he meant their mutual lustiness or his desire to wed her, but too much anxiousness had already been spent. Zaklina reached high and brought him down. She had to curl his back to reach her mouth, but he came willingly, meeting her without hesitation. He drew her in, crushed her, and kissed her with a passion that felt like it spanned eons. Their mouths crashed together, devoured, and mingled, and their hands spun and shifted along the whisper of the clothing between them. He pulled her in so tightly against his chest she wondered if he thought to combine their skins.

The whistle of the wind across the tops of the trees cut through them soon enough, and even protected by his bulk, she felt the chill of it and shivered once, hard. He paused their embrace and glanced at the pines and snow, then at the madly swirling clouds, which felt much closer than the treetops. She thought if she held up her hand and stood on her tiptoes, she might pull down a handful of their whisps.

"We should continue," he said, looking pleased in some measure. The deep carved lines between his eyes and on both sides of his mouth were less deep, and there was a lightness to his step as he reopened the door into the bowels of the castle's lower levels. "Do you wish to walk or shall I continue to carry you?"

Zaklina tested her weight on a few more steps, and took in a bumpy breath. "It seems healed. I will walk, but..." She intertwined her fingers with his. "If I might?"

"Please," he said, so quietly but with a soft pride she could not miss.

As they walked back into the darkness, which ate the bit of grey light and seemed to go fathoms below the horizon, she glanced back at the quiet lands beyond. Once again, the crows pierced the sky and shot back down, though she was certain they were even closer than before.

When the Gargoyle opened the great doors, sanded to true white and embossed with pale images of lotus and marigolds and wide irises, she was prepared for another dim room of long thin windows, or perhaps one of rusty, jewel-crusted scepters. But instead, it was a room filled of dust and light, looms and yarn, and the smell of old woad and dead fish.

"It is the room of tapestries," he said, gesturing with something that could only be called excitement. "Where stories are always remembered and woven, put to cloth and bone, tattooed into flesh and picked into ribbon. Do you see them?"

Zaklina let go of his arm to wander the great hall, for that was the only word for the cavernous room, which echoed with each step she took. It was a room of whispers, of long-silent shuttles and gossip of a thousand women of a hundred different ages. She could feel their weighted presence, though it was not so very piercing, more a curiousness no more harmless than the glance of another at a market stall. She was of no interest here to the lost memories. All that mattered was the slow flow of story and verse, exchanged and remembered though the looms were dead, and their strings withered to spiderwebs.

The walls between the huge windows, which she imagined once were filled with sunlight rather than the gloomy darkness of clouds and fog, were hung with massive tapestries. On each loom was a half-finished tale written in silk and satin, cotton and wool, and the gentle softness of many animal hairs.

She saw unicorns embraced by maidens, and seven crowned sisters fleetly fleeing a hunter in the navy night sky. There was a great eye weeping children, another watched over all, while a green-faced god slumbered and his wife wandered, swollen with child and surrounded by many golden scorpions. Another was of a great crane who held a translucent cloth spun from a wheel, with the rivers of Asia beyond it. Zaklina paused at the third loom, which was mostly brilliant reds and oranges, but faded near to pale apricot and rose. A massive dragon twisted on the partially finished tapestry, enfolding a willing maid between its claws. But the girl looked fuzzy, and the dragon drooped, even though it was clearly meant to be crisp and freshly made.

She felt him step behind her, though his leather boots seemed to make no sound here, as if he was half-specter.

Half-god?

The idea fell into her mind, and she quickly brushed it away.

A god would be indifferent to a woman. They only wished for unwed girls, who were tender and untried. She recalled just enough of the older myths, there. Indeed, she saw a faded tapestry beyond of a white bull and an equally rose-fleshed girl in an unseemly embrace.

"It is coming undone," he said, shock and loss crisscrossing his voice. "They are fading and melting so quickly!"

She spun to face him, unprepared for his surprise. "They are different from when you last were here?"

"Yes!" He strode beyond her, his cape swirling in great gusts and kicking dust into the air so the hall soon filled with the haze of it. "They are all turning to nothing!"

When he spoke with such fear, she looked closer at the weaving, and realized he was correct. These were not long-lost carpets, given away to time and disarray. They were decaying as they stood – both the finished and unfinished – and were turning to motley rotten threads. Some were even black with mold along the edges, and the few with metal balls to hold the threads were rusted and eating one another, turning into chunks of unusable iron.

"What can it mean?" she asked, running to catch up. "Is it very bad?"

He whirled and stopped, causing her to catch up her skirts and forced her ankles to halt too fast, and she nearly buckled with the cost of it. The Gargoyle gripped her elbows to stop her from toppling, but he released her the moment she was steady to spin around the massive weaving room in dismay.

"They are losing their power. I did not believe it. I could not. Not even with the anger of the castle, the emptying of the halls, the quieting of the forges. There was always something bigger. Some hope. But this? This is more than paper, it has a longer life than ink for a story dyed in the wool lasts beyond ages, and even here, in the most active hall of whispering and tales, where the gossip leaks into every inch of the room, preserving it all..."

He suddenly went to his knees, and she was at a full loss to calm him. Once again, he seemed more creature than man, an unknowable force that threatened to lash out in fierce anger, unseeing and filled with despair.

"Can it be fixed?" she asked.

"Fixed?" His eyes found hers, but she was certain he did not see her. "It is the place of remembrance and memory, it is where history is made and magic is knit, and without it, my place in the world weakens further."

"But you are made of stone," she said, not knowing if it was actually true, but going on the strength of what she believed and saw. "You are not a tapestry to be eaten by moths and time."

"I am a being of tall tales and folk stories, of magic and emotion, woven in and out of myth and lore as long as there are people to speak of love, no matter its face. I can and will crumble should all truth be buried and stories lost. Should the shout of the mob silence those who will question tradition, and should rumors be told enough that they override long-known reality. Should the world become the sound of only few voices, spreading easy and flowery stories to suit one or two preferences and needs, no matter how unethical or bloody they be...then I am nothing."

Zaklina looked wildly about them, certain such a place could not be good for him, if only his morale. But how to move him? How to pull him from his stupor? She was not strong enough to pick him up, and she could not fix the tapestries or change what he saw unraveling in front of his very eyes. What did they say? *Miłość jest ślepa. Love is blind.* If she could make him see her, and only her, perhaps she could pull him out of the gloom stopping his mind and yank him out of such a terrible place.

But he did not love her.

Even if perhaps she was already half-way to loving him.

"There are other fabrics," she said, desperate to break through his pain. "I have seen them, and they are lovely and pristine."

He looked up at her, dazed. She pressed her palms to his cheeks, shocked that his beard felt more like a man's and less like carved stone, as if this discovery wore down his otherworldliness and drew out the last vestiges of his strength.

"In my bedroom, I saw them, still silken and they speak of love and even of passion. There are several tapestries in my bedroom. I am sure there are others."

"But it is these...these that matter."

"Come. Come see. Perhaps there are enough in other places to sustain the stories. Between the paintings on ceilings and what I can show you, the stories will not wither. You are still here, and I am, too."

She leaned down and kissed his forehead. Her lips found it feverish, and he trembled under her hands.

"I will show you. Let us go together," she said, speaking as a lover would into his ear.

Zaklina pushed herself under his arm and shoved, hauling his bulk to standing. They walked out together slowly, for he seemed to feel the pull of gravity for the first time. As they exited, she watched the threads and yarns on the looms snap and fray faster and faster, and she hurried them out before he might notice, too. But all she knew was they must go up, and he was unable to guide her. The stairways spiraled higher than she recalled, and the cracks on some of the landings crumbled as they walked across.

Up they went, further and more, following the winding trail until they could go no further, for she could not leap the largest crevasse and bring him with her.

"Gargulec," she said, shaking his arm hard. "You must jump across."

He swung his head, his eyes more brown than black, with a flash of white along them. "What about you?"

"I can leap myself over," she said, not sure if it was entirely possible in her heavy brocade skirts, but not wishing to worry him or ask too much of his weakened state. "But not with you about my shoulders."

Finally, he seemed to see how heavily he leaned on her and jerked away. "You are so pale. How long have I been so?"

"A few hours is all."

"Hours!" He cast about with a sense of disarray, then noticed the deep crack. "This one was not here on the way down."

"I don't know if I've brought us right," she said. "I could not remember."

He looked about harder, squinting. "There are not too many staircases to get lost if you only go up." As he looked at the crack again, it crumbled further, black rock bouncing and crackling as it fell to unknown depths.

"You go first," he said, once again the chivalrous gentleman. "For you are correct. I do not believe my strength can carry us both yet." He turned to her and pulled her tight, briefly. "I did not expect such a blow. It means... it is—"

"Don't dwell on it. Besides, I am taking you to view the others that still are good and whole. You'll see." She offered him a small smile, gathered up her gown, and took a running start against the distance before the crack could widen even further.

As she went, she knew at once she had miscalculated the distance. It did not seem too far from one side, but it was far enough for a woman who did not have full use of her legs under the embroidery of skirts and chemise and slippers on a still-healing leg. She let go of the fabric to reach out, scrabbling at air, catching the edge of the opposite ledge only at the last moment, and even that crumbled under her fingertips.

There was no time to scream, and no time to think, only to hope her arms could hold her for another second, and then another, for it was all that kept her from tumbling into the dark unknown of the hungry castle.

The whoosh of the Gargoyle's shape above her happened with such speed, she only sensed the air moving as he near flew over her, and then his rocky fists were around her upper arms, holding her in place. His breathing sounded like panting, but without a rhythm, as if he was going to lose his lungs and their purpose completely.

She looked up at him in the dimness of the wet stone and saw what looked to be sweat beading on his forehead, a strange human thing that was all she could notice as she hung over the depths of the castle, her slippers dropping silently into the black. He gripped her harder, leaving bruises, but hauled her up with extreme care so she did not scrape too hard against the jagged wall. When her legs were visible, the Gargoyle let her go, falling backward flat. Zaklina collapsed forward, her stomach scraping the inside of her corset and the roughness of the fabric scratched her nipples. She gasped at the impact, her cheekbone hitting the floor, cracking the skin so blood poured down the line of her jaw and dripped off her chin.

Crawling, she inched across the narrow landing to his side, where he gasped shallowly. Her hands found his stomach, then his chest, and she lay next to him, winding her arm about his great width, finding her own breathing to match. His hand slowly found her elbow, pulling her tighter.

 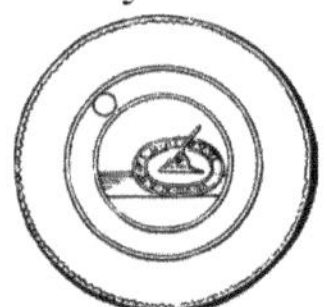 

He did not rise for untold minutes, his eyes closed, as if the rescue had taken the last of his powerful build. As they lay together, her heart began to ache. But it was not the physical pain of straining. It was the realization of what had happened already deep inside.

She reminded herself of his earlier words. He'd loved other maids, who had long since left. Two of them, over the centuries, and his own heart was hard. And he had not again asked for her hand. Perhaps he had gotten what he needed from her. Perhaps he did not need to beg for her hand in marriage. Perhaps that was only required a few times by the castle's magic, perhaps her obvious affection and desire was not enough to compel him. She didn't know if he paced the nights in frustration and uncertainty, hoping she would accept his offer.

She curled next to him, her wound finally congealing. As the sun slowly traveled above them, a mist between clouds and heat, she tried to gather fragments from the past, to remember how the stories always went. Could she save him, if not the castle? Could she help, even if she was not enough?

Was he in correct form, or was it she who was to transform?

Did the man burn the clothes of the woman, or did she kiss him to break a spell?

Who needed wings?

A swan, a snake, a frog, a pig, a hyena?

It was all muddled, all gone, spirited away as splinters of tales even as she thought them, as if such memory was forbidden.

"What is it truly like out there, beyond?" he said, breaking into her reverie. "I wonder…"

"You mean beyond this dying castle?" she asked, her voice flatter than she'd planned. It was a question she had not dared to fully form since leaving the meadow.

He shifted slightly, as if he could start to move again. "Is there still some small magic where you are from?"

"No…and yes. It seems it is underground. Hidden and secret, but yet right in front of everyone's face. People seek it. I did, in my own way, through the words of stories." She thought to offer him more to go with, something to sustain him. "There are stories of you, though. Or at least, stories like this."

He jerked a little. "People know of me?"

"Creatures like you, yes. Myths. All the lands have the tales, in various forms, from East to West. They are slightly different, depending on the country, but there is always a tale, even though I cannot remember it. Very old stories—some go back centuries and eons. But real magic…the way you speak of it? It is different. Lost. Wandering."

"It is the demons, then, and all other goodness is fading." He sat up, a gust of air pushing out of his bellow lungs. "But you say the stories are still woven? Somewhere?"

She stood, finding her leg good, and waited for him to join her. They walked up slowly, the light going faster, but they were closer than she had expected because they were at the great jewel studded door before too long. He pushed it open, and the hearth fire there spat and snapped at them, and filled the cool room with rose gold. She took him first to her changing screen, tracing the fine lines of the bathing beauties and peeping satyrs. All the eroticism in the rounded hips and bosoms, the obvious, aroused beasts, felt more lifelike than during the morning, and she flushed to show him, even as the vision of story put to silk seemed to give him strength. He stood taller when she took him to the tapestries around the back of her chambers, which hid the dripping castle walls, but were of nature and humankind. He stopped completely in front of the last, with the queen-like bee woman in the center and the others about her.

"This one is of you, for I have not seen it before."

"No, for I am not this goodwife," she said, tracing the rosy cheeks of the fat lady-bee in the middle.

"Goodwife? She is a crone with the face of a maid. A woman with the mind of the ancients," he said, pointing to the same woman, frowning darkly. "Do you at least see the insects? The hive of wasps—"

"Honeybees."

"But they turn to blood, which rains on the fields and crops to make them bloom, and in turn feeds them. It is a cycle. Anything that disrupts it...you are right, it is not for you, but a warning. The castle has offered you a glimpse of the future." The Gargoyle put an arm about her waist again, though not for support but to offer comfort.

"You tried to break the cycle," he said, staring at the tapestry. "You built and created a new tale."

"I could not," she said, wanting to laugh. "I am not enough to do so."

"What is the root of your name?"

Zaklina shook her head. "What? The meaning of my...it means *the one who supplants.*"

"And you tried to change the way of the rumors – you challenged them – in your Miódshire. You asked too much of the woman in charge of it all. You offered reason to the stories, you stopped the cycle of sustenance."

"The food...it began to rot," Zaklina said, staring up at the woven image. "You mean, stories are our bread, and if we change them, we die?"

"If we forget them, supplant them with something else, then yes, we notice when the stories sustaining us die. But it only matters if that which we are eating is false. People may try to live too long on untruths, and they are like a sickly sugar, though an easy thing to ingest. Eating false rumors and stories of lies is like eating rotten food. No matter who feeds us, then, their ambitions poison it all."

He sagged with the telling, as if the words forced him to use up his inner light, as if he fought against the silence of his tongue to say such things.

"Come. You must rest," she said, pulling him to her bed. "And I will not let you do so alone. You will stay."

His fatigue was so deep he did not even attempt a protest. She fussed over the pillows under his head, and the ties of his boots. At first, he did not allow her to remove anything but his cape. She dared to glare at him as he lay like one entombed, his hands clasped at his belly. His dark glance warmed her before he closed his eyes against his lethargy. She looked at him in the middle of her bedclothes and was struck with the foolish hope that it would be like this always.

"Comfort is as comfort does. Allow me to take care of you for once. You forget you do not need to guard me from your form. I have been wed," she reminded him, putting her hands on her hips in the age-old posture of a woman meaning to get her own way. "I did not mean for you to sleep in my bed with your boots and trousers on."

"What of my desire for you? Shall I protect you from that?" He did not even open his eyes, and she realized he truly was drained beyond measure if he was so bold. "Suppose I am unable to restrain myself?"

"You seem too tired to do much harm," she said lightly, and commenced to take off the boots, and then his coat. Below it was a vest and a shirt, all of the same stone grey, but she discovered the actual feel was very much that of fabric, though one she did not know. His breathing turned ragged as she peeled everything off, not planning how far she meant to go, but could not find it in her to stop once she'd started. Removing all the layers did little to change the palette, for his skin—if one could call it skin—was near enough a man's in texture, with only slight, near serpentine pattern-ing faintly etched across it all. It was truly as if he was carved and then brought to life, or perhaps so very old he had become like rock. The details were alarmingly real, even the hair spreading over his chest, trailing his navel and disappearing into his trousers. Mesmerized, she ran her fingers through the fuzz on his pectorals to convince herself it was not a trick of the light. Under it, his skin was very warm.

"You're going to undo me," he rasped suddenly, gripping her hands. "You must...stop."

"Do you wish me to do so?" she asked, stung at once. "I thought...I must apologize." She shifted to leave the bed, but his hands held her in place and his eyes finally opened.

"Do not think I am so diminished that I will not act. I've been wanting to ravish you since I met you."

Her heart felt as though it sat on her tongue. If she spoke wrong, she could bite into it and crush it all.

"Why didn't you?" she asked, inching back to his side, all of their fingers still intertwined.

"Would you have let me?"

"Not at the first," she admitted. "But then..." Embarrassment glued her voice near shut.

"And then?" He seemed frozen on the bed, poised to move suddenly. Was he struck down yet or full of that hope he harbored?

"Then I...I've become afraid of how..." She couldn't say the rest, knowing she would be rejected. "I'm afraid of my curiosity. It's why I asked such logistical questions."

"About my anatomy?"

"...yes."

"And yet you have more questions."

"Always, I'm afraid."

"I do not understand completely how you are here, and how you have chosen to stay, but I will continue to wait. I have waited this long."

How many nights had he asked of her?

Six?

Seven?

She had somehow lost count when the nights bled into the days, and her own extreme tiredness tugged at her eyes.

"I will go get some fruit," she said, looking him over again. "You might need nourishment in a more traditional manner, and I am at least good for providing food when it's at hand. There are some oranges still on the tree in the garden, and I think I will have enough time."

The Gargoyle's head raised up as she left the chamber, but he did not call out to stop her. It made her move all the faster. She hoped by staying at his side all night, she might be given one to sleep. Even in his state, she felt he would offer her all the protection she needed.

In the garden, the light of the sun had already slipped below the tops of the castle, casting it in green and grey shadow, with deeper grey-blue ones along the edges. The ponds were black with silver edges, and the pavement a cool sparkling white when it peeked from the carpets and moss.

She knew where the citrus trees clustered in the middle and to the side, a small grove of orange and tangerines, with two peach trees mixed in between ones holding limes. The lemon trees were all to themselves even further in and closer to the overrun garden herbs.

As she plucked a few of the squishy ripe ones, holding them in her fine skirt, she looked up and saw the sun had moved even faster, casting the garden in starlight, with the promise of a near-full moon to come.

She must hurry.

And then the slam of the garden door boomed, and she dropped the oranges, all plans and all hope scattering below the palms and vines when she heard the first small steps in the dark, the patter of a single pair of tiny feet, hunting with surety in the dark.

Zaklina wanted at first to hide, and then thought to climb a tree. The fear that burst inside her was more than she could bear, the terrible, irrational fear of the rabbit hunted by the wolf. She was powerless, without any knowledge of what haunted her, and without the stories to guide her, she was lost.

Trembling through her bones, so they clattered between all her sinew, she turned and waited as the gloom settled on her skin, and listened to the footsteps pick through the little gardens.

At first, one would be deceived, for it was only a child, padding through the thick foliage, parting the waxy, glossy leaves. The tiny girl looked at Zaklina without blinking out of huge dark eyes in a pale face pinched with hunger. When she opened her mouth, it was a black hole without teeth, a maw of unfilled need, and the child's voice was low and broken.

"Feed me."

Zaklina frowned and gripped her head. Something twisted, a thread of confusion that still linked the old folklore together. "Are you not the goddess of winter? Do we not throw you in the river?"

The child-creature drew back, hissing. Her garment, white and stained with pus and old wine-colored patches, gapped open to show a skeletal frame wracked with pustules of plague—black and ready to burst.

"That is what they call me now, fool. But before—"

"Mara? Mar...Marzanna? The plague maid," Zaklina whispered, stepping backward, her heel crushing one of her dropped oranges.

The scent of food propelled Marzanna closer, her head whipping unnaturally fast one way and then the other. Her nose widened and her mouth opened wide again. The scent of feces and vomit, putrid skin and the sickroom filled the garden, blocking the sweet scents of jasmine and lavender and lemon.

"Feed me!" the child demanded. "Feed me and I will depart. Do not, and I shall stay and devour all!"

"I...I have only oranges. Limes and lemons. You may have them, each one," Zaklina said, yanking down the fruit as best she could in the dim blue moonlight peeking between the overgrown trees and without taking her eyes off the slow advancement of the plague girl.

"Feed me or I will stay and kill with the disease of the damned. You will feel hunger and thirst, you will die!"

Zaklina poured the fruit into the girl's overeager, bony hands. She tried not to touch the peeling flesh and globular nobs of fluid trailing along Marzanna's knuckles or the open sores of the gangrenous palms. The bright oranges poured down that black hole of a throat without chewing, and the next handful, too.

Time began to stretch as Zaklina pulled all the oranges she could reach, and then all the peaches. She half-climbed into the branches, which swayed with her clumsy attempts to scale into the flimsy twigs at the top of the shorter trees. When she could reach no further, she went next to the pears, which were taller and had fruit hanging heavily on the lower boughs. Her heels crushed some of the overripe ones, and they fell to the ground, though Marzanna ignored everything except that which Zaklina handed over willingly. She followed Zaklina around, sniffing and inhaling the citrus, not tasting and not caring, a ravenous, unfillable hole in the body of a child demon.

Zaklina would have liked to strip down to her corsets and chemise but there was no time, for she did not think Marzanna would hesitate to start eating Zaklina's own flesh if there was a pause to the actual food. There was a pinched look in the plague-maids eyes, a hard edge to the way she held her skeletal frame, as if she could and would pounce if given a chance. But Zaklina did not pause, harvesting the tangerines next, and then the limes. She stripped the trees bare and looked up at the sky. How much time had passed? How long was the actual night?

She raced to the lemon grove, glancing at the herb garden as she passed. It was overflowing with oregano and lavender, mint and tarragon. Would such simple fare be enough?

As she pulled the lemons down, sweat poured between her breasts and the line between her shoulder blades, bumping down her spine. Her mind spun with fatigue, for carrying the Gargoyle had spent her more than she had expected, and her arms ached from the earlier fall and his great bulk. Was he awake? Did he think of her? Did he wonder where she had gone? Could she keep up the pace of feeding the demon child the rest of the night? If she finally dropped with exhaustion, would the creature just set to eating her from the feet up?

Marzanna took the lemons, plunging them into her mouth, swallowing with a single gulp. Though Zaklina took care to only offer one at a time, soon enough she was hauling herself up and pulling down the higher fruit.

It was gone sooner than she had hoped.

Breathing hard, she dropped to the ground and hurried to the herbs. Tearing it up by the roots, she snapped off the pale crunchy tubers of the mint and offered them to Marzanna, who inched even closer. It was enough, for the demon ate them without complaint. She tore her hands on the woody stems of the thyme and the rough ends of the lavender. She ripped the leaves off the basil and sprinkled its flowers into Marzanna's waiting mouth.

And soon enough, that, too, was gone and the herb garden lay bare.

Zaklina could not breathe fast enough. She could hardly move her body, the fatigue turning into a nauseous heaviness. Her chest felt as though it was moments from exploding, and the muscles of her neck were strung so tight she could not work her jaw. All she wanted was escape, and the sun. She just wanted a moment to stop moving...she wanted to flee the garden and find the Gargoyle's arms and the comfort she was sure she'd find.

"Is there any more?" the demon child rasped, stepping closer. Some of the enormous black pustules on her stomach and arms had burst. Maggots squirmed inside the wide gaping sores.

The scent of her decaying flesh filled Zaklina's own nose and crowded her mouth, making bile slip like slime between her gums. She choked it down and looked about wildly. There was nothing, nothing left on the trees or in the garden, nothing but inedible plants.

Marzanna's eyes gleamed in the half-light. "There is nothing?"

Zaklina could not answer. She could not get enough air.

There was not enough...

Not enough air...not enough food...

"Then you will rot. You will die and decay. My pestilence will devour your flesh and leave you as bones."

Marzanna stepped closer and reached for Zaklina's hands, bleeding palms dripping onto the lovely brocade of the skirt...the skirt which the Gargoyle had selected for her, which she had used to gather up oranges for him...

The other fruit! The ones she had dropped...

They had rolled everywhere...

Zaklina ducked away from Marzanna, who screeched with fury. It was the sound of a banshee and a forsaken woman combined, ghoulish and forever unending.

Scrabbling on her hands and knees, Zaklina tore through the beautiful garden back to the bare orange trees and searched frantically under the low bushes.

There!

One of the oranges!

She pulled it out just as Marzanna attacked. Lunging up, Zaklina shoved the fruit into the demon's mouth, jerking her fingers away just at the last moment before the demon could swallow those, too.

She went back to it, seeking the last few, knowing there were less than a half-dozen to be found if she could find them at all—another!

And another!

And...the last...

And then there were no more.

Zaklina climbed to her feet, lungs heaving, her dress stained with the spray of lemons and limes, her knees bloodied and her hands ripped along her lifelines.

There was nothing else, and the sun...the sun still did not rise...

Marzanna chuckled, and it was a familiar sound, one that cut through the haze of Zaklina's thoughts, a reminder of something earthy and of wet tea leaves, black...

Black, like the demon child's rotten corpse.

Black like the sores lining the great wide mouth, rising up to Zaklina's own, to offer a kiss of death, to infest her bones and body with—

The morning sun shot through the canopy and pierced Marzanna's head.

The demon's head exploded without warning, followed by the whole body, into pulp. It laid about in chucks of rancid meat and gristle. Bloated flies flew out from it immediately, and the flesh went from putrid to grey, then ash.

Even on Zaklina, the stains turned to dust, which fluttered off her skirts as she shifted.

Exhaustion pooled in her stomach, and she hoped the garden door would open…and where was the Gargoyle? He was always there, always waiting for her…

She moved to the entrance, gripping grape vines to stay upright.

"Gargulec?" she called through the dryness of her throat. It hurt to speak, but she asked for him again. There was no answer, and she pressed her body into the door to open it on moss-cover hinges to an empty hall.

Though wearied and battered and terrifically sore, she climbed the stairs up to her rooms as fast as she was able, sometimes only able to do so by using her hands on the wet, slick castle stairs. Her hair, tangled in knots and filled with twigs and bits of leaves, fluttered in her face, and her skirt frayed along the edges.

"Are you here? Are you well?" she asked weakly, opening her chamber door and squinting in the castle's gloomy morning. "Gargulec?"

The softest sound came from across the great rooms, and she hurried to the bed. He lay there, still alive, breathing, and deep asleep. She did not think he needed to eat nor sleep, but her mind was fuzzy on the ends and her memory less clear than ever before. Zaklina yanked at her overdress and wiggled out of the corset. Climbing up next to him, she draped an arm about his middle, slung a leg over his thigh, and nestled her face into the curve of his neck and immediately fell asleep.

In the early afternoon glow, she woke. They'd shifted in slumber, and now laid curled together, her back pressed into the bare expanse of his chest. Though he still slept, she felt the hardness of his arousal against her buttocks, and the realization of it was torture and happiness at once. Happiness, because she knew now that she roused him in some fashion.

And torture because she knew it was only his body, and not his heart, that caused the response.

She wanted to relish the joy and warmth of their closeness but could hardly manage her own desires in such a position. Had she ever wanted another the way she did for Gargulec? When Narcyz slept in her bed, had her body wound itself so tightly?

She did not think so. She did not remember it so.

Spinning carefully in his embrace, she traced the lines along his mouth, carefully, lightly touching his skin. Heat still poured from him though he was once again marble-cool first and then warm. If he was a man in the typical sense, he would be one of harsh features and covered in a virile amount of hair. She found she did not care either way. It was he who she wanted, in any shape he had.

"Zaklina," he said softly, catching up her hand with his and kissing it without opening his eyes. "You are here."

"I was waylaid in the garden," she said.

That woke him further. He seemed to come into his body and once again shifted away from her. She clipped her fingers into his trousers – the only thing he yet wore – and tried to hold him near. It did not work, as his strength had returned. He flopped onto his back with a thin hiss, but she held on and ended up sprawled half on top of him, the inner dent of her knee a centimeter from his most sensitive area, and her chemise pulled down on one side.

"I do not think I can manage it," he said, frozen. "This ease between us. It is a comfort and beautiful, but it is something I want so deeply that I do not think I will survive if it is only the castle's trick."

"What part?" she asked. "My affection—my desire for you? Here it is I who thinks it cannot be true."

"I will never play you false," he said, his voice raspy and rough, as if he was attempting to control his deepest emotions. "But if we truly mean to consummate this...if we start, I will be unable to stop. I am not the shape of a human man in some ways, but I am still male."

"Then you'll give me this?" she asked, her fingertips finding the waist of his garment, as his own pads played with the front tie of her chemise. "Please do. I want...you. Though you do not love me as you did the others."

That stopped him. "The others? There was only the other one. And she was long ago. I believe I needed that rejection to fully understand you now." He lowered his head to her neck, then gently caressed the side of her breast over the fine cotton of her undergarment.

"But you said…" Through the haze of desire, she recalled he'd said he had loved two.

Two…

Wild hope jumped into her bones, and she clamped it down, unable to fathom, unable to believe. Clutching him close, she closed her eyes and let him touch her. His hands ghosted over her bare hips and buttocks, and the backs of her thighs before he drew away, his breath ragged.

She opened her eyes. He stared at her as if she was an impossibility. Questions poured from his very being, even as their lust was not sated and he obviously ached for her. If it was not their first time so near to lovemaking, she would have reached across the silence and the moment to touch him, to release and stroke him. How had they fallen to this, and so quickly? Did time pass differently in such a castle? Was there magic in the very air, forcing their feelings to the surface?

"If I asked you again…" he suddenly said, perhaps gaining courage from her embrace. "If I offered you marriage…"

She froze, wishing and willing for him to stop. She didn't know if she could refuse him again, and didn't know if she could manage the pain if she allowed herself to love him. This way, this suspended, physical way, they could be together without any type of spoken promise.

"Don't ask me," she pleaded, and pressed herself close, hoping a clear distraction of her body and her breasts would silence him.

"When may I ask again?" he asked, urgency coloring his deep tone. "What else could you fear?"

"I am afraid I will agree, and it will be devastation," she admitted.

He shot upright, pulling her out of bed so they stood facing one another in the dim murk of afternoon. All desire between them hung suspended, forgotten in the intensity of his manner. In the soft grey and blue of the shadows, his eyes pinned her, begging, pleading.

"How?" he demanded, pressing her hands together with his. "How can marrying me devastate you? You have said I am a man to you, that I am handsome. What else can you mean?"

She closed her eyes against the truth, and nodded. "I have said those things, and I meant them. But… Well, but you do not love me. And I have promised myself I will not love again. And marrying you? I can see it now. I will love you, and I will lose you."

Saying the words caused the pain to rip itself through her chest, binding her breath and crippling her feet. If he had not gripped her so tightly, she might have sunk to her knees. She felt the rejection already, simmering in her future.

"You *will* love me?" he asked, and his voice sounded ripped and tortured.

"I suppose I already do," she told him suddenly, opening her eyes to his. "Not that it does any good."

It was done.

The words were spent, in a roundabout way, without actually putting them into existence. There was no mistaking her meaning. Had he not continued to grip her, she would have used her fists to tear into her own neck and yank into her ribs, to pull out her heart as if she could scratch it out and let it crumble in her palm.

"But Zaklina!" he said, the sound now ripe, as if his words were finally released from a dam. "I too know rejection. I, too, know pain. Why must you think I will be the same as the man who cast you aside? Are you like the other girl, the maid I once loved who left? Who was not strong enough for the trials of this existence? No, and I thank all the other gods for that. No. You are mine."

"Am I?" she asked, weak against the maelstrom of her own emotions and the power of his. "Am I, indeed?"

He stared at her for a long minute, then pulled her out from the bed-chamber, out of the rooms, past the great door. Their feet chipped on the black stairs, the slippery nature of it not mattering under their bare soles as their toes gripped the edges in a desperate climb up. They only went a short way, and he pushed at the wall of the castle to their left, a secret passage she would never have found on her own. Even with wearing nothing but a thin bit of cotton and silk, she was not cold, for they moved quickly—so quickly she felt the thin sheen of sweat cover her skin in a fine layer of salt.

They burst onto a little used castle rampart, so long forsaken that the entire walkway was covered in brilliant sage moss, so thick it was spongy to walk on. The Gargoyle's feet, odd in their bareness, sunk deep with his weight, leaving imprints as he went.

"You are my other half. Together...we can do more. You must see it."

He flung out a long, thick arm, uncaring at the wind whipping across the stone, the sheer, slick height of the mountain above, the impossible depth below and the glare of the sun all around them. It was so bright she could hardly focus, but tried for his sake, for he was overwrought in a way she had never thought to see.

At first she only saw the tall towers of rock with discoloration, until she put shape to the red ochre and the black pigment swirled on it, which marred the grey surface of a dolman structure propped up in deference to long-lost life gates. From there came a tablet shoved into the castle's wall. It was of lines and strokes, and then there were hieroglyphics chiseled into yet more stone with the original color swept away by time. There was no real link to everything, but he watched her walk on that springy moss with such eagerness. So she moved on as the sun blistered the part in her hair and the tip of her nose.

And then she saw other bits, faster, reminding her of the stories she'd only recently remembered. The bull, the hyena, the frog. A crow, a snake, a pig. A large bison, a tiger. And others, much more explicit. A dark long crocodile-headed god, making love to a woman in a river. A bright prince emerging from the feathers of a bird, his arms stretched out to hold a maid. A snarling beast protecting another girl from demons. And then the last, a winged man, carved in marble, with arrows tipped in gold and silver, shooting them across the lands ...and then the same man embracing a woman, kissing her, enveloping her—

She caught her breath sharply.

It could not be.

Zaklina shoved down the desire and lust, the love and hope simmering under her bones. She grasped the edge of the castle wall and looked out to where the clouds below met the blue of the sky dome. There was no sound on the moss and lichen, but she knew he approached for he blocked the unyielding sunlight. The coolness was a blessed relief, but when she turned to look up at him, he was only a shadow against the glare.

"You...I can't...what shall I...your name. What ought I really call you?"

"What you have always," he said. "I don't know if I will ever be different again. The changes happen so slowly, over time and tale, and there's no knowing how it will affect my form. Now you see it all. You see what I have been, what shapes I have been given, what I am."

"But you are always the same," she said, her voice a hoarse whisper. Every stretch of her muscles, every twist of her ligaments seemed to push toward him, for all she worked to stay apart from him, to keep from finally collapsing under the enormity of the knowledge he offered, the depth of his past.

There was no possible way a mere woman could be enough.

She did not deserve it. Him. Truth. Love. Something must have gone all wrong.

He inclined his great head slowly, once. "So you see. Love...I cannot exist in a void. It cannot be alone. I cannot stay like this forever and fight against the lies and hate of the world. I need help retrieving my arrows and the demons I sent with them. I need help preserving the stories. And I do not wish to do so without the other half of my soul."

"I do not plan to love again," Zaklina said, searching for the staunchness of her character and finding it flailing. "I swore I would not."

"Yet you have said you do anyway," he reminded her, his hands cupping her cheeks.

"But you haven't," she said, wondering if he could use the word at all if it was his very essence. Perhaps he was forbidden to name the feeling, as it was too close to his person. Perhaps he could not speak of himself.

He looked choked, but bent down to capture her mouth, kissing her with carefulness and bottled promise even as he did not offer the words she needed to hear.

It was too much to bear, too much to hold onto, too much to ask of one single, simple, damaged woman. She could not continue, balanced on the edge of the glass, wondering.

"Tell me what you wish of me," he said, pulling back slowly, his eyes seeking hers.

"I thought I made myself quite clear before. If anything, *you* are the hesitant one."

"I disbelieve my hopes could ever come true."

Zaklina stepped back, the action a searing tear. Her bare feet sank into the peaty moss below them, and the loss of his shadow meant the sun once again burned her flesh. She gazed at him, fighting herself, his revelations, and yet the surety of it all. It made her itchy and angry and lusty all at the same time.

"I do not like how the magic here tugs at my eyes and erases the stories. I do not like being without you, nor how dependent I am upon you...while at the same time I adore the attachment. Can you answer at least that you care for me in some small fashion? You only ask one thing of me. It is something I doubt you do of your own will. Does my place not matter? What of my own desire?"

His arms had dropped as she backed away. He suddenly seemed more rocky and carved than ever before. Her body ached to move back into his embrace, to warm him and make him real. But she could not completely disregard her own core, not when things had spiraled so very fast. She would lose herself in him if she did not try once more, desperately.

"You wish for me to marry you, but you won't say that you love me even though the word and sentiment is buried in your every fiber. Do you even think to ask if I love you in return? Do you need my words said exactly, so you might repeat them?" she asked, and turned away again, away from him and the sun, to gaze over the sun-bleached blanket of clouds far below.

His silence was so hard, she could not bear it. She glanced over her shoulder, against the sunlight. He had not moved, rooted, and suddenly she feared she had somehow turned him into a statue. Had she?

After all they'd managed, each night of suffering and each morning of slow building comfort and passion and...no, surely not!

She took the few hurried steps back to him, putting her hands on his bare chest. Under her fingers, she felt the stirring of a breath and a flutter, the barest hint of a heartbeat, the throb of blood and veins, as if he truly was a real being, not something of smoke and stone. When she looked up at him, into the shade his bulk provided, he was staring at her, poised and coiled, and she realized he wished to ask her of her own heart precisely, and yet would not.

Could not.

Forbidden?

Her voice caught and snagged, but she forced it out, anyway, feeling as though she was betraying herself while unable to deny him this last bit of herself, for all she was afraid to do so.

"You must understand I have my own worries, though they are small in comparison," she said. "Am I enough? Too much of the other world where I was born? Do I belong? Will you still want me as the years pass? You'll... leave me." She paused and closed her eyes. Old pain laced her throat. "I cannot bear it if you left me. If you cast me off."

"Never," he said, and it was so stoutly said with so much determination and honesty, she believed him before reminding herself she had no proof but his word.

And yet...

There seemed no point in holding it in. She was cursed.

She was lost.

"I...will offer it, then. All I have...the only thing I can give. I do love you. Desire you. You need not disbelieve or doubt me, for I am here. I have not left. I will give you my heart, if you swear you will not break it."

The Gargoyle's reaction was immediate. The moment she uttered the word, he fell to his knees, and the sun seemed to burst into a thousand crystal lights. The ground under their feet tilted, and she stepped forward and clutched him to her, hugging his great head to her bosom, closing her eyes against the bright heat that burned the moss beneath their feet.

Power. Might. Magic.

He stood and pulled her into the pale blue-grey shade of the dolmen perched on the side of the mountain, a space of both earth and man, built of one by the other, a doorway between. It too had a thick floor of spongey moss, with debris and long sticks and sharpened reeds scattered in the corners, as if it was a bathhouse of old.

Everything between them had somehow broken, and yet it was all she wanted, for he turned and was upon her, bearing down on her with a kiss that didn't feel like it would ever end, and his hands roving around her hips with abandon, rubbing her skin through the cotton silk and curling his fingers around curves.

He broke their kiss only a moment, clenching at her chemise. "Will it come off easily? Otherwise, I am strong enough to rip it."

"Like this," she said, untying the bodice laced at her collarbones, letting it pool on the thick unburnt moss, and brought up her gaze to meet his. He walked back a pace further into the stone house to better survey her, his eyes—familiar and yet feral—cloudy with something she believed was affection and lust combined. He seemed dazed, uncertain, and yet in full control as he stalked back towards her, and pulled her nakedness against the lines of his form.

"I have wanted you," he said. "As yourself. No matter how uneasy you say you are."

She reached inside his clothes and gripped his length. He swayed, almost staggering, his eyes closed. He was thick and long and hot. Smooth and iron, silk and rock. She wanted to taste him, feel him. It was the same, as if nothing had changed from hours before. The recognition of such passion was a relief. The familiarity of their touch was a caress and permission.

"Never doubt me," she whispered. "I would have let you ravish me, if you had asked. I nearly released you from your clothing constraints this morning, ached to see you, feel you within the cradle of my bones." She slowly wound her palm around him, and then, quieter. "I ache to hear you say you love me..."

"I may not be very gentlemanly," he said suddenly. "I now find I'm too far overwhelmed."

"I don't think I need much romancing," she agreed. "And you forget I am no shy virgin, and am not a...a nubile—"

"If you think I want some young thing barely into adulthood, stop now," he told her, staring hungrily at her bosom. "I'm not young or necessarily agile at lovemaking either, and I'm certainly glad I don't have to mince about carefully. Not after all these years."

He lowered her to the softness of the ground and put his attention to her bosom with reverence first, then moving his lips to her stomach and lower. It was a worshipful thing, and something her first marriage bed had never offered. Zaklina arched toward the offering, feeling as though she was not in a castle, not in her body, and certainly not in the world itself.

"I have been waiting to do so to you," he said, breaking into her glorious numbness, his voice rumbling against the soft skin of her thigh. "To offer you pleasure after the nights of pain."

He descended again, and she tried to think of something to say, but the bliss won over, and soon she couldn't help but clench at the moss, tearing up fistfuls of it.

"Wait!" she gasped, pulling her hips up slightly, suddenly, recognizing the signs of her body, desiring more before she was broken. "Wait. I don't want it all, not without you."

"I'm afraid...It's been too long, and..." Though they were in a carnal embrace, it seemed he still held onto the old chivalry, and even older notions of lovemaking.

"You seem to think a woman will not take her pleasure from the act," Zaklina said, determined to strip down the careful, stilted layers of frozen language however possible, finding the root of the truth between them. "I have ached for you as well, and I swear you will give me all I need." She said it with certainty, knowing her body, her preferences.

He slid away from her in one movement, staggering slightly, as if the release of desire had unbalanced him. But his eyes were on her, her body, her face. She sat up to watch while he drew off the last of his clothing. It was such a manly, human thing to do, she realized she had stopped seeing him as a gargoyle, a carved being, and was only himself. A big male, a shape of eons, formed by tale and tome, story and fable, carved into reality and larger than life because of it. In the ligaments of his arms and legs, the greatness of his limbs, the width of his chest, she saw only gentleness. When she looked at his face, she only saw *him* – the man and the creature, the echoes of both. And he was ready for her, hard and straight.

"You're a god!" she whispered. "Truth. Love."

"Do not think of me as such," he said. "Unless you allow me to call you a goddess, for you are that to me." He tested his weight, those dark eyes still trained on her. And then he lowered himself, his elbows at her shoulders, her face in his hands, finding her center in one fluid movement.

"My Zaklina," he said, sincere and earnest. "My beauty. My life." He kissed her soundly. It was an age-old dance, a rhythm they fell to as if listening to the same music. She hadn't misled him – her body was ready, her limbs quivering as she climbed.

Above her, she could hear an echo, as if his heart boomed in the cage of his ribs, and then his breathing hitched as he paused.

"What is it?" she asked, holding her breath against falling, yet wanting desperately to feel him press hard into her hips, knowing she would be undone in another movement.

"I told you, I am unable...you are..." He was incoherent, his eyes closed.

She felt the tensing of his muscles, and pressed herself against his pelvis where she knew it would undo her. Thus, deeply intertwined, they crashed without inhibitions, as if their bodies could not contain their desire or their hearts and must flee. His body strained against hers and she pushed to him, riding it, pressing against the air itself as they rocked.

She had known a man's embrace countless times before her husband turned from her, but never like this.

It was heat.

It was knowledge.

It was a communion, a splitting of souls, an explosion of white light in darkness that turned purple and yellow, a cacophony of impossibilities.

Zaklina felt as though her heart had once again been torn out, pierced with sticks and the sharpened reeds, and perhaps it had, for the slickness between them seemed coppery and smelled of iron. Pain and pleasure shot through her ribs as if she was branded. The depth of her love for him, the power of it made the scattering of stars in her forehead burn.

She was certain she was dying, certain she had somehow torn out her very life breath and offered it to him. She had given him her entire heart, willingly...did this now mean she would die without him? Would he hold her love with regard, or press the organ between his two stone palms and crush it?

Crush her.

Destroy her.

Part 3:
The Demon

THE FOREST

SHE WOKE AT THE CUSP of twilight.

And she was alone.

Her mind felt shattered, her body bruised in a proper, full way – a way she had always longed to feel, and yet could never fully receive when she had wed Narcyz. Perhaps because his name alone meant numbness...

Zaklina was not numb now.

She felt so alive it was as if her skin crackled, and a lifeforce stronger than the sun lived within her breast.

And yet...she was alone.

Had she broken through, then, only to lose him? Had the Gargoyle been given all he needed? Her love. Her body. The taste of her womb?

He had called her his beauty. His life. Had his words meant nothing?

Then again, he had not professed his love in return.

What had she reminded herself, so many days ago?

It felt like years had passed.

Ah, yes. She should guard her heart.

For if even the Gargoyle, a creature built of nothing but truth and love... if he did not love her, who or what could?

She was the fool.

Slowly standing, she picked up the discarded chemise and let it flow over her head, snaking around her shoulders and hiding the evidence of their embrace. When she stepped out, the sun had dipped to the tip of the mountaintop, soon to disappear and cast the world into shadow. Below, the clouds simmered and boiled, now so close she was certain she could taste their bitterness if she reached and grasped a handful.

And yet, there was an unearthly silence. Her neck felt heavy, and she wanted nothing more but to slump inside the walls of the ancient dolman, hide her face, and wait for whatever evil would find her.

She did not think she would have the will to fight so very hard this night.

Why fight if she had given all, and it was still not enough?

Why stay and endure?

Yet she wished to find him. To grasp his jaw and scream at him. She wished to force a confession from his lips, to rail against his lack of love, to hold him near and feel his comfort about her own limbs.

To what end? To beg? To plead for something he would not give?

And then, Zaklina realized she could leave now. Before the night fell.

She moved as though in a trance, a lost woman if ever there was one. Where had he gone, and why had he left her? Why take her if only to discard her?

She had given him her heart...

As she moved down the stairs, she saw the door of her chambers still open, when he had flung the door wide to race with her. She went inside the rooms, and found them the same, as if the castle had not become aware of their passionate embrace. A staleness filtered from the dead hearth, and the dresses on the rack behind the screen hung limply. Zaklina chose the simplest, one that reminded her of homespun and brown. Leather slippers were the best she could find, though she did not think they would protect her feet from mud and snow.

She wondered, for the first time in long hours, if Milena missed her.

Would Marek wish to make a match for her with hot-eyed Ludoslaw, a man who loved glory more than he might ever love her? Was that to be her true destiny? Was all of this a dream of some addled state?

All she knew was she had to go down.

So down she went, holding the wall, watching the evening seep across the sky, and for once not caring what found her on the many stairwells or landings. With no interest to peek inside the decaying rooms, she was thankful that the castle had either repaired itself or had never cracked open this particular set of stairs.

Down and down she went, dizzy with the spirals and the darkness, and the way the fog seemed to creep through the slotted windows.

Down into the clamminess of the castle's lower halls, where she had not wandered, for the Gargoyle had first brought her to a top rampart.

Down, as night filled the halls, and she went by feel alone, keeping a hand to the soaking walls and weeping stone.

Behind her, she thought she heard him. *"Zaklina..."* His voice deep and mellifluous, sounding hoarse and tired, an echo of a hope she dashed at once in her soul. She wondered if she only imagined she heard her name.

That would be like her to do so, a fool of a woman who thought stories could sustain her. Who had dreamed up this madness in the confines of an overly-lonely mind.

If she had stayed silent and listened to the rumors of Mrs. Staryski, would all be well, or would they all have starved without realizing it?

Every step was harder, a struggle.

Every move toward the exit of the castle felt impossible.

It loomed above her, a massive wooden door the height of ten men, inlaid with bronze and gold, with brass fittings and iron hinges. The many images danced across the panels, stories and whispers that congealed in her mind, filling it so fast with the lost and splintered stories she almost fell. Fairies with crowns and apples of curving flesh, snakes and speckled cakes, eggs and hawks, trios of maidens and brothers, dragons and horses. Giants battled princes, the sun and moon destroyed each other, moose and bears pranced in the sky while a coyote laughed, a pipe sang and snared hunting game and another that ensnared children. There were mice and chimeras, and a great host of gods and goddesses, jinn and monsters watching over all. It was a door made to awe and made to withstand the bashing of a cannon or the push of a ramming rod.

And yet, it opened at the press of her fingertip.

The road leading out of the castle was covered in green grass, slick with overlarge mushrooms, strewn with last year's leaves, while grit-rusty pine needles that crunched under it all. She took the path toward the great black forest, her feet begging her to reconsider, to turn back to him.

Zaklina wondered if he looked for her. If he remembered her at all.

If he cared that she had finally, finally departed.

Likely not, she told herself. Likely he would forget her as time passed. Likely she had played her part. There were always these old stories that would speak of an ardent man, a lover who would chase his woman to the ends of the known world and beyond, but such tales did not have a used woman at the center with a scar carried on her flesh and nothing to offer.

The only trouble was the part she'd played in this story had left her with a broken existence, a cracked soul, a lost heart. Yet she still lived. How was it she still lived?

I loved him.

Love him.

Love.

...love...

The clouds overhead blocked the moon, though somehow grey light filtered from the immense trees above, dusting the pines with a faint crystalline dust. Snow and ice mixed with mold and mildew, soaked earth and dead bark, and the scent of meat left to sit out in the wet. Zaklina picked out the path, risking a look back and expecting the castle to have disappeared or melt into the face of the mountain. She had a sudden fear that she would not find her way back, that it would disappear forever. Should she not return? Beg the Gargoyle to keep her, even as he did not love her? Live her life in terror of the nights?

As the light dimmed further, the snap of branches above made her pause and look to the sky. Wind crept around boughs, gathering strength and whispering in circles. The mud oozed up the sides of her leather shoes, leaking into the seams so every step felt unsteady. She stopped again to listen and to wrestle with herself.

She should return. What was she doing? Where was she going?

She did not really want to go back to Miódshire.

But to stay? After declaring herself and being rejected yet again?

Zaklina sank to her knees. Would she make it through the woods if she kept pressing on? Would a barrier exist, or would she tumble back into the village at the edge of the yellow flowered field, as if she had never left? Would the woods be filled with wild cats and crows, bears and beasts? Could she face life again, knowing the Gargoyle could not—would not— save her? Fear and agony wound themselves in her gut.

Would she survive? The pain of loneliness, the ache of an empty bed, the knowing she was cast aside once again? Perhaps she ought to just kneel and wait for the evil festering among the trees to find her, to truly tear her heart from her so she would not have the anguish for the rest of her life.

Unable to choose, but unable to go back, she pressed her forehead to the spiky bark of the nearest tree, her nails digging into the roughness of its trunk. Dry, hacking sobs wrenched from her, twisting her stomach and trembling down her fingers. She thought perhaps she might be ill, but they had not eaten, and she was empty.

The forest grew quiet, as if putting itself to bed...or perhaps it held its breath. Zaklina looked up, suddenly feeling blind in the growing darkness, which seemed to leak between the trees like smoke, but blacker, sootier, and smelling like aging roses and thick pollen, like sugary propolis, sticky and heavy. It grew, blocking the bit of weak moonlight pushing through the clouds, and the scent of it choked her, squeezing the life from her lungs and filling her nostrils and eyes until they felt full of mucus.

She wiped her nose and eyes, realizing that the slime glistening though it was not clear, and the smell of blood hit her, cutting through the floral. It was not the scent of a long-rotting kill – it was new and bright. She struggled to her feet, the sodden skirts tripping her movements, knocking against her knees. Limping, she took a step backwards, only to trip on the hem and fall, her back landing on a rock and jarring the breath from her.

In the moments she tried to find it, shadows of a dozen figures crept out of the woods, inching toward her as if lured.

"There she is!"

The shout was a yell and a screech, the sound so sharp it pierced the night itself, a white-hot arrow of malice and anger, fear and power. It curdled around the shapes, and as they hunted closer, she saw the wild, fury-filled eyes of the men. Their eyes were over-bright, their faces caked with scratches and muck, their boots covered in an inch of clay. Ones she did not know – Czicbor and Emmilian – and those she knew too well – old Gnegon and intense Ludoslaw, and Marek staggering behind them all.

"Get her, capture her, save her!" The voice was female, and Mrs. Staryski appeared at Marek's side, her pale face round and full, her mouth ringed with blood, her bulk bursting at the seams, as if freshly gorged.

"Grab her, before she is lost to us," she hissed, her eyes finding Zaklina's in the dimness. "Do not let him find her!"

The fury inside each of the men rose up, their breathing haggard and frenetic. Zaklina scrabbled back and found her feet, leaving the leather shoes behind.

"He has done nothing wrong!" she shouted. Above them, a thousand crows rose up and swirled, adding further darkness to the night. "He has harmed no one!"

"Lies!" Mrs. Staryski scream back.

"He has attacked us each night," Marek's voice boomed. The fear in it, the statement itself, made Zaklina freeze. "He has come as we searched for you, thwarted our rescue. As we looked, starving and hungry, we woke each morning still able to go on, but one of us missing. He killed us bit by bit, for nothing but our desire to see you home safe!"

He crept closer, Mrs. Staryski a shadow following him behind.

"You are my wife's sister, and my family by that bond. Will you not take my hand? We would see you home." Marek held out a palm. It was creased with dirt, chunks of old food stuck between the fingers. A maggot dropped from his sleeve.

Zaklina took a step back. "You say the men were killed each night?"

"Every night, one disappeared, and only one being would hunt us so," Marek said, sounding appalled and resigned at the same time.

She could not deny them this story, for had the Gargoyle not said he would not come in the night? Had he disappeared each evening, leaving her to the castle's attack? Is that what he did then? Disappear to wreak havoc on these men who sought to save her? Who only did their duty as expected of them?

Had he stolen them, one by one?

"And yet you have survived," she said softly. "Without food or water, you have survived all this time and all this way and found me."

Marek looked confused at her statement, and the other men paused their creep toward her position on the rough path.

"Yes," he said, suddenly uncertain. "We...survived. Without food or... water." He glanced around, as if looking for said sustenance, and then at his hands, which reeked of meat.

"How did you find me?" she asked. "The meadow stretched to a forest that spans in three directions. Who would guide you so well?"

Ludoslaw scoffed, and it cracked among the men. "Of course we found you, Mrs. Staryski lead us. She knows the way."

"How?"

With each question Zaklina asked, the men wavered, a weakness dragging on their bones, their cheeks sinking inside their jawbones. Mrs. Staryski grew gaunter.

"We...we found you," Marek said, his voice now a rough rasp. "We will... take you with us."

"What if I do not wish to go?"

As she asked the question, faced with the future, she finally had her answer.

She did not want to go.

She would not go.

Spinning suddenly, the forest floor offering purchase on bare soles, she sprinted away, back down the path, toward the castle buried in the side of the mountain. As she ran, she prayed the building hadn't melted into the sheer slick obsidian of rock, that she could find her way home.

Home!

The door still shone, its many panels gleaming in the night, a beacon even when there was no light to make it gleam. It stood open, an embrace waiting, and even though the space beyond was a hole of nothingness, she hurtled herself into it, trusting and not caring what might greet her within the castle walls, as long as it was not the grasping hands of the Miódshire men or the overly-familiar eyes of Mrs. Staryski.

She took the stairs with hands and feet, clawing at the rock, blindly moving upward and up again. Below, the sounds of clumsy men climbing jumbled and echoed—the smack of wet boots and too many people trying to squeeze narrowly, the shouts of shock at entering a pitch-black space.

Mrs. Staryski's screeches were wordless, too-high, and careened into the hallways, filling each room. The rumble of more rock falling growled in the depths of the castle, and Zaklina prayed she did not hear the tell-tale crack of the stairways yawning to the depths of nowhere.

Where was the Gargoyle? Did he not know his realm was invaded? Did he not care? Or did he think it justice for the terror he had brought the men of Miódshire?

Did she really believe Marek? That Gargulec would do such a thing?

She could not imagine him hunting them, could not imagine him killing.

It was impossible.

It was not his nature.

Her palms bled, her elbows scraped, her knees battered against the rocks of the stairs until she stumbled onto one of the widest landings. She could not see the next way up, did not know which of the doorways would lead up, always up. It was impossible to think, so she kept going, unable to count, until she smacked into the gem-studded door of her own chambers.

Had she come up so far? A stitch under her left rib made her think it possible. Could she hide inside? Bar the door from within? She had never been safe in the rooms before, but perhaps, this time...with only humans, not demons, chasing her...

The sounds of the men seemed closer than before, as if they gained strength with the climb. How had they followed her so easily? How had they known?

She shoved open the door to the stale air of the rooms, the ashy hearth, the cool marble. Candlelight, which burned low and pale, a blue-green

  Sara Dahmen

watery color that held no safety or warmth. Turning to shut the heavy door silently, so they would not know where to look, she met resistance. Had the castle decided to betray her? The door was pushed open with such vehemence she went sprawling on her back again, barely stopping her head from cracking on the stone of the floor.

Mrs. Staryski led the charge of men, a skinny skeleton of a wasted witch, all arms and sinew, with blood pouring from her own eyes and nose and mouth. With a crazed yowl, she leapt, attaching herself to Zaklina's throat with both hands, squeezing so the bones under her crepe-skin knackered together and pushed into Zaklina's windpipe so she could not move.

"And now, you will be silent!" Mrs. Staryski spat, blood spraying across Zaklina's forehead and landing in her eyes.

With her knees on Zaklina's hipbones and one hand holding Zaklina's throat prisoner, the Mrs. Staryski dug her nails into the soft flesh under her collarbones.

The crackle of cartilage cracked through the room, freezing the men around them, who watched as if starving, panting, waiting to be fed.

It was as if she was ripped again, torn apart again, sliced open again.

Eaten alive.

Devoured.

The pain went deep, snapping long blood vessels and blue-purple veins, spidering across her shoulders and into her gut. It was a fire that left ice in its wake, a death by anger and hunger and hate. Mrs. Staryski's eyes burned with a thousand colors, as if trapping all the light in the watery room and beyond. Her lips pulled back, revealing loose gums and narrowed teeth, a tongue covered in white fuzz and smelling of fetid flesh.

As her fingers curled under Zaklina's ribcage, snapping the bones, yanking upward, the pain filled her mind so sharp, so fresh, her vision narrowed, first to white, then grey, her brain swelling with fear and shock, and yet a deep resignation.

She'd stopped caring.

She gave up.

Let Mrs. Staryski tear out her heart, for it was useless.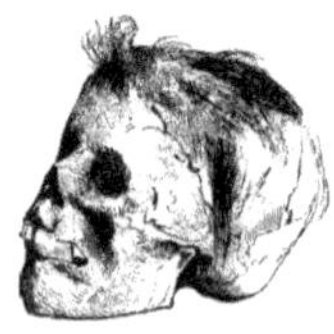

Unwanted.

Unloved.

Let them suck on the valves of it, chew on the entrails of her stomach, drink the pus of her kidneys.

As her chest gaped open and the blood pooled below her scapulas and

matted the hair behind her neck, Mrs. Staryski reared. The old goodwife—
or was it witch? Crone?—scrambled up, seething with tremendous wrath,
and threw back her head. The tendons of her neck popped so hard they
looked as if they'd rupture, and her skeletal limbs whirled.

"Where is it?" she howled. "Where is it!"

Mrs. Staryski roared once more.

And then, she disappeared.

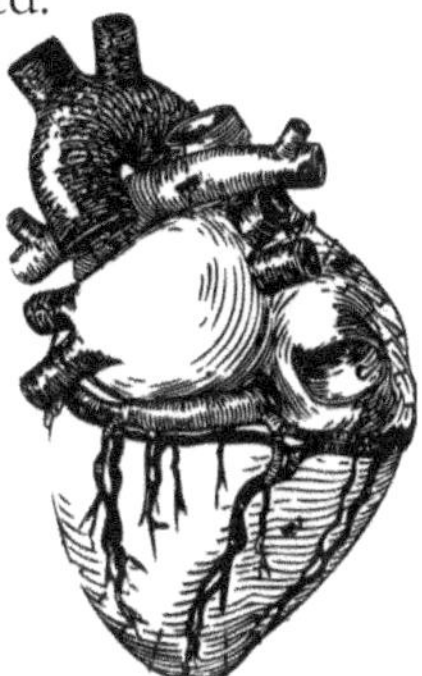

Marek let out a breath. She heard it, though her vision would not clear
enough to see him clearly, and knew his sighs and noises from the weeks
spent sleeping in his kitchen. Ludoslaw gasped. Old Gnegon choked.

"Where are we?" Ludoslaw asked, his voice low and worried. "What
have we done?"

"She was like this, we found her dying," Marek said, sounding uncertain.
"I'll tell Milena. We are too late."

"A pity," Gnegon wheezed. "She should not have wandered so far."

"A woman in the woods alone," Ludoslaw's voice had already moved to
the door. "It never bodes well. The panthers will tear out her heart."

"We could hunt them," another said.

"There are always beasts and monsters in the woods. We cannot kill
them all."

"Poor girl. She did not know."

"Too used to living in the city."

"Her head in the clouds, speaking of stories and aught else."

"We must get back," Marek said. "I would see my son."

The footsteps of all the men shuffled out, muffled by dust and darkness.
Zaklina could not call them back. It seemed her voice had fled completely.
And it didn't matter, for each moment marked another trickle of blood,
as it pumped slowly, slowly, and spreading.

"Zaklina!"

The shout came from very far away.

She was blinded, uncertain if the sound came from under or above, or from deep in the castle.

It did not matter.

Perhaps it was Milena, calling her back to help…

But no, did not Marek say he already had a son?

Or it was Narcyz…?

"Zaklina! No!" The voice was ragged, punctured with pain. "Come back!"

She had no interest in pulling herself up out of the weight pulling her down, but it was the sheer panic in his voice, coupled with the anguish, and the obvious desperation that made her struggle against the fog.

She was jostled, her shoulders pulled up from the cold marble, her skin sucking at the blood below her. The Gargoyle cradled her to his chest, and she wanted to say it was too late. Her heart had been torn out, she had been left for dead, she had given up. Under her, she still felt the strength of his thighs, the tremble of his limbs, and she knew that she could not stop loving him, even though she had left.

Even though she would die.

"Wait," he said. "I have you. I have kept you safe. Do not go."

Her eyes fluttered, and she tried to see him one last time, but it was no use. Her sight had fled. And yet…his hand pressed into the open cave of her chest, pressing gently but firm as impossible warmth spilled into her and shot through every fragment of her remaining blood. In one hard jerk, her heart burst into action, pumping and throbbing, aching and pulsing.

She took in a ragged breath, made thick by the blood clogging her throat and nostrils. The Gargoyle lifted her up higher, so it could all drain out and over her mouth and chin. She took another breath, this time a cleaner one, and then another.

It was impossible.

She should be dead.

Yet her heart worked.

"You ran? You…left me?" he asked, his voice haggard, his breathing fast and tight as he held her closer.

"I'm sorry to have fled," she admitted, her voice a rough whisper. "It felt...safer."

"Safer than me? Than my arms?"

Her eyes finally opened, the lashes gritty and partially glued together. When they unlocked, she looked up and into his eyes. The moment for fleeing—from the castle, from life itself—was gone. In his face, and his eyes, she saw a pure esteem, an earnest emotion on a face more deeply carved than she remembered.

"You gave me back my heart," she said.

"I had to do so," the Gargoyle explained. "I would not have you die."

"She looked for it," Zaklina said, sitting up further, clutching her hands to the center of her body. The skin was blemished with a jagged scar from her throat to her belly. "She wanted to eat it."

"All demons wish for the hearts of men and women. It is how they live. How they sustain themselves and those under their thrall."

"And you? I gave it to you. You do not want it?"

"I would keep it as mine always. But to save you, I will give up all chance of your love."

She swayed and found her knees. The Gargoyle stayed at her side, his arm about her waist. Slowly, they stood as one, though she felt she might faint if she moved too quickly and he seemed clumsier than she recalled.

"You have it," she said, as if he needed affirmation again, after all she had done for him already. "It's yours again to take. If you wish it."

"You're my wife," he said bluntly, determinedly, and her breathing stopped. He noticed at once, and pulled on her palms, so they were hand-fasted while standing in the stain of her blood. "That is...you will marry me, won't you? You cannot leave me... If you do...but you cannot. You're mine. I am not whole without you."

"The curse of the meadow, of the castle...it ends if a woman agrees to marry you?" she wondered, thinking it too trite a thing to bind. Would not their lovemaking do more? Or the fact that she had ripped out her heart and given it to him? Should she do so again?

"No," he shook his head. "It is love, true and returned, pure and strong. You have torn away the demon in the midst of this place, who crept ever closer, who shadowed the last stronghold of stories closest to this land and weakened me from my watch and my abilities to go out. She sucked hard, eating away the love and the tales of Miódshire which have sustained me, even as much of the world loses hope."

"So it is not a wedding or a marriage then."

"In the beginning, I had thought if I kept a woman, married her, showed her...she might grow to love me, and I her, and thereby begin to heal the stories themselves. But it is just love itself. I was not sure...the stories... they have been dying and melting so long, I could not recall what exactly needed to be done. I only knew I needed...you."

The realization of what he offered her struck hard. "We both needed to love one another? As equals?"

"Yes. Only then. It is...the magic kept my tongue silent. And then...the night came and ripped me from your side before I could find a way to say the words, to tell you how I love you, to make you believe it, so you did not think my profession merely a response to your offering of body and heart."

The relief washed over her, but before she could respond, he pulled her out of the swirling emotions.

"Zaklina," he pressed her hands. "For all this, you haven't answered my question yet."

"What question?"

He was anxious. "You...left. I suppose you could – nothing is holding you here. With what we have shared...clearly you love me as strongly as I do you, even if you do not wed me. But...please. Don't leave. Will you marry me? Be mine...forever, in the truest sense of the word? I will not ever put you aside. I love you with a pureness and a desperation that will never fade. I promise you this. And if I ever cease to love you, may I finally turn to stone, and all the true love of the world disappear."

His earnestness was palpable and washed over her like a wave. The words she needed, the promise she'd craved. It was there, laid out and spoken. Her answer spilled.

"I...of course. Yes. Yes, I will. I will marry you." She bent her forehead over their hands, giving in to the weight of her admittance.

He lifted her up. "Then we will marry now, in the old way, if you are amenable to something so soon."

"Today?" She did not know if she could stand that long without falling back down.

"I would marry you before the sun sets another day, before the seventh night falls," he said. "If you will have me."

Zaklina realized she, too, would like to be rid of the unknown and set her next path. Choosing him, changing the status quo again, giving in to the magic...

"Let us do so," she agreed. "Now."

"I would marry you this moment of course, but you may wish to change?" he said, and gestured to the rags of her dress, drenched in darkening blood.

"Oh." She looked down. "Don't go. It won't take me long."

He helped her limp over to the table and chair in her bedchamber, settling her carefully and putting a blanket across her back. She stared at her reflection, the caked blood across her face making her skin look deformed and blotched with infection. The Gargoyle stood behind her for a moment, his hands light on her shoulders as she wiped it away. There was heat there in his nearness, and she leaned into it, into his familiar cooling warmth and bulk, and pressed her ear to his waist.

"If you are looking to hear my own heart, it is gone," he said. "I gave it to you long ago."

"You love me," she said, needing to hear it again. "Truly?"

"I will never tire of telling you how much I love you now that I might say so. I desire you. Wish you to be my partner in all things." He looked at her in the mirror, his dark eyes searing. "I feel it in my bones, Zaklina. We are meant to fit—in all the ways."

She gripped the table and stood back up, turning to him. Physically drained, aching and sore, she needed to forget the feeling of ripping flesh and breaking bones. She needed be real, but floating. She needed to be reminded. "Show me." Pulling on the quick laces of her ruined gown, it all fell to the floor, leaving her in nothing but the rags of her undergarments, which she removed with a few jerks and tugs.

"I admit I had almost forgotten the ways of men and women until I met you," he said softly, his voice a rumble as he traced the outline of her body with his eyes alone.

"Didn't you allow yourself pleasure in all these lonely eons?"

"Are all women—"

"Yes, some are this brazen to ask," she cut him off, all patience for the dance coming to an end. "And you should know that you are joining with one of them."

"It was different. I...rarely had such desires. Until...you...and then..."

"Then you did. Tell me you did." There were fresh marks on his torso, still bare from their last meeting, his only clothing once again his trousers, hastily worn. She reached to touch the crisscrossing lines, realizing there were others, fainter, longer, thinner, all layers within layers.

She met his frank stare, simmering with need and lust and an offering of something even more revealing.

"What is this?"

"Where do you think I went in the nights when you were trapped and hunted, torn and tortured? I was bound. By the rules of magic, the might of the castle, the hatred of humankind. It doesn't matter, though had you called for me, I would have died trying to come to you. And though you said nothing, and you faced each trial without failing...I still strained my confines. And each day, they left their mark in the morning, fading slower and slower, until..."

She stopped him with a touch to his lips, pulling him down to kiss her. He made a low sound when his chest touched hers. His arms were iron again around her, one hand finding her bottom as well, the other holding her so tight it was as if they were melted together. He picked her up with ease, swinging them to the bed so they collapsed together into the vast plushness. There was no fumbling this time, no prelude to their joining. They fit together indeed.

"Zaklina..." He buried his face in her neck as he moved with her, so deep his physique cradled the soft flesh of her pelvis. She pushed back, finding the pressure easily, still filled with desire and need, if not more so. The flush of life, of near loss, turned the pleasure into something far more desperate.

It did not take long before she fell into the void she craved. It blinded her from the night's devastation and fear, pulsing and black and delightful. As she bridged into another, and then another, as if the waves would not stop, she felt him pause before shuddering, his shout wordless, but the meaning clear.

They lay, dazzled with one another as their heartbeats calmed, though he did not move away from her, instead staying within, holding her face in his hands and gazing at her as if she were the culmination of every love and mother goddess ever formed.

Perhaps that was the way of it, then. Love allowed such devotion. And with it, possibilities.

"We shall marry in the old way, under moon and stars," she said with relish, needing to find some grounding in the whirling. "But then what?"

He softly sighed. "I'm not entirely certain. I only know us together— questions and truth—we will have strength."

"I'm not magic, nor worshiped. I am not a god," she said.

"You are here with me," he reminded her. "There is enough magic around us, and we have shared our blood and bodies. You are me, and I am you. What is it the one religion says? One flesh? You will live always, now, as the embodiment of your essence."

Zaklina did not feel any different. She decided not to press logic for the moment. "So now – we hunt demons? Cure the world of its twisted stories and untruths?"

He leaned over her, a looming that felt like security.

"We will hunt my missing silver arrows and the demons who wield them. One by one. Perhaps we will find more gold and restart the forges. You might tell the stories as you remember them, to save them."

"Did we save my sister?" she asked. "Did we save Miódshire?"

The Gargoyle shifted his head, the creases on the side of his mouth deepening as he thought and his brow had a line down the middle as he frowned, considering, then deciding.

"We can be sure."

"How?"

"There is a way. It ought to work, now that we are...now that we have joined. Now that you and I are of one skin."

He drew on the bits of clothing left to him, and she threw on a dress without a corset. His eyes widened when she did so, as if it was the token of a peasant. But when she reminded him that she planned to take him to bed after their moonlit wedding, he did not protest. The Gargoyle took her out to one of the lower ramparts, but not so low that the trees kissed her fingers if she reached out. The clouds had cleared for the first time all week, so the bluebell of the sky smashed into the forest horizon. It was so colorful it seemed to burst her sight. Were the tree boughs always so chartreuse along the ridges? Was the sky always the color of pea flowers? Did the mountain behind them always look imbedded with diamonds?

This rampart held carved boxes all along the row, as far as she could see, and where it stretched and curved around the mountain's contours, there were countless more. They were all wood, somehow untouched by time and weather. Warm oak, pale beech, bright cherry, and even others she could not name. They were unadorned with anything other than their simple shapes and a single symbol on the front of each. She could not name most, but she recognized some of the alchemical symbols for their multiple meanings and uses.

Gargulec went to one made of knotted pine, peppered with so many curls in the wood that it looked to be spotted. He lifted out a golden scepter, slender and tapered.

"We will have visions with that?" she asked, trying to come around to the notion that she might be filled with wonder every day. How would she learn her way around the castle if she was constantly turning around to the next wonder. Here was a golden tool she would never have known existed until just now, and it was a beauty, with a white gem sparkling at the top.

"There are stories that say this scepter allows its owner to rule over all the jinn of the world, to call demons, to determine the end of the battle of ages. But it really is only a way to see whatever you wish."

He held it up to his eye and twisted the gem. It caught the light and winked, blinding Zaklina for a moment. When she'd blinked away the white, the Gargoyle was holding it out to her.

"There. You shall see. Miódshire is well. We have saved its people, chased the wicked lies away, and the demon with it."

"So there is hope?" she asked, taking the gold in her hands. It was oddly warm, as if it was alive. "That is what we are doing. Finding truth and sowing hope by our love, the power of it, and telling the stories with their ageless, buried questions, forging it all to last...it will all come together, will it?"

"There is always hope that truth and beauty and love will be enough."

"And when we are gone?"

"There will be children," he said, and his eyes were gentle and perhaps a touch joyful.

"Ah. The other kind of hope," she said, and smiled up at him.

His hands closed over hers and lifted the scepter to her eye. It acted like a lens, a far-seeing eye, and after a moment of scrambling focus, Miódshire came into view. The same bumpy streets, thatched roofs, bursting gardens, and long thin fields. Milena sat on her front stoop with a babe in her arms, her cheeks radiant as Marek arrived with a basket of cheese and bread. Quavering on the edge of her vision, the yellow meadow suddenly flickered, and then disappeared in a flash of sunlight. All that remained were the dwarfed huts of Miódshire, where it stood at the edge of a great forest, as if it had always done so.

As if the stories had always said so.

IN ANOTHER LAND, WHERE THE *soil lay rocky and weak, and rocks had to be picked from the narrow farms in order to shove tubers and seeds into the clay and sand, a small village called Bitki-özü clung to the hills. The people hunted the boars and deer of the deep woods surrounding their narrow streets and scraggly chimneys and told the old tales when the winds howled. They spoke of the fairyland realm to be reached on the back of a pegasus or with the aid of the peri-birds, and of the seven spheres below the skies and the seven below.*

Mrs. Staryski walked out from the trees to the market, a fat goodwife with the glint of hunger in her eye. Behind her, a great meadow spread, filled with heavy roses and fluttering lavender, feathery poppies and wide dahlias, and sharp yellow grass, as if it had always been there, and the stories had always said so.

NOTES

So it begins...

This is my first foray into historical fantasy, though it won't be my last. In the many years of research for all the novels I write, I've stumbled across folktales, myths, lore, and more across every culture and continent. What became interesting is how interwoven these stories are, no matter the culture. Places that seem like they would never touch - Japan and South Africa or Peru and Russia - have similar stories. The same holds true for mythology and pantheon stories from ancient Ur to Lakota tribes of the American plains.

This has opened a whole new adventure for building novels imbedded with history and magic, and holy cats, have I had a blast doing so! It's my hope you have enjoyed this play on a very old Polish folktale called "The Crow", in which I've also embedded what I know of bees as a beekeeper, references to countless old symbols and tall tales, subversive commentary on society's evils and faults at large, and a healthy dose of the traditional Beauty and the Beast story in a very unusual format. For example, if you were able to catch it, you may have noticed this is, in some parts, a sort of retelling of Psyche and Cupid.

I must thank Valerie Johnson, for her editing work on this book, as well as Ben Coles, my editor at the publishing house. Also, a shout out to my manager Noah Jones, who is very keen on this book as a movie (in Polish?!), so we'll just keep our fingers crossed about that.

I'm grateful for my children, who let me write in chunks of silence even during their summer vacation, and to Julia S and Lanora S who read a much earlier version of this story (even though it wasn't on audible...). And without John, this book would never exist, as he absolutely always believes in me without fail--what more could a woman need?

BOOK CLUBS

1. Did you think the townspeople were more afraid of the monster or of Mrs. Staryski?

2. Does Zaklina's lack of "sheep" mentality help or hurt her? Or both?

3. Why do you think the townspeople went along with the rumors and stories, even when they didn't make any sense, and it was killing them to do so?

4. Do you recognize any of the demons from each night of terrors? Which would frighten you the most?

5. When the Gargoyle shows Zaklina the different places in the castle, which is your favorite? Why?

6. What do you believe is the author's underlying social commentary about society in this novel?

7. What symbolism in the novel spoke to you the most? For instance, are any gods or images familiar?

8. Compare yourself to Zaklina in the role of 'heroine'. What would you have done the same or differently in her shoes?

9. Do you recognize the many renditions of the Gargoyle in his previous forms, as shown on the carved dolman? What was the point you were able to understand his true nature?

10. Did you expect a different "happily ever after"? Why?

OTHER BOOKS BY SARA DAHMEN

Fiction:

The Flats Junction series
Tinsmith 1865
Widow 1881
Outcast 1883
Medicineman 1884

Wine & Children

Non-Fiction:

Copper Iron and Clay: A Smith's Journey

Learn more at: www.saradahmen.com or www.housecopper.com

Find Sara at @saradahmenbooks on Twitter
or @sara_dahmen & @housecopper on Instagram